Short Stories
By
Crazy Joe Mama

A Man From The Bronx

 For information, address: Josephbaybayron@gmail.com. Twitter: @JosephBayron. Facebook: Joseph Bayron. Registration No. TXu 2-246-535.

First Edition

My name is Joseph Bayron. This is a Puerto Rican family's journey from Puerto Rico to Harlem, the Bronx, and Hawaii. I also have fiction and non-fiction stories.

Begin

Table of Contents

I lived in an area called Boston Secor Housing projects. I was a resident for seventeen years. It is located in Bronx, New York. It was not a joyous life. Welcome, welcome to section 8 housing.

SMACKDOWN

I was a sixteen year old kid. My brother was 10, an easy target. It was a hot summer day in the projects of the Bronx. My friends and I were playing catch on the baseball field. Rumors circulated around the neighborhood. A 16 year old teenager named Paulie decided to beat my 10 year old brother for fun. I saw my brother at the water fountain. I waited for the first punch. Paulie punched him twice in the face. He laughed when my brother hit the ground. I went to my brother's aid. A fight ensued and I lost. I lost badly. However, my brother was safe.

The next day my brother was punched three times. Again, I fought and lost badly. On the third day I decided, FUCK THIS!! My brother was punched, I pushed Paulie to the ground. I punched him repeatedly. He laid there stunned. I grabbed my brother. We went upstairs to the fifth floor apartment. I put him in his bedroom. I began to realize that this will go on all summer. So I went to my parents bedroom. Inside the closet was a rifle. The rifle was inside a brown leather case. I took the Winchester Model 70 out of the leather case. I proceeded to the entrance door. My Mom and two sisters guarded the door. My sisters were four and six years old.

They pleaded in tears, "Put the rifle away!"
I said, "Get out of my way!"
"I am tired of Chris being picked on."
Emotions were running high.
Then my mother said, "Put the rifle back or I will tell your father!"
It was my way out. So I decided to put the rifle on top of my parent's bed.

I went to my bedroom and began to sob. I heard my mother grabbed the rifle. She put it back in the leather case. She left the apartment and gave the rifle to a neighbor. She returned and waited for my father to return from work. When he arrived, my mother screamed about what I did. My father looked at me. I was expecting the worst. But he turned to my mother and said, "I'll take care of it."

The next day my father went to work. When you are a blue collar worker. You realize that some of your co-workers are low level criminals. Louie was a bookie. He knew my father well. He would ask my father once or twice a week to punch his time card at the end of his shift. He was leaving early to go to the horse track. In return, he would give my father one hundred or two hundred dollars. One day my father went to Louie and said, "I don't know what to do?" He explained the situation. "I might lose one or two of my sons."
Louie said, "John ,I'll take care of it."
My father stated, "What are you going to do?!"
Louie said, "You do not need to know."

Three days later, I was sitting at the kitchen table. The table was facing the window. For some reason, no one was home. I know that sound travels up. I saw Paulie laughing with his friends, "I'll kick both of their asses."
"I will kick their asses all summer long."
Then two big Italian men approached Paulie. They were both wearing long black leather jackets. They told Paulie's friends to scatter. They left quickly. The Italian guy to the right said, " I heard your having problems with the Johnson brothers?"
Paulie replied, " I don't know what you are talking about."
Then I hear the italian man say," I HEARD YOU ARE HAVING PROBLEMS WITH THE JOHNSON BROTHERS!!
Again Paulie said," I don't know wha---SMACK!!"

The smack was loud. I mean loud. Paulie was stunned and felt his left cheek with his left hand. Again the italian guy to the right said, "Are we going to have problems with the Johnson brothers!!''
" I don't kn-- SMACK!!" This time Paulie's legs were getting shaky.
The guy took Paulie by the back of his collar and shook him like a rag doll. They walked him through the park and baseball field. They went behind the rocks. For the next ten minutes, they were out of sight. I did not dare to go there and see what was going on. Then I see Paulie walking alone. He is holding his left cheek with his left hand. He was walking through the baseball field like a drunken sailor. He proceeded through the park. He passed by my building. He never bothered my brother and I again.

RADIO!!
RADIO!!

I was a twenty year old kid working at a gas station in the Bronx. It was the summer of 1980. I saved my paychecks to buy sneakers and cassettes. Then I bought a JVC radio with dual cassettes. The neighborhood would call this radio a boombox. It needed eight D batteries to operate. While everyone was playing hip-hop and R&B. I was playing classic rock. I would share this radio with all three of my brothers. Then I made the mistake of letting my fourteen year old brother use it.

My brother was playing AC/DC on the cassette player. A sixteen year old Jamaican kid decided he wanted the radio.
My brother said, "No!!"
The Jamaican kid broke a beer bottle and began to stab my brother. My brother tried to grab the bottle from the kid's hand. Instead, my brother was cut badly on his neck and forehead. He went upstairs to the fifth floor. My mother opened the door. My brother was crying and bleeding like a pig. My brother told my dad what occurred. Everyone went to the bathroom. My mother went to the medicine cabinet and took out the first aid kit. My dad used his thumbs and index fingers to close the neck wound. My mother used the white adhesive tape to cover the wound. They did this to his forehead as well. My father said, "Take Chris to the Hospital

Miriam. He will need at least fifty stitches." My mother said, "Angel that kid will bother him again." My father said, " I know, just take him to the hospital. Chris where did the kid go?" "He went to the Plaza pop." My father said, "Ok."

My father went to the master bedroom. He sat on the queen size bed and heard the front door close. He looked in the closet. He saw his long black leather jacket. It had big pockets. Then he went into the closet and opened the black trunk. He took out his 9mm gun. He put the magazine into the gun. He laid the gun across the bed. Then he put his black leather jacket on. He put the gun in his right pocket. Then he walked to the Plaza.

He approached the back end of the plaza. Then took out his 9mm with his right hand. He put the gun near his heart. The index finger was on the trigger. He made sure the handle was in full view. He turned right and approached the sixteen year old kid and his two friends. He said, "Give me the fucking radio back." The kid said, "Please old man. What is that a BB gun?!" All three laughed. My Dad said, "Last warning!" The kid said, "Go home old man." My Dad took out the 9mm and put it to his head. He shouted, " GIVE ME THE FUCKING RADIO BACK!!!" He quickly grabbed the radio and told the kid, "Talk to Paulie. He has a story to tell. It involves visitors."
"DON'T FUCK WITH MY SONS!!!" Then he left.

Later on that day, I came home from work. My dad approached me. He said, "Do not give the radio to your brother again! Leave the radio in the apartment from now on." It was understood. I kept the radio for three more years. Then I gave the radio to my three brothers permanently.

$400,000 Question

I

There was a call about a shooting in an abandoned building. The first police officer named O'Reilly arrived at the scene. Two dead drug dealers were on the floor. Each drug dealer was holding a black briefcase. O'Reilly opened the first briefcase. It was full of cocaine. The second briefcase was full of cash. O'Reilly estimates $400,000. He goes to the next room. He finds a locked door. O'Reilly finds a key in the first drug dealer's pocket. The key opens the door. He quickly puts the briefcase full of money in the room. This is done in two minutes.

The other officers arrive. The ambulance takes the two dead drug dealers away. Then the officers snoop around. They walk to the back and realize the door is locked. They wonder what is behind the door. They decide to leave it alone. Two days later, O'Reilly arrives in a $500 dollar car. He dresses like a homeless guy. He then takes a two wheel shopping cart out of the trunk of his car. He fills it with clothing and a blue shower curtain. He takes the shopping cart up three flights of stairs. He opens the locked door. He wraps the briefcase in the blue shower curtain. He puts the briefcase in the shopping cart. He returns to his car. He puts everything in the trunk.

O'Reilly drives the vehicle back to his house in Queens, New York. He puts the briefcase in a locker in his garage. He then drives the vehicle to a dirt road with high grass. The location is twenty miles away. He takes the license plates off. He puts them in the back of his pants. Then he proceeds to burn his car. He walks to the end of the road and takes a taxi ride back to his house. He smiles and realizes that he his $400,000 richer.

II

"You motherfucker!!"
"Why do I have to go to the roof?!"
The cop says, " Creole get the fuck up there!!"
Creole was a small black man. Four officers realized that every Saturday, Creole carried his cash in a briefcase. Creole has a bodyguard. The bodyguard was told to leave or die. He left and Creole was on his own. One police officer said, "Let's visit that building." The three officers begin to push Creole to the building. One officer says, "Let's visit the roof."
Creole says, "I am not going to the roof! Take my money! I can always make some more!"

They enter the building. The officer says, "Get the fuck upstairs Creole!" They put a gun to his head. Then they push him up the stairs. Creole pleads with the cops to take his money. It falls on deaf ears.

The officers reach the roof. They open the door and throw Creole out. The fourth officer had a silencer stolen from the evidence room. It had no vin numbers. He pointed it at Creole and shot him in the head.

They opened up his briefcase and counted the money. The cop who shot him got $15,000 more. The other three took $95,000 each. They all left with a smile on their face. One cop says, "Thanks for the early Christmas gift Creole." They left the building in three separate cars.

WHICH STORY IS TRUE?!

WHICH STORY IS FALSE?!

BOTH ARE TRUE!!

EMPTY WINDOWS

It was a muggy summer night in the projects of the Bronx. I decided to walk my sister's dog Shags. It was a stressful day. I walked Shags for over an hour. I entered the lobby. The alarm from the elevator was on. That meant they were urinating in the elevator or having sex. In the lobby, a crack cocaine dealer was arguing with a customer. I decided to take the stairs to the fifth floor apartment.

The next morning, I grabbed my briefcase full of resumes and headed downtown. The elevator was working. I went to the lobby. The elevator door opened. I walked out and saw the horror. The windows were all shoot out. Glass was all over the floor. I walked toward the windows and heard the crackling noise of broken glass at my feet. I looked down and saw no shell casings. I looked right and saw four bullet holes embedded in the wall. Then I looked down at the glass at my feet. An ugliness took over my whole being. I grabbed my briefcase and walked to the train station.

PLYWOOD

I was reading the Daily News. It is a very popular newspaper in New York City. On page seven, there was a drawing of a bank robbery. It involved six men with machine guns. There is nothing unusual about bank robberies in the Bronx. But this bank robbery was only a ten minute walk from the projects. I went to that bank so many times. The bank tellers were a friendly bunch of young women. Their young faces are still in my mind. The terror they faced was so primal.

The robbery took place on an early Monday morning. I knew that the girls would get their coffee from the greek diner. The diner was a popular place in the plaza. They would order coffee and blueberry muffins. The muffins had a nice buttery taste to it. I know. I had them from time to time. The bank teller Tina recommended them to me. It was a Tuesday morning, there was no muffins to eat. The diner closed for the day. I could not say my usual hello to Tina. She would be at the diner. Everything changed. I stopped by the bank. The windows were shot out and covered with plywood. I hit the plywood with my right hand. I was surprised how thin it was. It was so quiet. I left and walked to the train station.

The next day I talked to the manager of the diner. He told me that five black men with african accents entered the bank with M16 machine guns. The employees in the bank were terrified. The police were there in two minutes. A gun battle ensued. The police were badly outgunned. The windows of the bank were shot out. The bank robbers got into their cars and took the 95 North Highway. This is all he knows. I thanked him and left for the subway.

It was six months later. The bank never reopened. I never saw Tina again. In its place, was a medical supply business. I asked the owner if he hired anyone from the bank. He said, "No this is a family- run business." I left with a feeling of sadness. My life had changed. I did not ask for this. But the world said so what.

HECTOR

I was waiting at a bus stop. I just came from the unemployment office. I recognized a man from the neighborhood. His name was Hector. He had his four year old son with him. The kid was named Jose. Hector also came from the unemployment office. We did some small talk. I found out that he lived with his mother. The child lived with his girlfriend. He invited me to his softball game in the South Bronx. It was an early Sunday morning. So I decided to go with my girlfriend.

I arrived at the softball field. Hector informed me that he was batting fifth in the line up. There was about fifty people in the stands. In the second inning, he popped out. In the fourth inning, he had a double. The seventh inning, he had a single. He played right field. During the game, he caught over ten pop outs. It was the bottom of the ninth, two outs. One man on second. One man on third. The batter hit the ball between center and right field. Hector and the centerfielder insisted on catching the ball. They collided. The ball dropped. Two men scored. Their one run lead vanished. They lost. Hector and the centerfielder got into a heated argument. Emotions were running high. You can hear them screaming. Everyone in the stands was nervous. The man took out a stiletto knife and stabbed Hector three times in the stomach. The people in the stands were horrified. The centerfielder continued to scream at a dead Hector. The police arrived and the man was arrested.

Today at Boston Secor Housing Projects there is a mural of Hector. The mural is on a wall on Bivona Street. The mural informs you that Hector was born in 1955 and died in 1985. His son never knew his dad. I hope the mural is still there. I wish I was a better friend. He seemed to be a decent guy and a good father.

TABLE OF CONTENTS

I worked for the National Park Service for five glorious summers. The parks were Yellowstone, the Grand Canyon, and Yosemite. Then I traveled to Alaska. There I worked at Denali and Glacier Bay. I also have a story of my Brother Ed at Katmai National Park. I hope you enjoy these chapters.

Denali

Janet knocked on the door. Bang! Bang! Bang!
She screamed, "Joeeee!!!''
I said, "Whatttt!!!'
Janet screamed, "There is a bear down the road eating a deer. We have some rides." I grabbed my coat and went out the door.
Janet screamed again, "Joeeee!!!"
I said, "Whattt!!!''
She was at a distance and pointed in front of her. To my right, was a big moose. The moose was seven feet high from the shoulder down. It was chewing something. It had no antlers. I said, "Christ what an ugly horse!!'' Then I proceeded down the trail.
I approached the four cars. There were sixteen of us. We got inside the cars and proceeded fourteen miles east. There was a crowd of over two hundred people. They all were watching a bear eat a deer. The bear was at least two to three miles away. There was only a rib cage left. The meat was bright pink. I watched the bear rip the meat off the rib cage. Then he put his front claws on the bottom of the rib cage and pulled a big piece of meat with his teeth. He put the meat down and bite into it. He began to chew.

The bear looked to his left and noticed fourteen wolves waiting their turn. The bear and two wolves locked eyes. Then he began to eat again. Finally, seven minutes later the bear left. The wolves went to the dead deer. They started to sniff. Two wolves pulled some meat off the rib cage. Then three wolves began to fight over the meat. You can hear the yelping and barking of the three wolves. Then the rest of the wolves began to bark and pull the meat with their teeth. The eating went on for fifteen minutes.

The wolves began to sniff and realize there is no more meat to eat. They left the dead carcass on the dry riverbed. Then proceeded to walk back into the forest. The two hundred people began to leave. I stated, “Boy am I hungry. Let’s get dinner.” Then sixteen of us got into our cars and proceeded fourteen miles west.

FIRE

It was the summer of 1991. I was leaving the Yosemite Valley. I was driving toward Tuolumne Meadows. Before I entered the tunnel, I looked to my left. There I saw an area with no life at all. It looked desolate and barren like a napalm explosion.

I returned to the Yosemite Valley the next morning. I went to the fire department. A friendly fireman decided to feed my curiosity.

In the summer of 1990, there was a bad fired. Planes were dropping tons of fire retardant in the west side of the Yosemite Valley. The fire could not be controlled. Eight firemen and four firewoman were surrounded by fire. Then Captain Dougherty received some terrifying news from the plane.
"John this is Jack."
"We cannot get to your crew.
"The fire is too intense."
"We will drop you a fireproof blanket to cover your crew."

John looked to the sky and saw a wooden box being dropped with a parachute. Inside the wooden box was a fireproof blanket made of silicaflex. It hit the ground and Captain Dougherty and crew grabbed the blanket. Then they walked to the valley and put the blanket over themselves. Afterwards, they laid to the ground and waited. Then the time came when the fire went over them. They felt the heat of the fire. The firewomen began to be terrified. The heat was getting worse. Suddenly a firewoman was screaming, "OH MY GOD!! OH MY GOD!!! OOOOH MY GOD!!!" Immediately Captain Dougherty covered her body with his own. He told her, "Joan!, Joan! Stay calm!" You can hear the planes up above. Then they felt the fire roll on their backs. The only thing that kept them from burning alive was the fireproof blanket. More screaming, " Oh My God!! OH MY GOD!!"

Then they felt the fire passing their back. It took several hours to put the fire out. The exhaustion and fear put the firemen and women to sleep.

Morning came, it was quiet. There was some smoldering and the smell of smoke. The twelve awoke. They crawled out of the blanket. They began to walk. Underneath their feet was a crunchy sound of ash. The ash was one to three feet deep. No one said a word. They walked the valley and found the main road in two hours. The paramedics were waiting. They were checked out. There was no serious injuries, just exhaustion. They rode back to the firehouse with pride and hunger. They had one hell of a feast.

The Winds of Yosemite

It was the summer of 1990. The Santa Ana winds were over sixty miles an hour in the Yosemite Valley. So all the visitors and employees were at the Ahwahnee Hotel. The dining room had plenty of food for everyone. Then everyone looked outside the windows. Because you see nature decided to pay a visit.

Ten coyotes surrounded a female deer and its fawn. They separated the two animals. The fawn was helpless. People in the dining room were watching. The anticipation of horror was about to take place. Four coyotes got their teeth on the fawn. The fawn was kicking and fighting. They began to tear at the fawn. Then the fawn split in half. The people were speechless. The young kids were crying. Then the female deer is attacked and killed. They start eating her. Then the managers of the hotel yell at the employees to close the blinds. They remain closed until nightfall.

Morning came. I walked to the location of the attack. The rangers already paid a visit and took the remains of the animals away. So I went to eat breakfast. Life moves on. Yep I'm cruel.

GIRL TROUBLE

Yep! Another Yosemite story. Patti was a short stocky nineteen year old woman. She had a white complexion. She decided to breakup with her live-in boyfriend. I was drinking a few beers and here comes Patti talking about her D cup breast. She stated that they were playboy worthy. She repeated herself over and over again. Playboy worthy. Playboy worthy. I put my beer down and looked at her. There must have been over thirty people at the party. I walked toward her and made out with her. So I said to myself, "I am going to have some fun." So I laid her on top of the picnic table. She did not seem to mind. I continued to make out with her. The guys at the party started to scream, "Oh my God. Holy Shit!!" Then the laughter started. We acted like we were alone. I started to dry hump her. She returned the favor. So I got off the picnic table and went to her place.

The next day she moved out of her boyfriend's place and moved to the otherside of the Yosemite Valley. Before she left, she told me to visit anytime. My new place will be in Boystown. It is located at Camp Curry. The next night, I ate dinner and decided to visit Patti. The buses in the valley were no longer making stops. It was dark. But I wanted to see her. There was plenty of light from the lampposts. So I walked the valley. Then I saw a twenty pound coyote. He was by himself. He looked at me. Up ahead there was no light on the road. He began to look at the dark area. Then he began to look at me. I said to myself, "There is only one coyote." So I began to walk. Then a second coyote came into the light. He looked at the dark area, then looked at me. Then he bowed his head and licked his teeth. Then a third, a fourth, seven in all. They were waiting for me to approach the darkness. They had their tails wagging. Two coyotes were bowing. Then one came on the paved road. I was approaching the dark road. I saw a silhouette of a small church. All of the coyotes were to my right. Now three coyotes were on the paved road. I said to myself, "You know what. Tomorrow is another day." "I think I should return to my campsite." So I did. The coyotes did not follow me. It seems they felt more comfortable attacking me in the dark.

My Brother Ed at Katmai National Park

"Hey nimrod!!"
"What is with the Moses look!"
"Where is your prophet stick!"
"Are you gonna say behold in an echo!"
"Fuck you Joe!!"

Then we hugged. My brother spent the summer in Alaska. He was working at a place called Katmai National Park. His job position was a park ranger.
To arrive at Katmai you must first fly into Anchorage, Alaska. There you catch a propeller plane and travel to a place called King Salmon. Then get on a plane that lands on water. This plane ride last about an hour. You land this plane on Brooke Lake. Then taxi to the pier. The area is called Brooks Range. What makes this park so unusual is that the grizzly bears are over one thousand pounds or more. They roam free. There are no barriers between tourists and bear. The fishermen and bears eat from the same lake. There is a famous waterfall were you can watch grizzlies eat salmon. The best bear to watch was a grizzly named Diver. He would go underneath the water to grab a salmon.

Like all bears they hibernate during the winter. During hibernation a bear can lose three hundred pounds. The duration can last up to six months. So when they awake they must eat a great deal of salmon. By the end of the summer, they must gain six hundred pounds. They eat all day. The summers of Alaska have 24 hour sunlight. This is the land of the midnight sun.

As a park ranger, my brother's job was to stand by the lake. The bear would be in the lake eating salmon. If the bear and a fisherman had the same fish, my brother would cut the line. The fisherman would reel the line in. The bear wins. The fisherman then proceeds to put new bait on the line and then throw the line back to the lake. Sometimes he would work the visitors center. There were days when my brother kept tabs on the whereabouts of the bears. This was done on walkie talkies. The summer was uneventful. Then that day came.

My brother was watching a female bear nursing her two cubs on the banks of the waterfall. Then he heard a female ranger scream. He went to investigate. A bear chased the female ranger up a tree. He was shaking the tree. The ranger was terrified. My brother called it in on his walkie talkie. The bear heard him. The bear turned around and stood on two legs. He looked right at my brother. The walkie talkie was yelling, "Ed, Ed please respond!'' This irritated the bear. He went on all fours legs and charged my brother. My brother looked down and made sure that he made no eye contact. The bear stopped in front of my brother and roared. You can feel the heat from his mouth. My brother saw the mucus on his fangs. He said to himself, "I am in total mercy of the bear. I hope to God this a bluff charge."

The rangers ran to the shed that holds tranquilizer guns and several rifles. They grabbed them and went to my brother's aid. Wild animals are unpredictable. The bear was about one hundred yards away. My brother was shaking badly. The seven rangers kept their distance. Four rangers used their tranquilizer guns Three pointed their rifles at the bear. The tranquilizers worked. The bear feel asleep. They called for a helicopter. They informed the helicopter crew they have to remove a dangerous bear. Before the helicopter's arrival. They took a blood sample. Then they collared him. The collar had a number and a location device . He was weighed. The male bear weighed 1100 pounds. He was measured. He was seven feet from the shoulder. The head weighed 100 pounds. His claws was three feet in length.

The helicopter arrived. They put the bear in a hammock. The helicopter picked him up and left for a location three hundred miles away. Within three minutes, there was no sound. The helicopter was at a distance. My brother stopped shaking. The girl came down from the tree. The rest of the summer was extremely tense. The rangers started to go gray. Every movement from a bear was intense. It wasn't the same. However, the rest of the summer was uneventful.

KILLER WHALES

I was working at Glacier Bay National Park in Gustavus, Alaska. During the summer months, there were twenty four hours of sunlight. The alaskan beer was tasty. You can feel the sugar around your lips and the tip of your tongue. I was at the pier drinking beer and watching the still waters of Glacier Bay. The dangerous part was falling in the water. It was below freezing. Your whole body would collapse and then you would drown. You must respect nature. Otherwise, you will not feel at peace with it. The sun and the moon were out at the same time. I watched a seal swim by. Then I saw a black bear swim across the bay. Once he got to the shore, he began to eat blueberries in the bushes. Then I watched three moose swim across the bay. It looked so peaceful. I watched the ripples of water from their necks. They had algae on their racks.

Then in the distance, I saw twenty to thirty killer whales in a pod. It was the biggest pod I have ever seen. They surrounded the three moose. Then some of the killer whales went underwater. Then I heard the frantic cries of all three moose. One moose made it to the shore. However, his organs were hanging outside his lower body. He began to die slowly. The other two moose were taken underwater. Blood began to surface. Then the two torsos began to float on the water. The killer whales came out of the water. Then ripped into the torsos and left only the heads and antlers. The antlers began to resemble branches from a tree. Then the bay went quiet.

Two days later, I went back to the pier. The moose on the shore was removed. I never saw the killer whales again.

COMEDY

TABLE OF CONTENTS

I did stand up comedy for four years. I enjoyed it, if it went well. I visit it like an old friend. Sometimes there is an awkward silence in front of the audience. I just talk and wait for the jokes to come. My sense of humor lies in these eight stories.

SHAGS

Jack and Annette were dating for three years in Brooklyn, New York. Jack was 33 years old. Annette was 30 years old. They made a decision to move to Venice Beach, California. They sold their cars and left to California with twenty thousand dollars in their pockets. They arrived in Venice Beach thirty days later. Upon arrival, they unpacked at a hostel. Then started to look for an apartment. They found a two story walk up, three blocks from the beach. The landlady Janette was friendly and extremely helpful. She informed them that two restaurants are always looking for help. So Annette called the owners of the restaurants. She set up interviews. Jack was hired as a bartender. Annette took a job as a waitress. They began to build their lives. They decided not to buy a car since parking in Venice Beach was nearly impossible.

One day Jack is walking to work and he saw a twelve pound dog. It looks like a walking gray mop. He looked desperate and hungry. But Jack continued to walk to work. The second day it rained. Jack saw the dog walking and shaking. Again, Jack continued to walk to work. A week later, he once again saw the walking gray mop. This time he was barking and shaking. He was surrounded by three coyotes. They were closing in. The dog was panicking. Jack looked around his surroundings. He found several bottles. He picked them up and threw them at the coyotes. They looked at Jack. He threw more bottles. This time they scattered. He worried about the coyotes returning. So he told the dog, "I'll take you to my apartment. Great I'm talking to a dog!"

They walked side by side. Jack approached the apartment. The dog could not make it up the stairs. So he picked up the dog and went up the stairs. He told the gray mop, "I'll clean you up and find a family for you. I have to stop talking to the dog!" Then kind hearted Annette came home from her afternoon shift. Jack told Annette, "We have a new friend." He told her about the coyotes. Then Jack bent down to see if he had a collar. His name was on it. It was a small gold plate saying, Shags. Annette opened two cans of beef stew. She feed Shags in two seperate paper bowls. Her eyes began to water. Jack looked frightened. Then he said, " No-No-No-Noooo! Please, Please don't!'' Jack paused. He sat down. He put his hands in his face. He said, "O-H-H G-O-DDD!!!" He looked at Annette and said, " I have to go to work!'' The walk seemed longer than usual.

He arrived at the bar with a long, long face. The waitress said, "Problems at the home front."

Jack said, "I took in a stray dog. Annette's waterfalls began to flow.''

The waitress said, "O-O-O. I guess you have a permanent guest. His name is?!"

"It's Shags."

"Nice Name."

"Congratulations, it's a boy!"

"It's not staying!''

"Yea-okay!"

The waitress began to laugh. Jack says nothing.

Everyone in the bar heard the conversation. So, the tips were good. The bar closed. Jack walked to his apartment. He saw the three coyotes sniffing around the same area he found Shags. They looked at Jack. Jack said, "Hello scumbags!" Then he threw some bottles at them. Then the coyotes ran off. Jack returned to his two story walk up. He opened the door. Shags was fast asleep. Annette was watching TV. She shut it off and went to bed with Jack.

The next morning, Jack borrowed a car from a co-worker and took Shags to a pet store. He asked the employee to give the dog a haircut. Jack told the worker, " Check for infections or any little creatures."

The worker said, "Creatures?!"

"What kind of creatures would that be!"

Jack said, "The creatures that don't want to leave. How long?!"
"Comeback in two hours."
"Do you want his creatures in a little baggie?!"
Jack said, "No minimum wage!!
Jack left and did some errands.

When Jack returned, he passed by a very thin dog. Jack said, "Christ what a skinny poodle!"

"Excuse me, where is my dog?!"
"You just passed it !"
"No that's a poodle!"
"Very good mastermind !"
"That's your dog!"
"Ummm it can't be !''
"I mean its i-t-t-sss from France."
"That's right!''
"It's not Norwegian!"
"It's not German!"
"You know Germany has shepherds, G-e-r-m-a-n S-h-e-p-h-e-r-d-s!"
"What does sheep have to do with it ?"
"Pick up your fucking dog !!"
"By the way, the price for Mr. France is eighty dollars."
"Okay here."
"I'll be right back."
"Don't leave your fucking dog here!!"
"Don't worry Frenchy!''
"I am going to the store to buy some bottled water and a steak for him."
"The worker said, "You mean the POODLE!!
"Yes the poodle.''

I returned to the pet store. I decided to cut the meat outside the pet store. I used a pocket knife. I returned to the store and opened the cage to my new friend. To my amazement, the employee of the store said nothing. The poodle ate and drank the water.

"The worker said, "Hey poodle owner!"
"You need to buy a harness."
Jack said, "How much?!"

The worker said, “Thirty dollars.”
I gave him my credit card. I put the harness on my poodle. Then I said, “Take care minimum wage!”
The pet store employee said, “You see that front door. It is a beautiful door.
“It looks even better when you fucking exit !!”
Jack said, “I hope you enjoy shit duty!”
“Relax I’m leaving!

I walked to my apartment. I opened the door. Of course Ms. Waterworks was in full swing. Of course, we kept the dog.

It was one year later. We bought a car and had new jobs. I was an assistant manager of a hotel. Annette got a manager job at a small retail store. Of course, Shags became my buddy. People would give me looks. But I never put a harness on Shags. He was always at my side like a little kid. He wagged his tail and ran everywhere. He had one problem. The damn dog had an enormous penis. He weighed twelve pounds and his penis was bigger than mine. Something was not right in the universe. I mean he hung like a goddamn horse!! Jesus Christ, I remember the first time I witnessed my nightmare. He was barking at the door. I yelled, “SHAGS!!” He immediately goes on his back. There in all his glory a penis that should belong to me. I put my right hand in front of my face to cover his glory. Then I looked left. Then I said, “Jesus Shags put that thing away!!” So naturally, I gave Shags a nickname. I called him Pornstar.

Annette came home.
“Hey, I have a nickname for Shags !”
“It’s PORNSTAR!”
“Jack this isn’t a porn movie from your smartphone!”
“Oh really. Hold on.”
So I screamed, “Shags!!”
Shags goes on his back.
“Look at that thing, it covers two states!!”
Annette says, “Why are you looking away?!”
“Because it is a big PENIS!!!”
“I’m sorry if a great dane with five nipples showed up at our door.”
“Feeding her young with double Ds just swaying in the wind!”

“You would not find that uncomfortable!’’
“No Jack!”
“She is feeding her young!”
“But there swaying in the wind!”
“No discomfort!”
“No Jack.”

Then Annette said, “I almost forgot, your sister called. She wants you to visit and see her new dog.”

Then Jack said, “ did she buy another meat puppet?!”
“Just visit her and bring Shags.”
“Okay.”
“Come on Pornstar. Pornstar you want to make movies?”
“Jack shut up!”
“Shags we are not wanted!”

Jack walked outside. Then Jack looked at Shags.
He said, “Jesus Christ Shags, is that thing scraping the sidewalk. Get in the car Porn Star.”

So I visit my sister in Marina Del Rey. She lets me into her apartment. I hear the dog barking. The dog makes an entrance. This THING is tiny. I mean a tiny little skinny hairless white dog . I can’t make out her features.
“Sis, what type of dog is it?’’
“I don’t know. It does not matter.”
“It does not?” I decided to go no further.

The dog is so tiny, you can cup it in your hands. Shags is getting Jack nervous.
Jack says, “Shags stop sniffing.”
Jack hesitates to ask. However, Jack needed an answer. So Jack said, “Sis what is the name of this hairless skinny white dog?” My sister says, “Cracker!” I said, “Of course it is! Then she yells, “ keep Shags away from my dog! He’ll rupture Cracker’s vagina!”

I began to wonder if Shags will fuck and eat Cracker. So I put Cracker on the shoulder of the coach. I am preventing Shags from going after Cracker. I sit down and feel the breeze of an open window. A giant condor enters the apartment and takes Cracker. Suddenly, I hear my sister yelling. She yells, "OH MY GOD!! OH MY GOD!! Cracker was taken by a condor!" Then she continues to yell, "CRACKER GOT TAKEN BY A CONDOR!! OH MY GOD!! OH MY GOD!!" Then Jack could not stop laughing. Jack yells, "Farewell Cracker! Farewell you tiny little shit! Farewell!!" Then my sister yells, "What is so funny you four eyed fuck?! Cracker is no more!"

Jack continues to laugh. He hears his sister yelling. She says, "Get the fuck out! Get the fuck out! I am in mourning for Cracker!" Finally Jack says, "Let's go Pornstar. The condor might come for you.
Jack leaves the apartment. He hears his sister slam the door behind him. Jack is laughing down the hall with Shags barking nervously. He leaves the building and enters the car with Shags. Shags begins to scratch the passenger seat. Jack yells, "Shags stop scratching the seat." Then of course Shags goes on his back. Jack feels uncomfortable. Jack says, "Pornstar please go on all fours." Shags obeys and waits for the passenger window to open. Jack opens the window. Then Shags puts his head outside. Jack starts the car. He then puts it on drive and leaves Marina Del Ray. Good old Shags barks and fells the wind against his face.

Jack arrives at his apartment and explains to Annette what occurred to Cracker. Annette is horrified and Jack can't stop laughing. Then things begin to settle down in the apartment. Annette looks at Jack and says, "Tomorrow will be a better day." Jack looks bewildered. He decides to keep his mouth shut. He will figure it out. They watch some television and then go to sleep.

The next morning, Jack realizes that they have been dating for four years. They were eating breakfast. She was drinking her orange juice. Then she asked, " Jack where is this relationship going?" Jack got tempted to be a wise ass, but he held his tongue. Annette deserved a serious answer. Then Jack made a big mistake. He was honest. Jack said, "I thought when I was a kid, I would be ready by thirty years old. Now I am 33 years old. I am scared. I love you. But I am really scared." She looked at him with hurt in her eyes. She got up from the chair and said, "Enjoy your day off Jack." Boy she sounded real sad.

Jack's day off did not go well. He walked for hours on the beach. He even put Shags in his harness. He was pacing and sweating. So Jack decides to walk to her store. There he sees a man she was friendly with, his name was Joe. Jack knows Annette. She will be dating this guy in about a year. It was tearing him apart. So he decides to go to the mall and look at some engagement rings. Scared out of my mind, he puts a two hundred deposit on a $3000 ring.

The next day, Jack takes Annette to a restaurant called Duke's. It is located in Malibu, California. After dinner, Jack drove to the Malibu Pier. They walked to the end of the pier. There Jack proposed. She accepted. She cried and Jack lost four pounds from sweating. They went back to the apartment. Shags was barking up a storm. Jack took a shower. Then he went to the bedroom. There he made love to her with the ring on.

One year later, Annette was pregnant. Jack opened up a burger joint in Venice Beach, California. Of course, he borrowed money from eight people. Then there was the bank loan. He also borrowed against the car and used Annette's credit cards. He called the place, Fat Bastard with bitchin fries. He held Annette's hand and watched Pornstar sniff a white poodle's butt. Jack said, "Shags be gentle!" Of course, he wasn't. Boy did that white poodle yelp. He looked at the sign of his burger joint. Jack said, "I like the fat guy's tight shirt. That is one big belly button." Annette laughed and called Jack an idiot. Pornstar approved. Apparently, he was done with his conquest.

ROSA

Her name was Rosa. She came from a far, far away land called East L.A. She was traveling on a white horse. She had long bronze legs and silky black hair. Bluebirds and beautiful blue butterflies surrounded her. She traveled through the forest for three days.

She came upon a medieval castle door. She saw a knocker. She disembarked from the horse. She knocked three times. The door fell and three miles away was the mall. She returned to her horse and rode to the mall. She entered on horseback. Trumpets were playing. Unfortunately, much too loud. So the birds and butterflies dropped dead. People from the mall shouted, "Rosa is here!! Rosa is here!!"
"How the hell do they know my name?!"
"Oh well, pretty girl problem

The ugly girls began to mumble. A little Mormon elf named Yoddy looked at her. Rosa said to herself, "Virgins are so weird."

She entered a big hall made of gold and glass. She announced on a bullhorn, "I AM SINGLE!! I HAVE NO BOYFRIEND!!" She sat on a chair with a computer in front. Once again, she heard the mumbling of ugly women. Rosa said, "Ahhh, the fuglies never change.

Men from far and wide came to take Rosa's hand.
They chanted, "ROSA PICK ME!!" "ROSA PICK ME!!"
The chants of Rosa were heard throughout the mall. Men came from everywhere. Then two men could not take it anymore. They smashed through two windows. Luckily, Yoddy broke their fall. Ahh yes virgin cushion. Boy was he fat!! Suddenly, the dead birds and butterflies came alive. They were zombies. They ate the two men. They screamed in agony, "ROSA!! ROSA!!"
"HELP ME!!"
"HELP ME!!"
Rosa was getting angry.
"Shut up!!"
"Rosa is getting a headache!"
"People do not die quietly like the old days."

The men get coming and coming. The King of the mall decided to put her on the second floor of the ivory tower. Her long black silky hair was sticking out the window.
"All this attention is so tiring for Rosa."
"But someone has to do it."
"It is so hard to be pretty."
"Ahh the attention is relaxing."

Down below was a man named Joe. He always stood by the side watching the men asking for Rosa's hand. He decided to wait and said a simple hello to Rosa. The next day Joe saw Rosa alone. He decided to talk to her. He talked about his big apartment. It had a big, big bed. It was king size with seven big pillows. You can put your body anywhere on the bed and have room to spare. You should come and try the King size bed. Rosa looked away and said, "Whatever makes you happy." Joe felt very foolish. You see Joe realized he accidentally got creepy. So he did not talk to her for three days. He stood by the side.

The third day came. He knew that she was thirty years old. All women by thirty had at least one broke boyfriend. They vow to never, ever date a man with no money. So naturally, joe talked about money. Rosa was pleased. The next day Joe said, “Hello!” Then he said nothing more. Joe smiled, he had her attention. Joe went back to the side.

Finally, the day came. Rosa went to the podium. Men from all over the mall were screaming, “Rosa!! Rosa!! Pick me Rosa!!” She banged her hammer.

“Order!!”

“Order!!”

“IOTA!!”

Slam went the hammer!!

“I have made my decision on a man to date.”

“ROSA,” they screamed. Four men panicked and smashed through windows on the second floor. No Yoddy the virgin to land on.

“I have chosen the nerdy rich kid from Burbank.”

Two more men smashed through the second floor window. This time they landed on Yoddy’s fat brother Yahtzee. Then Yoddy ate them. Boy, were they salty.

Men screamed, “The rich kid shocking, I say I say shocking!!”

Then men said sarcastically, “Oh I didn’t see that coming!’’

“Joe you came in second.”

“You would have came in a stronger second if you had a car and an apartment.”

Joe said, “Isn’t second still losing?”

Joe smiled and said to himself, “That won’t last. Joe stood by the side. He calmly went to work and continued his life.

That night the victorious nerdy rich kid gave a ride to Joe. Joe was quiet. He cried in one eye. The nerdy rich kid said, “Are you crying?!” Joe said, “Who cries in one eye!! “What am I, the fucking indian!!” he slammed the car door. Joe said, “ Mr. One eye says buy a fucking american car!!” “Many Mexican auto workers would be happy!!” The nerdy rich kid laughed and sped off in his Mazda. He went to his apartment. He quietly opened the door. He entered.

He cried and cried. “Oh mother, Oh mother she is so pretty!” There was a picture on the wall of his Mom with Mom glasses and peanut little titties. (Wow this is a disturbing statement!) Each side of the Mom picture had a lite candle. Suddenly, Joe shouted, “She is so PRETTY, SO PRETTY.” He ran for the thick sliding door window. SLAMM!!! He fell down and saw the grease spot of his forehead, on the window.

His mother’s spirit appeared.

“You fucking loser!!”

"You fucked up another suicide!!"
SLAMMM!!! Joe's mother hit his right cheek with an iron skillet.
SLAMMM!!! She hits him on the left cheek.
SLAMMM!!! She hits him with an uppercut.
"Can't you find a nice girl and settle down."
"You mean an ugly woman!"
"I 'd rather be alone!"
SLAMMM!!! She hit the left cheek. Poor Joe got dizzy and fell to the floor. It was covered in beautiful 1970s carpet.
"What are doing with an iron skillet ?"
"I got it from your illegitimate son, you fucking loser!"
SLAMMM!!! She hit the top of his head.
"You are not so special dickhead!"
Joe was expecting another hit, but mom's spirit disappeared. Then he smelled smoke. The paper under the candles caught fire. The sprinkler system went off. The fire alarm went on. Joe laid on the floor.

The next day, Rosa did not appear at work. She left the mall. She rode her white horse, never to return. Joe went searching for her.
"Rosa!"
"Rosa!"
"Where are you?!"
Joe went to the crying cave of Puerto Ricans. He went inside and cried for Rosa. There were other Puerto Ricans crying for their girls. One was crying for Juanita. One was crying for Roberta. One was crying for Maria. Their cries echoed throughout the cave. Then the fat guy Santiago was crying for his mother. No girlfriend. Then Joe left the cave. He once again was searching for Rosa. He looked far and near. He even went back to East L.A. No Rosa. Then one day he crossed a river to get to a far away land called Pasadena. Then he found her.
"Rosa!"
"Rosa!"
"It is me, Joe!"

He ran to her. He was met with a net and many stun guns by the police. Rosa's nose twitched, the foul smell from Joe was intense. Joe started twitching and drooling. One policeman said, "You look like a reasonable man." " There are other pretty girls out there. So leave so I can hit on her." Joe left twitching profusely.

Thirty years have passed. Joe is in an old folks home with Alzheimer's. He thinks the pretty girl of long ago. He finds out that the nerdy rich kid of Burbank marries an unattractive Asian woman. He still lives with his parents. He lives there with his unattractive kids and a screaming wife. Joe sits on his rocking chair at the old folks home. He is talking to himself. He talks about the imaginary date with Rosa. They are sitting at a steakhouse. Over and over again, he tells Rosa; "Eat the filet , eat the filet side of the porterhouse steak." A black orderly screams, "SHUT THE FUCK UP WHITE BOY!!!" Joe repeats, "Eat the filet; eat the filet side." "White boy shut up!!" Joe replies, "Excuse me but I am spanish." SLAMMM!!! The orderly hits him with an iron skillet. "There's your filet side motherfucker!"

Joe's mother spirit appears. She looks at her son.

"I give up!"

"What a fuckiing loser!"

She takes the iron skillet away from the orderly.

"I need this iron skillet!"

"My other son is fucking around on his wife again." She appears to her other son George. "SHE HAS TWO JOBS YOU IDIOT!!!" SLAMMM!!! Right to the balls. I was going to say the family jewels. But fuck it.

MIKE TYSON

I was at Honolulu Airport in Hawaii. I was picking up a passenger. You see, I was a limo driver.

"Hey Joe."

"Yea John."

"Did you know you are going to pick up Mike Tyson?"

"My sign says James."

"That is his assistant."

I was stunned. People do not realize the responsibilities I have as a limo driver. As a limo driver, I did tours around Pearl Harbor and the island of Oahu. I also picked up very powerful people. This included movie stars, ceos, and dignitaries. They came on commercial flights and corporate jets. I needed a ramp license to pick up people from corporate jets. But my favorite pick up was Mike Tyson.

Mike Tyson came in a commercial jet. He was built like the Hulk. He said very little. He came with two women. A dominican and the third runner up of Ms. Canada. We went to the to the limo and a bunch of Japanese reporters came rushing to the vehicle. They asked me if Mike Tyson was in the limo. I said,

"No. I have an accountant inside the limo." They stood there, twenty in all. Then Mike Tyson came out. He conversed with the journalists. They asked Mike if he is excited about the K-2 fights. He stated, "I am looking forward to the K- 2 fights at Aloha Stadium."

The K-2 fights are very popular in Japan. They take popular fighters from all over the world. They would put sumo wrestler against a kung fu artist. A boxer against a Karate fighter. A professional wrestler against a Tae Kwon Do fighter. The most popular fighter was a 7 ft. 2 inches tall wrestler named Giant Baba. They were trying to entice Mike Tyson to become a K-2 fighter. The whole trip was sponsored by the K-2 organization , so they put him up at the Kahala Hotel. When the limo arrived at the hotel. Mike's assistant left the vehicle. He went to Room # 242 and paid two hookers to leave the hotel. Then he called Mike on the phone and said, "Come on up." Mike went up with two giant hotel bodyguards.

Mike stood at the hotel for four days. On the second day, he went to the K-2 fights at Aloha Stadium. He was accompanied by his two lady friends. On the third day, his lady friends left the island of Oahu. On the fourth day, I went to pick up Mike at 8:30 A.M. Of course at 11:30 A.M., I am still waiting for Mike. Then at 11:35 A.M. a beautiful black Mercedes Benz GLS550 SUV arrives. It is customized with lots of chrome. The sound of the muffler is throaty. It arrives like it owns the parking lot. It is of course parked in front of the Kahala Hotel. The driver's door opens. A fat, fat white girl comes out of the SUV. She gives the key to the valet guy. She waits in the lobby. I say to myself, "This can't be for Mike!" Mike comes out and says, " Hey Pickles!" You see she was so fat that she was shaped like a pickle. Hence the nickname Pickles. She got in the limo with Mike. Then we went to the airport.

We arrived at Honolulu Airport at 12:35 P.M. I parked my limo in front of Continental Airlines. I opened my door. I went to open the passenger side. I opened the door six inches, Mike slammed the door. He almost took my arm off. Ten seconds later, the limo starts shaking. I didn't know that shock absorbers could be that squeaky. Then all is quiet with the limo. Mike comes out with his belt unbuckled and his zipper down. He says, "That was great Pickles!!" Then he drops $800 on fatso's lap. Mike looks at me, "Hey Mr. Limo, drive Pickles back to the hotel." I said, "Yes sir Mr. Tyson!" I returned to my vehicle and put the divider up. I figured a girl this fat might have a gas problem. I returned to the hotel. Of course, no tip was involved.

MAMA'S BOY

There was a forty year old man who lived with his mother. She would talk about the evils of women. The forty year old virgin would listen. Therefore he was terrified of the ladies. My great grandma Bonita Ribot thought this was hysterical. The virgin had black curly hair, beady black eyes and wore black rim glasses. He would comb his little black mustache all day long. He was five foot four and of course never worked. From time to time, he would peek through the beige blinds. Bonita would wave and smile. He would stare and panic. Then Bonita would laugh. He was so pathetic. He would leave the window in a hurry. Then his mother would scream, "What is that woman doing to my boy?!" Bonita would laugh and say, "That woman screamed the man out of him!" Then she lit her cigar and made some smoke rings.

Everyone was in the house. My grandmother Isabel was cleaning the rooms. The three children were doing chores. My grandfather Jose was cutting oranges and putting them into his glass jug of ice tea. There was Mr. Peek-A-BOO again. Bonita said, "Shhh!" She puts the shade half way up. He combs his little mustache. He puts his black beady eyes between the blinds and looks at Bonita's ass. She knows and puts her cigar down. Then she plays the radio nice and loud. She shakes her ass like nobody's business. She puts her right index finger in the air and shakes that too. Isabel is screaming, "Madre! Madre!" The ass was moving faster and faster. Then the song ended. She thrust her ass out. He fell on his ass. He broke some of his mother's figurines on the way to the floor. Bonita was hysterically laughing. She listened to his mother scream at her stupid son. "Get up!" " Your shirt will get dirty!" Bonita is laughing even harder. My grandmother was yelling at Bonita, "Madre!! Madre!!" Then she points at her two daughters. Bonita can't stop laughing. My grandmother looks at Jose, he is just laughing and laughing. He calls Bonita a crazy woman.

Well Mr. Peek-A-Boo got up again and of course broke more figurines. His mother screams, "Sit down you idiot!!Tuck in your shirt!!" Bonita COULD NOT STOP LAUGHING!! Then Mr. forty year old was told to go to his room. Bonita finally calmed down. She took her cigar off the counter. Then lit the cigar. She walked to the porch and sat down on the rocking chair. She called her grandson, " Angel, venaca." My Dad sat on her lap. He looked at her with his four year old eyes and said, "What the hell is wrong with him?!"
"Ahhh, Angel he is a Mama's Boy!"

BATBOY

My dad was an eight year old boy. He lived in a small town. One day he was walking and came upon a yellow house. He looked underneath the porch and noticed a brown bat. My dad looked surprised. Then he decided to go to his father's grocery store. He went to the liquor shelf and grabbed a pint of clear Bacardi. He returned to the yellow house. He went underneath the porch. Then he opened the bottle. He poured a little Bacardi into the cap. He took his right hand and put the cap next to the bat's mouth. The bat's tongue came out and drank the Bacardi. The tongue looked like a pink stick of bubblegum. My father thought it was the coolest thing. Then the bat fell on his face. My dad laughed. Then my father had an idea.

He runs to his house. He grabs the canaries and throws them out of the cage. They chirped in a panic. My Dad runs back to the yellow house. He grabs the drunk bat and puts it in the cage. He runs back to his house. He enters and sees a table at the end of the hallway. He removes some pictures from the table. Then he puts the cage on top of the table. He waits for the bat to recover. Then the bat hangs upside down on the perch. Then my Dad puts a black dish towel over the cage.

My dad leaves the house. He runs down the street and yells, "Bat Show!!" " Bat Show!!"
"Come and see my Bat Show!!'
"I will charge one penny for the Bat Show!"
Twenty kids show up at his house. The show begins. He announces to the kids, "I will now have the bat smoke!!"

My father grabs his grandmother's cigars in a draw. The wooden matches are next to the cigars. He has seen his grandmother smoke so many times. He knew what to do. What he didn't realize was how disgusting a cigar can taste to an eight year old. My Dad begins to get sick. However, the show must go on. He takes his right hand and puts the cigar near the cage.The bat leaves the perch. He walks to the cigar. To my Dad's surprise, the bat begins to smoke. The girls scream. The boys laugh.

My Dad puts the cigar down. Then he unscrews the cap from the Bacardi. He fills the cap with liquor. Then he puts the cap near the bat. Once again, the pink tongue comes out. It drinks the Bacardi and falls in the cage. My Dad looks puzzled. The kids begin to boo. My father begins to panic. He opens the cage, grabs the bat. He throws it in the air. The bat is flying drunk. He hits the walls of the hallway. The kids are screaming and running out of the house. The bat falls to the floor. The bat begins to vomit. My dad is puzzled, "Is the bat sick?!"

His mother returns from her errands. She looks on the floor and sees a drunk bat. The canaries are flying around the house in a panic. There is a lit cigar on the table. A bottle of Bacardi is opened. Then there is a face of a frightened eight year old boy. He stands next to the bat vomit. And so the ass whipping begins.

UNCLE BENNY

Uncle Benny was a pot smoking nut. He lived in Miami Beach, Florida. He graduated high school in 1975. In the summer of 1976, my brother and I went to Miami Beach for two wonderful weeks. He picked us up at Miami Airport, barefooted. We drove to a bar, Uncle Benny entered barefooted. We drove to a pool hall, Uncle Benny entered barefooted. The heat during the day was unbearable. However, Uncle Benny continued to walked barefooted. Oh, I forgot to mention. I was 16 years old. My brother was 14 years old. Uncle Benny was 19 years old. I tried to walk barefooted but the Florida heat said put your sneakers on.

Florida had over five thousand people a day moving into the state. This did not include the snowbirds. The state was overwhelmed. My uncle had a lot of unpaid parking tickets. He decided to decorate his wall with 300 parking tickets. I know, I counted them. Then he told us that he works at a gas station. Occasionally, someone would forget their credit card. So one Friday afternoon he calls the house.

I answered the phone. "Hey dickhead! Today my name is Michael Schmidt. I'll pick you two idiots up in two hours." When he arrived he said, "We are going to buy a few things." We went to the store and bought a 12 pack of beer, styrofoam chest and ice. We filled his car with gas and went to the beach. We meet his friends and drank. The beers were done. So Uncle Benny threw out the cans and styrofoam chest. We went to another store, bought a new styrofoam chest and a case of beer. This time he bought ten pounds of ice. We went to another another beach meet more friends. Then we finished the beer. Then we went to a record store and bought seven albums. We went back to the house, took showers and went to his friend's house to get fake ids for my brother and I. Then we went bar hopping. We picked up some girls and went to the diner. We ordered quite a bit of food. Mr. Schmidt left a hell of a tip.

The next morning we went to a gas station to fill up his car. The credit card was still good. We went to another beach. Then I discovered Uncle Benny does not pay tolls. You see some of the toll booths had no crossbar. So Uncle Benny would get to the toll booth and make a ping noise. Then continue driving down the road. Then we got to the beach. Uncle Benny threw out Mr. Schmidt's credit card. It was so sad to see that card leave us. Christ we had to buy lunch. Later we went home of course Uncle Benny did not pay the toll.

It was day three. Uncle Benny said, "Let's go to the dump." He pulled up his mattress and beneath it was thirty rifles. He took three rifles and some ammo. He put them in the trunk of his car. Then I said, "Are they loaded?!" He said, "Of course dickhead! Okay fuckface!!" Then we drive to the dump. We arrive and start looking for empty clorox bottles. We found six empty clorox bottles. Then we hit paydirt and found a moldy watermelon and some wine bottles. We put them on top of an abandoned car. I asked Uncle Benny, "Did ummm Mr. Schmidt pay for the rifles?" He said, "No dickhead! Just asking Buttmunch!"
"Mr. Carter paid!" We laughed and started shooting.

The next day Benny returned from the gas station with two credit cards. He said,"We are going to Disney." We packed our bags and decided to leave in the morning. We took the back roads to avoid tolls. Then we arrived at a motel with a pool. Benny uses a credit card. I said, "Why thank you Mr. Flaherty!" Benny gave me such a look. When we left the check in desk Benny looked at me and said, " SHUT THE FUCK UP MORON!!" I did not challenge him. We go to the room

and notice some girls at the pool. We are about to put on our bathing suits. Then Benny says, "Let's go in the pool naked!" I said, "You mean commando!'Won't we get in trouble! No shit!" I was mad, I wanted to talk to the girls. But we went commando. We ran to the pool and did a cannonball.
I said, "Hey ladies what's shaking?!"
Then I said, "Hey Ben my dick is floating!"
"Is this a medical condition?!"
A girl screamed, "You are a dickhead!"
We could not stop laughing. Then we noticed a guy just sitting there.
I said, "What is your name?"
He said, "My name is Dick."
I said, "Why do parents name their son Dick?!"
"What is your mother's name, VAGINA!!"
"Oh I'm sorry is it PUSSY!!"
"How is your Dad, MR. PENIS!!"
"Why sir is that acne!"
"No this is HERPES!!"
We were hysterically laughing. So we dragged our naked asses back to the motel room.

There was a knock on our door. Then a voice said, "Security!!" Uncle Ben put his finger to his lips and softly whistles. The security guy knocks three more times. Then he leaves, there was an awkward silence. We packed our bags and quickly leave the motel. We ride for two more hours and arrive at another motel. We are about to check in I yelled, "We have arrived Mr. Flaherty!" Uncle Benny gave me such a smack. I did not talk for over an hour.

We finally reached Disney World. In the parking lot, we smoke a joint. Then we take a kiddy train to the waterpark. We had so much fun that we went to the waterpark a second day. Then we went to the amusement park for three days in a row. Compliments of Mr. Jensen's credit card. We left and did two more motels. Uncle Benny was getting nervous about the credit cards. However, we arrive at Miami safe and sound. Uncle Benny threw out the credit cards twenty miles north of Miami. For the next week we never go to IHOP sober. It was a miracle that no food fights occurred. This is because we had to PAY FOR OUR MEALS!!

One afternoon, I helped Uncle Benny change his oil. Then we played monopoly. Of course everyone cheated. We laughed so hard. Then my grandmother made us some dinner. We ate it sober. It felt weird. However, my stomach thanked me. The next morning we went to the airport. As always Uncle Benny was barefooted. We said our goodbyes and took the flight to New York City.

A year later, Uncle Ben gets laid off by Ford. So he joined the Army. He was stationed in Germany. So he decides to be a hashish dealer in the Army. He makes about a thousand dollars a month. He takes the money and goes skiing in Switzerland. You can ski in Switzerland all year long. Of course, Uncle Benny never gets arrested. However, he could no longer walk barefooted.

EIGHT

Uncle Benny was eight years old. He was only a nut. He was the youngest of four children and a spoiled brat. He was only two years older than me. I loved him like an older brother. Every Friday I had a ritual. I combed my hair with the same black plastic comb. Then I would get my little blue suitcase and fill it with good play clothes. I knew my dad washed the 1965 Chevy Impala every Friday. I would run to the car and stop. Then I would see how shiny the car was. I would open the back passenger door and put my suitcase to the left of me. My Dad would start the car. When he started that engine, then I got excited about going to grandma's house.

Yep going to grandma's house. Every Friday felt like a new vacation. First, we go to grandpa's grocery store. Every weekend I would look for toys. Every weekend there were no toys. It is a grocery store. But don't tell that to a six year old boy. Well grandpa would close his grocery store and ride with us. Grandma's house was on Ryer Avenue in the Bronx. It was near a police station. It was a light green two story house with a beautiful garden. My dad would drop us off and grandma always feed me a damn good meal. When morning came we went to the park. My uncle always insisted that I call him his cousin. Then we would hit a rubber ball against a big cement wall and catch it. I loved throwing that ball as hard as I can. Afterwards, we would watch the teenagers play basketball. Then we would have lunch at grandma's house. After lunch we would put our bathing suits on and go swimming in a neighbor's pool. They would feed us and then we return to grandma's house. This is where Uncle Benny became a pain in the ass.

Grandma would give the idiot money to get ice cream for the both of us. Instead, mister pretend cousin would buy an ice cream and a comic book for himself. I would put my hands into my empty pockets and watch the brat eat his strawberry shortcake ice cream and read his comic book. When we returned to grandma's house, I would go to the refrigerator and get ice cream. Of course, it was not a strawberry shortcake ice cream. It was something grandma liked. I learned to move on. My weekends at grandma's house was generally exciting.

Then one weekend my uncle found a key to the apartment upstairs. We went up the stairs and opened the door to the apartment. The place was spotless. You can eat off the floor. Uncle Benny would open up the refrigerator and get some ice cream for the both of us. Then we would sit on the recliners and read the stacks of comic books on the table. Afterwards, we would play with the train set. Then return to the recliners and watch tv. This went on for three weekends.

Then one sunny sunday my grandmother was making me lunch.
I said, "Hey Grandma?"
"How come you do not go upstairs to eat?"
"Your apartment up there is really nice."
"It has nice recliners. Grandpa's train set is really nice."
"The refrigerator has cool ice cream."
Suddenly, my grandmother had a puzzled look. I sensed something was wrong. So I cease to talk. My grandmother said very little for the rest of the day.

It was 8pm. My uncle and I were tucked away in our little beds. I heard grandpa opening the door. My grandparents were speaking spanish in a certain tone. When a spanglish child hears spanish this meant TROUBLE. The grandparents went quiet. My grandfather entered the bedroom. Boy did that door open fast. He walked fast to my uncle and beat him with his fists. Then my grandfather left the room. I pretended to be sound asleep. Then I awoke and pretended to be all confused. I said, "Whha what's going on?" I rubbed my right eye. Then my grandparents were arguing in Spanish. My grandmother went to the bedroom door. She inspected it. She discovered that my grandfather broke a hinge off the door. They spoke more spanish. Then the argument ended with my grandfather saying in english, "That kid drives me crazy!" My grandparents then went to their bedroom.

I visited that house every weekend for the next two years. Then my grandfather retired. He sold the store and the house on Ryer Avenue. One day we all went to grandma's house. I had no idea that they were taking a final flight to Miami,Florida. I saw grandpa in black suit, white shirt and gray tie. The slacks were black and cuffed. The shoes were black italian loafers. My grandmother wore a blue dress with white pearls. The shoes were 1960s style two inch heels. My uncle had a blue polyester suit with a white shirt. The tie was a plaid clip on. The shoes were buckle brown shoes. He carried on his right arm 12 comic books.

We drove to JFK Airport with luggage in my dad's chevy. My grandparents and Uncle Benny arrived earlier in a yellow cab. We finally arrived at American Airlines. I walked into the terminal with my mom and dad. My grandparents and Uncle Benny were waiting for their flight. I heard the intercom say, "Flight 24 now boarding for Miami Beach." We all stood up and hugged each other. Then I watched my grandpa, grandmother and uncle Benny board the plane. I stood there and watched the plane taxi out. My Dad then said, "Come on son time to go home.'' We got back to the car and my Dad said, "Joe, your grandparents and uncle Benny are moving to Florida." I was overcome with grief. I got in the backseat of the 1965 Chevy Impala and cried quietly. The drive back to the Bronx was numbing.

For the next three years, Benny and I wrote each other. I could not wait for the letters. Then one day, grandma and Benny came to visit the Bronx. We began to play fight in the kitchen. The fighting got serious. The friendship to my uncle ended. When he returned to Florida, he never wrote a letter to me again. Oddly, it did not bother me. Four years later the friendship returned. Then one year later it ended for good.

ONE MORE BENNY STORY

Dear old Benny. He never disappoints. It was New Years Eve 1977. We left the apartment in the Bronx and took the subway to Times Square. It was Benny, my brother Ed and I. We arrived at Times Square at 8 P.M. We went to the nearest grocery store and bought a case of beer. Then we walked to the center of Times Square, put our beer on the ground and began to drink. I asked the police officer if he wanted a beer. He replied, "Don't be an asshole!'' I just laughed and the officer said, "Just have a good night." Then the three of us grabbed a beer and began to drink. Then two attractive girls came to us. The blonde girl asked me for some beer. So I grabbed two beers and gave it to the girls. We made some small talk. They were not friendly. Then two guys started to grab their attention. The girls asked for more beer. I said, "Sorry! The beer is for us. Nice meeting you." Then we started to talk to other girls.

It is now 9 P.M. The crowd is getting larger. I noticed couples wearing party hats and glasses that said 1977. People were getting drunk and swaying back and forth. There was nowhere to move. I am 16 years old and having a blast. In a four block radius there are over 500,000 people. Then Uncle Benny starts screaming.

He decides to put his hoodie on. Then I watched the smoke of winter leave his mouth. Then his screaming was forming into words. He was drunk. He was high. He kept on screaming, "LSD, COCAINE, MARIJUANA, HASHISH, PCP, AAAAA!!! LSD, COCAINE, MARIJUANA, HASHISH, PCP, AAAA!! He said this phrase over and over again. Finally I yelled, "Hey Loser!! Quiet!!" Of course he did not listen. So I reached into his coat and gave him a nasty titty twister. He screamed, "AAA you dick!" So, I gave him another one. Funny thing, he tried PCP once. He thought the television set was going to swallow him. He hated the drug.

It was 10 P.M. The crowd was getting larger. All of the people were pinned in. You stayed in your position.I started looking at people who were not happy about being there. I watched some young girls screaming at their boyfriends, "Get me out of here! Please get me out of here!!" Then I watched other girls just crying on their boyfriends chest. Other people began to panic and rushed the police barricades. Then, just like that, it became calm.

It was 10:15 P.M. Fifty teenager boys were pushing through the crowd and punching people in the face. If you went unconscious they picked your pocket. This went on for three minutes. Then the police came in swinging their nightsticks and throwing muggers to the ground. I watched several teenage boys get arrested. Then I unexpectedly got hit with a nightstick. It was pretty painful. Then once again it was calm.

It was 11:59 P.M. There was over one million people in Times Square. I watched the New Year's Eve ball begin to drop. Then one million people began to scream, 10-9-8-7-6-5-4-3-2-1. The ball lights up and everyone shouts, "HAPPY NEW YEAR!!!" People blow their party horns. Young couples kiss. I gave another titty twister to my uncle. He yells, "Cut the shit!!" So I gave a titty twister to my brother. He just looked stunned.

We began to leave Times Square. Then a teenage boy ran to an elderly man and punched him in the face. The old man hit the pavement pretty hard. He was unconscious. The mugger took his wallet and ran. I decided to stay over the gentleman's body and talk to his wife. The police came within two minutes. Then I said goodbye to the lady and walked to the train station.

We took the number two train to 180th street. Then we waited in a heated room for the number five train. The train arrived at 2:00 A.M. We arrived at Dyre Avenue at 2:30 A.M. Then we walked to the projects. We arrived at our building and took the elevator up. I opened the door to our apartment. We went into our bedroom and fell asleep.

We finally woke up at noon. We went into the kitchen and heard my Dad say that the bedroom smelled like a brewery. We laughed. Then Benny, my brother and I had our first breakfast of 1977.

TRUE EVENTS

TABLE OF CONTENTS

The world can be a cruel, cruel place.

Brazil

Soccer is a serious sport around the world. This includes the country of Brazil. During a game against Columbia, a bunch of Brazilians went to the top of the stadium and dropped a refrigerator on the Columbian fans. The Columbians went to the roof to look for the culprits. Instead they meet some Brazilians on the way. A fight broke out. Then security came and assisted the police with arrest. Then more fights broke out in the stadium and water cannons were used to control the crowd. Finally, the soccer game began.

All referees in soccer carry weapons to protect themselves. They are under constant threat from opposing fans. During the game, an argument broke out between the referee and the Brazilian soccer star. The argument got intense. The crowd was starting to boo. The argument between the soccer player and the referee was getting worse. Then the referee took out his knife and stabbed the soccer player. The soccer player died on the field. The fans were furious. They began to enter the soccer field. Their star player was a thirty year old man named Josenir Dos Santos Abreu. The referee was named Jordan Silva. At first, it was a dozen fans. Then a dozen more men came on the field. Finally, over four hundred fans entered the soccer field. They trampled over the dead body of a soccer player. The referee was fearing for his life.

Finally, the crowd caught the referee. They stumped and beat him. The fear in his face was primal. Then they begin to stretch his body. They stretch and stretch. Then the referee's head and legs are removed from his body. The head remained alive for ten seconds. He saw his torso on the field. Then the fans began to shake his head and legs in victory. The broadcasters were acting like it was another day in soccer. It just stunned me.

What shocked me most was the Brazilian news. It was their top story. They go to an autopsy room. Then show a torso. They speak some Portuguese and put the guy's head on to identify him. Then more Portuguese is spoken. Then they put his legs on to say, "Yea those are his legs." Then they go to commercial break and then return to the autopsy room. This is repeated four more times. Afterwards, they calmly report that out of four hundred men. There were only four arrest. Yep, the world is coming to an end. The leader is Brazil.

KANSAS

It was nightfall. A small town called Lawrence, Kansas was burning. The bullets were flying everywhere. Fifteen slave traders lay dead in the streets of Lawrence. A man named John Brown walks slowly around the town. He observes the carnage and looks for more slave traders to kill. The barrel of his Winchester lays on his right shoulder. He has a militia of thirty men. This included five of his sons and six free black men. Jacob the oldest son speaks, "Father."

"Yes Jacob."

"Two slave traders ran into that building."

"They carry no weapons."

John Brown walks slowly to the building. He faces it. He takes the rifle off his right shoulder. He points the barrel of the rifle to the ground. Then he puts his right index finger on the trigger. Three militiamen make sure that the building catches fire.

Then John Brown yells, "SLAVE TRADERS!!"

"COME OUT!!"

"COME OUT OF THAT BURNING BUILDING !!"

"SO I CAN KILLYA!!"

He cocks his rifle. He puts the butt of his rifle against his right shoulder. His left eye is above the barrel. He waits patiently. The two men are beginning to cough from the smoke. They slowly come out of the building. They are about to put their hands up. John Brown shot them dead. Now there are seventeen dead slave traders in the town of Lawrence, Kansas.

Mr. Brown walks to his son. The son says, "Father tomorrow a dozen stagecoaches will be on a trail heading toward Kansas City, Kansas. There will be slaves with them."
Mr. Brown says, "We will meet them at sunrise."
The son says, "We can hide behind the trees and fire our rifles. The element of surprise will be to our advantage.''
Mr. Brown says, "No. We will fire our rifles face to face!"

It is sunrise. The militia is hiding behind the trees. The thirty men cock their rifles. Mr. Brown carries his rifle in his right hand. The barrel is facing toward the ground. All thirty men walk toward the stagecoaches.
Mr.Brown says, "HALT!!"
"HALT SLAVE TRADERS!!"
"Why are you putting God's children in bondage?!!"
A slave trader from the south is chewing tobacco. He says, "God's children?!"
"They are nothing but a bunch of niggers!"
"NIGGAAS!!" Mr. Brown says.
"WILL MEET YOUR ALL TIME FAVORITE NIGGER LOVER!!"

The militia begins to shoot. The slave trader who said the word nigger is shot in the face five times. Mr. Brown feels the vile hatred of the slave traders with every shot fired. Then a militia screams, "Gauntlet at two o'clock!" Four militia lay dead. One black militia is seriously hurt. Finally, the man shooting the gauntlet is killed. The blood leaving his body gushed like a firehose. The shooting continues. Then Mr. Brown shouts, "Ceasefire !"

He notices that all the slave traders lay dead. He walks toward the wounded black militia. Mr. Brown says, "Jeremiah stay with me, stay with me son." He tells another militia man, "Put a jacket underneath his head." "Jeremiah please stay with me." Mr. Brown and the militia approach the dead slave traders. They go through their pockets and remove some keys. These keys release the black men and women from their chains. Then Mr. Brown explains to them that there is a community of free slaves. They live twenty miles north of the trail. It is a two or three day walk.

He picked up the rifles from the dead slave traders. Then he gave them to the free slaves and said to use them to kill game. He wished them well. Then he returned to Jeremiah.

Mr. Brown asked the militiaman, "How much did he witness?"
The militiaman responded, " he only saw the first man being freed."
Mr. Brown said in a disappointed voice, "Ok. Let's give our dead a proper burial."

It is nightfall. Mr. Brown and his men surround a campfire. Mr. Brown's son Jacob lights a kerosene lamp. He approaches his father. Mr. Brown takes out a map of Harper's Valley. Mr. Brown's states, "Gentlemen Harper's Valley is located in Virginia." Immediately, some of the men show concern. However, Mr. Brown is in charge they will not question him.

Mr. Brown speaks, "Gentlemen here lies an arsenal of rifles and guns. This train station in Harper's Valley holds twenty thousand rifles and guns. The train cars will be full. They do not have very many guards. We can take these rifles and guns at 3 A.M. We will receive very little resistance. This will be done quickly. We leave at the crack of dawn.

They arrive at the outskirts of Harper's Valley at night. At 3 A.M., they quietly move into Harper's Valley. The scouts were right the arsenal is poorly guarded. They quietly strangle and stab the guards. They break the lock on one train car. They grab three hundred rifles and guns. Then they see a wooden box separate from the rifles and guns. They open it and see a large quantity of ammo. So they take the box. There were two guards that went unnoticed. One blew a whistle. The guards were killed instantly. However, the townspeople hear the commotion and went to investigate with rifles in hand. A gun battle ensues. John Brown and his men retreat to a firehouse for cover.

The confederate soldier's are informed that a gun battle in Harper's Valley is currently in progress. The soldier's arrive at dusk. The general in charge of the confederate soldier's is Robert E. Lee. Mr. Brown is badly outnumbered within a few hours he is defeated. Everyone in his militia lays dead before him. This included his five sons. The confederate soldiers made sure that Mr. Brown is taken alive.

The date was October 11, 1859. Mr. Brown is put on trial. The trail takes several weeks. The day comes for his verdict. The jury finds him guilty. The judge has Mr. Brown stand up.
"Mr. Brown!"
"The state of Virginia finds you guilty of treason. Do you understand these charges?" Mr. Brown responds, "Yes I do your honor." "Very well then. Escort this prisoner to a penitentiary located in Charlestown, Virginia.

On December 2, 1859. There are six confederate soldiers who arrive at his jail cell. They open the jail cell.
A confederate soldier says, "Mr. Brown, please stand up." Mr. Brown responds. The confederate soldier reads a letter from Governor Henry A. Wise. The letter states, "By the great state of Virginia, you are charged with treason. Today on December 2, 1859. You will hang by the neck until death. Do you understand this letter?" Mr. Brown says, "Yes.'' Then the confederate says, "Mr. Brown hands behind your back."

Mr. Brown is handcuffed. Then Mr. Brown tells the confederate soldier, " I have freed over eighty black men, women and children. I am ready to meet my maker." The confederate soldier says nothing. Mr. Brown is then escorted out of the penitentiary. Mr. Brown realizes that he has done well in God's eyes.

He goes down the stairs of the penitentiary. Then they put him in a small wagon. The two confederate soldiers sit Mr.Brown away from the horses.They hit the reins and the horses begin to move. Mr. Brown looks at his coffin. He shows no emotion. He has visions of free slaves enjoying their lives. Then he looks at 12 confederate soldiers following the small wagon.

They arrive at his hanging post. He walks up the wooden stairs. He can hear the sounds of his footsteps. He gets to the top of the stairs. He walks to the noose. The preacher ask God to have mercy on this man's soul. Then the preacher ask Mr. Brown for any last words. Mr. Brown looks at the one thousand soldier's before him.
He begins to speak, "War is coming!"
"It will be vicious."
"Blood will cover this great nation."

"Many men, women and children will die."
"Great cities will burn."
"One side will be victorious."
"Make no mistake slavery will end."
"Because it is evil."
"Okay preacher it is time to meet my maker."

The noose is put on Mr. Brown's neck. The lever is pulled. A small portion of the floor gives way. Mr. Brown's neck is broken. He is dead.

Throughout the north, church bells ring in his honor. In the south, they celebrate the death of a terrorist. During the Civil War, the Union soldiers arrive at the firehouse in Harper's Valley. Each soldier takes a brick from the firehouse. It is a souvenir to these soldiers. The war ended in 1865. There are over five hundred thousand people died in this war. The north is victorious. Slavery in the south ends. Mr. Brown becomes a folk hero. He is now part of American History.

THE CANNIBALS OF HAWAII

Two thousand years ago, the first settlers came to Hawaii. The archaeologist feel that they settled in Oahu and Kauai. They came from the Marquesas Islands. The Marquesas Islands were fifteen hundred miles southeast of Hawaii. They were polynesian. They were cannibals. The second group arrived five hundred years later from Tahiti. They were polynesian. They were not cannibals. They eventually became the majority. The Tahitians on Oahu became known a Oahuians. The Oahuians decided to put the Marquesas people on the west side of the island. There the Marquesas people practiced cannibalism. An agreement was made. If an Oahuian commited murder outside of war, he was punished. The punishment, you will now live with the cannibals. You were escorted to the west side of the island by warriors. They left you with a jug of water and three days of food. They point you to a trail and they would watch you walk. Within three or four days, the cannibals would capture and eat you.

By 1600 A.D., the cannibals were no longer happy with just prisoners. The supreme leader of the Marquesas people had a discussion with all seven tribes. He began his speech, "My people, we were the first settlers of Oahu. Yet we take scraps from these Oahuians. I am no longer happy with this arrangement." The leader of the third cannibal tribe spoke, "Supreme leader if we do not abide by this agreement they will kill us." The supreme leader did not like being questioned. " So you are happy with the scraps." The leader of the third cannibal tribe said, "We have an agreement."

The supreme leader was getting disrespected. So he gave a look to his most loyal warriors. They got up and killed the leader of the third cannibal tribe. Then the supreme leader ask, "Does anybody else disagree ?" There was complete silence from the other tribal leaders. The discussion was over and the supreme leader went to talk to his priest. The conversation ended and a religious ceremony began. Once the ceremony ended the dead man was consumed.

The supreme ruler discussed with his other leaders what village of Oahuains would he attack first. They decided to travel on a trail that led to the top of the Waianae Mountains. There they made a decision to attack a small fishing village of one hundred people. The supreme ruler stated, " there are about twenty men in that village. We will attack tomorrow at dusk."

They returned to their villages and prepared for the hunt. Weapons were chosen. The spears and knives were sharpened. Then four hundred cannibals went to the top of the Waianae Mountains and waited for dusk. When dusk came the supreme leader said, "They are eating now it is time for the attack. Remember we only eat the men, because the women are impure." The cannibals picked up their spears and quietly went down the mountain.

There were twenty huts in all. Each hut was attacked by ten cannibals. The men were taken out of their huts and killed. The women and children watched in horror. The men were stacked upon each other like dead animals. The hunt was completed. The cannibals stood guard over the dead men. They laughed and felt pride from their hunt. Then they tied the dead men's hands and feet to thick sticks. The cannibal leader told the frightened villagers, "Take care my Oahuians. We will return." Then they picked up the dead Oahuian men and walked back to the top of the mountain.

The cannibals went back to their villages before dark. They put their kill in the fish ponds that surrounded their huts. Then they proceeded to make a campfire. They drank and told stories about their hunt. Then they retired for the night.

The sun rose and the cannibals prepared for their meal. Some of them were making new tattoos. The others were filing their teeth. You see the Marquesas people made sure that all of their teeth looked like fangs. They sharpened them before eating human flesh. It was a ritual. When the meal was over they found many uses for the bones. For example, the leg bones were used to make walking sticks. The skeleton heads were made into buckets that hold bait for fishing. Then they would take the finger bones and break them in half. The top of the finger would be sharpened. Then the men would drink kava until their face was numb. Afterwards, the elders would make two incisions in front of the head. Then two incisions in the back of the head. Then the sharpened finger bones were put into the incisions and sealed.

Two days later, the cannibals attacked another village. This time the cannibals attacked with five hundred men. They killed thirty Oahuians. This time a fourteen year old Oahuian boy ran from the village and informed the next village about the cannibal attack. The village decided to get ready for an attack. Then they send a few warriors to the Kualoa Mountains. There they spoke to the supreme leader of Oahu. He was informed that there was at least a force of five hundred cannibals. He knew that not one Oahuian has any knowledge of cannibal country. So he decided to send four hundred of his best Oahuian warriors to cannibal country. However, he needed help. So he sent some of his commanders to the island of Kauai.

The commanders reached the shores of Kauai. They spoke to the supreme leader of the island. The leader decided to send his elite force of Kauain warriors. They were the best warriors the islands had to offer. They were mercenaries who handled very bad affairs. The cannibals of Kauai were killed off long ago. It was obvious that Oahu must do the same.

This elite force were hairless from head to toe. Their tattoos represented their lineage, speciality in warfare and the teacher who taught them. They have been in training since the age of six. They knew spear throwing, hand to hand combat as well as club and knife fighting. They were a force to be reckoned with. They numbered six hundred strong. The decision was made. They will help the Oahuains.

The morning sun of Kauai rose from the east. The elite forces of Kauai went to a religious ceremony. Then they did their haku dance in front of all the people of Kauai. Afterwards, they set sail for Oahu. They landed in front of the Kualoa Mountains. They were informed that two more villages were attacked. There was no time to waste. The allied forces of 1000 warriors walked to the west side of

Oahu. They make basecamp about five miles away from cannibal country. No one from Oahu or Kauai has ever entered cannibal territory. The commander of the Kauain forces made a decision to send scouts into cannibal country. No one from Oahu or Kauai has set foot in cannibal country.

Their mission is to locate the cannibal villages. The scouts kept their distance from the trails created by the cannibals. They decided to investigate the beach head that meet the Waianae Mountains. Their hunch was right. They saw seven villages in all.

They paid close attention to a particular village. There they saw a Marquesas man remove a dead Oahuian from the fish pond. He laid him on the ground then chopped his feet and hands off. Then he threw them to the pigs. A scout said, "The dead man has committed no crime. The cannibal has desecrated that man's body!" The scouts agreed all Marquesas men must die in battle. The cannibal then chopped the man's head off. The scouts have seen enough. They walk through the wilderness and find the trail that leads to the top of the Waianae Mountains. They decide to go to the top of the Waianae Mountains. There they see the carnage that the cannibals have caused. They return to the wilderness in disgust.

Then the scouts wait in the wilderness to see when the Marquesas men take to the trail that leads to the top of the mountain. The scouts see their enemy take the trail at dusk. A scout decides to take the cannibals. He is held back by the other scouts. They inform him that they must go back to base camp first. He agrees with mixed emotions. Then the scouts watch the cannibals reach the top of the mountain. Then they leave to base camp.

Upon arrival, the lead scout sees his commander. The commander then relays the information to the general. Then they discuss strategy to attack the cannibals. They agree to attack the enemy at the trail that leads to the top of the Waianae Mountains. Then the supreme commander informs his troops to ready their weapons. They will leave at sunrise to the trail. Then the commander said, "We will take no prisoners. All cannibals will die in combat." The cheers of all one thousand warriors are heard throughout the camp.

They patiently wait in the forest of the Waianae valley. The warriors know that every three days the cannibals take to the trail. The Kuaians lay their six hundred spears behind dozens of palm trees.They reach the open fields of the trail. Then they see 1200 cannibals walk up the Waianae trial. The cannibals have weapons of war and knives that cut into human flesh. The Kauain general speaks to the leader of the Oahuains. He says, "This is your aina. This is your island. When the spears are thrown. You will lead the way."

All six hundred spears were thrown in the air. When the spears made contact with the cannibals. One thousand warriors ran like deer to meet their enemy. Each warrior knew that now they must become lua warriors.

The battle was close and personal. Throats were slashed. Necks and torsos stabbed. Clubs layered with shark teeth are used on cannibal heads. Then there was hand to hand combat. The cannibals were no match for these warriors. However, primal screams of war were heard on both sides.

Finally, the battle is done. The cannibals are defeated. Not one is left alive. Unfortunately, some Kauains and Oahuians lay dead. A cannibal lays dead on a fallen Kauain warrior. The Kauain general yells, "Young one get this okole puka off my warrior!" The victors take care of their wounded and stay the night.

Morning came. They walked to the cannibal villages. They went hut to hut and killed any man who remained.Then the cannibal tools were put into a bonfire. The victors watch the cannibal tools burn. Afterwards, the woman and children were forced to gather in the middle of the main village. The commander of the Oahuains speaks, "Your practice of cannibalism will cease. Your husbands, lovers and brothers are dead. You are now slaves of the Oahuian and Kauain people." The commander of the Oahuains tells the oldest woman to speak. She replies, "We were the first settlers of these islands."

The commander replies, "I do not care. You are barbaric. The men who lay in your fish ponds will receive a proper burial. The cannibals we have killed will be feed to the sharks. Then we will have a ceremony. A kahuna will put a red tattoo on your forehead. This signifies that you are now a slave. You will not have new husbands. Your children will not be permitted to procreate as adults. The gods you worship will no longer be practiced. The idea of cannibalism will die with your children. The slaves who will go with the Kauains must be put in cages made of koa wood. They set sail in two days. Goodbye Marquesas people. Now the islands are in harmony."

The Oahuian supreme commander of the military tells his subordinates that they must send three hundred warriors to the west side of the Waianae. They must investigate each valley. The second valley had a cave. There they found fourteen male cannibals. They were killed instantly. The fourth valley also had a cave. They found ten more male cannibals. They were killed. Finally, they reached Kaena Point. No cannibals were found. Then they walked to the village of Mokuleia. They talked to their leader. They asked him if he had any problems with cannibals. He said no. The warriors of Oahu were pleased. They went home with a feeling of eternal peace.

THE KING OF HAWAII

The Mauian ruler meets with the religious leaders of Oahu. The meeting takes place at a religious site in the Kualoa Mountains. The religious leaders are called Kahunas. The Mauian chief speaks to the leader of the kahunas.

"Holy one. The Oahuian chief is a weak leader."
The leader of the kahunas speaks, "He is well liked in these islands."
The Mauian leader says, "Popularity will not protect him from war."
The kahuna speaks, "He may have alliances."
The Mauian leader replies, "They will not come if he is crushed. I am no longer happy with just Maui. I want Oahu!"
The kahuna says, "Do you want to speak to the Oahuian ruler?"
The Mauian ruler says, "No! I do not speak to weak rulers."

The religious leaders were concerned. They knew for years that he would be a problem. When the Mauian chief was a young man, he liked to put fear into his warriors for entertainment. He allowed only his left side to be tattooed. The tattoos were supposed to tell a story of his ancestors. Instead, he had violent acts of war. He was a thin man who stood at 6 ft. 7 inches tall. He weighed 210 pounds and had long wavy black hair. When he spoke many of his warriors wondered, will he torture me today?

The kahunas were alone. The head kahuna speaks.
"War is coming because of a bored King. Much blood will be spilled. The Oahuians are no match for the Mauians. The Mauians will come with an army of four thousand warriors. The Oahuians only have twenty five hundred."

Another kahuna speaks, "We must warn the Oahuain chief."
The seven kahunas returned to the Mauian chief. He looked at them and smiled. Then he waved his right hand. The kahunas looked concerned. Twelve assassins appeared out of the woods. They killed six kahunas. One kahuna ran for his life. He was no match for the assassin. The assassin swings his club and hits the back of the kahuna's skull. The kahuna falls to the ground. Much blood leaves his skull. Then the assassin hits the kahuna three more times. The kahuna is dead.

The kahunas are wrapped in wet banana leaves. Then put in fishnets. The fishnets are then tied to thick koa wooden sticks. They carry the dead bodies into the caves of the Kualoa Mountains. Then return to the island of Maui.

Two days later, a religious ceremony takes place in Maui. After the ceremony, a king must perform his strongest athletic feat. This must be done before going to war. For the Mauian chief, it was jumping from the highest point of Maui. He walked with his military commanders to the seven sacred pools. There he climbed to the top of the waterfall. He jumped one hundred feet. Then he swam to the shore to meet his commanders. There he speaks, "Gentlemen, tomorrow we go to war with the Oahuians. We will be victories!" He continues, "When the war is over. We will hunt down the Oahuain ruler and his eldest son. When found they will be stabbed to death. His wives and daughters will belong to me. Our kahunas will be the new religious leaders of Oahu."

The Mauians attack the island of Oahu on four sides. The Mauians are ruthless. Any warrior who does not attack with brutality is executed at the end of the battle. The war will last one month. Oahu is defeated. It is now under Mauian rule. The Mauian ruler speaks to his assassins, "You know your assignments! After the stabbings, I want the heads of the Oahuian ruler and his eldest son brought to me. Now leave my presence."

The Kona King of the big island received word of the Oahu war. The Mauian King was his grandfather. There was also another king on the big island. He was the King of Hilo. The Hilo King was his uncle. He hated both of them with a passion. They wanted war. He wanted peace. The people of the big island are called Hawaiians.

The Kona King speaks to his kahunas. He tells them, "My uncle has attacked my people three times. It is time to end these attacks. Kahunas gather my people. It is time to speak to my Hawaiians." The people gather and prepare to listen to the king.. The Kona King speaks, "I am tired of war. There will be no fourth attack. At dawn, we march to Hilo and defeat their king."

It was a four day march. They approach Hilo. The Kona King tells a stirring speech. Then the battle begins. The Kona King fights with honor. The Hilo King is defeated. The Kona King tells his uncle's troops, "You are now under my rule. Any attempt to reinstate the Hilo crown, will be met with deadly force." The King of Kona is now the King of Hilo. The whole big island is now under one rule. He consolidates the military. He now stands at eight thousand strong.

For one year, he prepares for the invasion of Oahu. He has many discussions with his kahunas and commanders. The discussions are about war and religion. Then one day he tells his commanders, "It is time to attack Oahu!"

The next day the warriors arrive at Kailua, Kona. The conch shells are blown. Then the warriors enter their outrigger canoes. All eight thousand warriors set sail for Oahu. They approach the island and attack from four sides. The biggest attack was Waikiki Beach. When they landed the fighting was fierce. The Hawaiians began to push the Mauians and Oahuians toward the Pali. The King of Hawaii set up base camp in Honolulu. The other three units consolidated in Kaneohe. The commander Aina informed the king that Kaneohe is now under Hawaiian rule. The war will soon be over. It is only a matter of time now. Then a problem arises.

Commander Aina approaches the war room. He enters and takes one look at the king. The king realizes that this is important. He leaves his other commanders and talks to Aina privately.
Aina says, "My king. Your first wife has taken a nineteen year old lover."
The King replies, "The Oahuians have an altar on top of the hill. Take him there. When the execution is completed, leave his body on the altar for one week. I will deal with my first wife."
Aina replies, "Yes my king." Then the king returns to the war room.

Commander Aina and a few men go to the hut of her lover. They grab and gag him. Then tie his hands and feet with rope made of coconut hair. The six warriors and Commander Aina drag the adultery to the altar. They take off his gag. Then release his hands and feet. Then put his back on the altar. The six warriors hold his hands and feet. Then Commander Aina grabs the club and smashes the skull of the adultery. The body is left on the altar. Aina and the warriors return to their duties.

The head kahuna goes to the King's hut and informs the first wife that she must meet the king in a hut for private affairs. He accompanies her to the hut. Then he informs her to sit alone and wait for the king. The king finishes his military strategy in the war room. Then Commander Aina meets with the king and walks with him to the hut were his first wife sits. Then the king enters the hut alone.

He speaks to his first wife, "If you were my second wife I would execute you. I have twenty two wives. You are the only one to commit adultery. So for one week you will live alone in this hut. Everyday you eat, you must pass by the altar of your dead lover. You will eat with common woman and eat common food. You will bow your head in shame. After the meal is completed, you will pass by the altar again. On the eighth day, I will enter this hut. Then you will immediately disrobe. The intimacy will be brief. I will then leave you. A common warrior will return to this hut and bring you back to my hut. Then you will apologize to my twenty one wives for your adultery." The king then returns to the war room.

The final plan of attack is completed. The king speaks, "We will have legions. Each legion will have one hundred men. The legions will be setup in Kaneohe and Honolulu. When the legion breaks they will fan out and go up the mountain. The jungles of the Pali will hide the Mauians well. The first layer of legions will have English rifles and guns. The second layer of legions will be the best lua warriors. Then the rest of the warriors will follow suit. We begin this attack at sunrise."

Sunrise came. The legions were setup. The conch shells were blown. The battle begins. The legions begin to fan out. A Mauian throws his spear at the neck of an Hawaiian. He goes down. Then more spears follow. The Hawaiians fire their english rifles. Afterwards, they run up the mountain. The fighting begins. Lives and limbs are lost. The fighting goes on for thirty days. The Hawaiians make it to the top of the Pali. The Hawaii king is informed that victory is at hand. The Mauians are cornered at the Pali cliff. There are five hundred left. Commander Aina tells his king they have 4000 men left. The king of Hawaii tells Commander Aina, "The Mauians have been brutalizing the Oahuians far too long. Do not take any prisoners push the Mauains off the cliff." Commander Aina states, "All five hundred." The king says, "Yes Aina and use the phalanx formation." Aina responds, "Yes my king." The order is followed and the victory belongs to the Hawaiians.

The king felt the warmth of victory. He then gives an order to his assassins. He says, "Find my grandfather and bring him to me alive!" He is found and brought to the King.

The assassins and the Mauiian chief enter the hut. The Hawaiian King looks at his grandfather.

The Mauian King speaks, "Disarm my hands and tell your assassins to leave."
The Hawaiian King speaks, "No grandfather I will not. The hands will stay tied and the assassins will stay with my warriors."

The Mauian chief speaks, " what is the meaning of this?! I am a King. I should not be in bondage. I will not speak again until the assassins leave my presence."

The king of Hawaii speaks, "Grandfather you are not a King. You are a murderer and a thief. This island of Oahu did not belong to you. The Oahuian chief was a man of honor. He was respected and loved by his people."
The Mauian king stated, "His military was weak and his belly was full. This beautiful island belonged to me. The Oahuian people were soft and easy to conquer. They would make such good slaves."
"Grandfather they are not slaves. Tomorrow at sunrise, you will die a criminal. The Oahuians will escort you to the altar where an adultery died. They will execute you. Then your body will be fed to the sharks."
The Mauian chief screams, "I AM NOT A CRIMINAL!! I AM A KING!!
The King of Hawaii speaks, "You are a murderer and a thief . Nothing more. Oahuians escort this criminal to his cage."
The Mauian chief yells, "You are no different than me. Who are...
"Goodbye grandfather."

The King of Hawaii helped to rebuild the island of Oahu. He also prepared for the invasion of Kauai. He was troubled by this invasion. The Kauaians were peaceful people. Their king was an honorable man. However, he could not predict the future. He decided to prepare for war. The King noticed that his warriors were dying from diseases brought by the English. He prayed to the Hawaiian gods. It did nothing to help his warriors. Then one year later, he went to sea. He was hit with bad storms. He lost many men. He decided to return to Oahu. He prayed to the Hawaiian gods. He lost more men. He felt that the gods did not want him to enter Kauai. So the king remained in Oahu.

Fifteen years later, the Hawaiian king realizes he had six islands under his control. It was time to set sail to Kauai. This time he reached the island. He went to speak to the Kauaian King. He told him, "I will make no war. I will leave some troops. Any uprising will be dealt with harshly." The Kauian King knew he was no match for the Hawaiian King. He agreed to these terms. The Hawaiian King talks to his most faithful commander. "Aina, I leave this island under your command. From this day forward The Kauiaans will say, "I am an Hawaiian from the island of Kauai. They must no longer say, "I am a Kauian." Aina speaks, "My King it

will be done.Aina, I will leave this island and never return. I am old. I will return home to the big island. The day will come when the gods take me.
Aina spoke, "I understand my king. Farewell." The Hawaiian King replies, " farewell."

The king went to his outrigger canoe and waited for the sounds of many, many conch shells to be blown. Then they set sail to his homeland. The year was 1810. For the first time in two thousand years, the eight islands were under one rule. There will be no more war. He felt that uprisings were easier to deal with then all out war. He was right of course. The peace throughout the islands made many Hawaiians emotional. They have never felt such harmony. The King of Hawaii felt their peace. He felt very humbled and pleased. Five years later, the King of Hawaii died in his sleep.

CHEROKEE NATION

Two men were driving a 1972 powder blue Silverado pickup truck. It was the summer of 1977. They were dressed like Cherokee Indians. They were listening to a song on the radio.

The driver puts the radio lower. He says, “Hey Anthony where is my wife again?” Anthony replies, “In Romania!” The driver says, “Are we married to our wives!?” Anthony replied, “Not this weekend! HA! HA! HA!”

Anthony goes into the glove compartment and pulls out a map. He opens it. John says, “How many towns did we hit?” Anthony says, “This will be our eighth town. It is called Littleton, Kansas.'' The name of the driver was John Romanov. His buddy was Anthony Gheata. They were con men pretending to be Cherokee Indians. They arrived into Littleton, Kansas. They stop at a gas station and ask for directions to the mayor's office. Then they drive their silverado to city hall. They go inside and meet the mayor's secretary. John always started the conversation. He would say to the secretary, “We are Cherokee Indians! We would like to speak to

your mayor." The secretary said, "Of course, of course!" Then the secretary got on the intercom and said, "Mr. mayor two Cherokee Indians are here.''
The mayor said, "Cherokee Indians! Bring them in! Bring them in!"

John and Anthony enter the office. John always starts the conversation. It is always the same. John says, "Hello Mr. Mayor, my name is Running Horse." Then Anthony says, "My name is Walking Deer. We are brothers and proud Cherokee Indians."
Then the mayor says, "It is a pleasure to meet such proud people!"

John shakes the hand of another smiling politician. He begins to wonder if he is banging the secretary. Then the two men would pretend to speak Cherokee. Of course, it was gibberish. Then they looked at the mayor and behold he was crying. They consoled him and laughed quietly behind his back. John says, "There, there Mr. Mayor." Then Anthony said, "We would like to know if your junkyard has any cooper?" The mayor called the junkyard and asked if they had any cooper. They of course had some cooper.

The mayor took a photo op. He started fucking crying again. John said to himself, like taking candy from a baby. Then John said, "Mr. Mayor. John and I will pick up cooper. Then sell it in the next town. The money will go to an orphanage in the Cherokee Reservation. I thank you Mr. Mayor." So Running Horse and Walking Deer would get into their silverado. Twenty seconds down the road they were laughing. They imitated the crying of the Mayor and laughed even harder. Of course, there was no orphanage. The money went into a swiss bank account by Western Union.

The ninth target was a town called Carson City, Kansas. John asked, "Anthony how much did we make so far?" Anthony says, "We made $180,000." Then John says, "I wonder how much crying the next mayor will do." They both started to laugh.

The mayor of Carson City, Kansas was a man named Jack Watson. Mr. Watson was a retired sheriff of Carson City. He was well liked it. He lived in Carson City, Kansas his whole life. He loved the city and its people. He always said hello to anyone who passed him by.

The two con men enter Carson City. Once again, they go to a gas station and ask for directions to the mayor's office. They arrive at City Hall. John turns to

Anthony and says, "Let's enter speaking Cherokee." Anthony says, "Sounds good to me." They knock on the mayor's door. The secretary says, "Come in." The con men enter speaking make believe Cherokee. They look at the secretary. John looks at her name plate. Then he says, "Hello Mrs. Wilson. I would like to speak to your mayor. My name is Running Horse and this is Walking Deer. We've come a long way from Tennessee." The secretary said, "Do you have an appointment with the mayor." John says, "No we do not." The secretary says,
"Let me talk to the mayor." She gets on the intercom and says, "Jack there are two Cherokee Indians who want to talk to you." Jack thought this was odd. However, he was curious. He said, "Ok Janet send them in."

The two men enter. They introduce themselves the usual way. John says, "I am Running Horse." Anthony says, "I am Walking Deer." But Mr. Watson gives them the you've got to be kidding me stare. However, John and Anthony keep talking. Jack interrupts, "Gentlemen I have a meeting with someone in five minutes. It will be brief just wait in the room with my secretary." The two men left the mayor's office. Then Jack called his friend Mike. Mike owned a grocery store. He knew Mike for over thirty years. "Mike do me a favor. Come to my office and pretend to have an appointment with me." Mike replies, "What's up?" Jack says, "There are two idiots outside saying they are Cherokee Indians." Mike says, "I'll be there in five minutes."

Mike enters the mayor's office. He says, " they have got to be kidding me.'' Jack decides to call the Cherokee Reservation in Tennessee. He talks to a man at the visitors center. Jack says, "Do you have an orphanage at the reservation?" The man says, "Yes we do." Jack says, "I have two con men pretending to be Cherokee Indians." The man replies, "I'll connect you to the orphanage.'' Jack waits. Then a woman answers. Jack says, "Who am I talking to?" The woman replies, "My name is Leotie.'' Jack says, "Hello Leotie. My name is Jack Watson. I am the mayor of Carson City, Kansas. Did you send anyone to collect money for your orphanage?'' "No I did not." Jack says, "Do you have anyone who speaks Cherokee there." She says, "Yes, my brother does." Jack says, "May I speak to him?" She says, "Yes of course." Her brother answers the phone, "Hello?" Jack says, "I have two con men claiming to be Cherokee Indians. They even pretend to speak Cherokee. I would like you to speak to them in your native tongue." The man replies, "Ok." Jack says, "I'll put you on hold."

Jack decides to call the sheriff. He tells him, "I need five deputies outside my office. I have two con men pretending to be Cherokee Indians. They are asking for donations for their orphanage." The sheriff says, "Ok Jack, I'll be there in ten minutes." Jack picks up the phone and says, what is your name? My name is Bodaway. Ok Mr. Bodaway, stay on the phone for five more minutes. I will put you on hold." Jack goes on the intercom and tells his secretary, " anet send the two men in." They enter the Mayor's office. Jack says, "Well hello my fine Cherokee friends. There is someone on the phone who would like a friendly chat!" He hands the phone to John. John says, "Hello?" So Mr. Bodaway speaks some poetic Cherokee. Well my fellow readers let me translate what Mr. Bodaway said.

"You motherfuckers. Taking money for the orphanage. How white of you. I hope you are in a town where the police beat their criminals." Then Mr. Bodaway says in english, "You are about as Cherokee as my white janitor." Mr. Bodaway hangs up. The face on John is priceless. Anthony says, "I think we'll go now." Jack says, "You do that and say hello to my friends outside." They leave the mayor's office.

Outside the mayor's office are five deputies. The sergeant says, "Hands against wall." They handcuff the two idiots and bring them to jail. They impound their truck. They take it apart and find ten thousand dollars in the glove compartment. Underneath the money is the map of all the towns they hit. Mr. Watson calls the mayors of these towns. They do not want to press charges against these men. They were afraid of their political careers. Mr. Watson was disgusted.

He went to the jailhouse and told the sheriff of the situation. The sheriff said to the Mayor, "Jack we have to let them go." Jack says, "I know!" The sheriff tells one of the deputies to park the truck in front of the jailhouse. The two men are released from jail. The mayor waits for them near their truck. They come out not wearing their Cherokee outfits. How odd. The mayor looks at them and says, "Here is your fucking money!" He throws it at them. Then says, "Take your ten thousand dollars and never come back to Kansas. In fact, never comeback to THIS COUNTRY!" If I find out that you did this in another town. I will take you into the woods AND BEAT YOU!! Now you will fucking leave!!"

John and Anthony get into their 1972 Silverado and drive off. John says, "This is an odd country." Anthony says, "Why?" John says, "We still have our money." Anthony counts the money. He says, "Yep it is all here." John says,

“All ten thousand?” Anthony says, “All ten thousand.” They ride non stop to the Kansas City Airport. They abandon their beloved Silverado at the parking lot and take the next flight to Romania.

MR. VERMONT

I went to college in Ithaca, New York. There I met a fellow student named Jack O' Connor. He was a ladies man. We immediately became friends. He came from a small town named Jericho,Vermont. He told me something I will never forget. He said, "I wish I was a black teenager who lived in Bedford Stuyvesant." This area is located in Brooklyn, New York. He told me this while I was dry humping the beer keg. I looked at him and said, "This is a cold bitch." Later on in life, I began to realize something. He was the biggest criminal I ever met.

During Christmas break, I had a month off. I decided to take a drive from the Bronx to Jericho,Vermont. I meet his mother and father. I slept in his younger brother's bedroom. We went to neighboring bars. Of course, the girls were not interested in me. All the girls knew that I was from New York City.
The girls asked, "Why are you up here?!"
"I am visiting my friend Jack."

They ask, "Why?!"
I said, "Why not!"

Four days in a row, Jack and I got drunk. The fourth night, I drank a lot at a fraternity party. I blacked out. I remember going to the second floor, something happened. My friend immediately rushed me out. We drove back to his friend's house. I slept on the couch. The sun came up. I awoke. My friend and his buddy started laughing.
My friend says, "Hmm, do you have any memories of last night?"
I said, "I remember you rushing me out of the frat house."
My friend says, "Nothing else?''
I said, "I remember talking to a skinny girl with curly hair."
He said, "That's it?"
He starts laughing and says, "You don't remember making out with a girl who was holding hands with her boyfriend?!"
I said, "WHAT!!"
He said, "That skinny girl with curly hair was holding hands with her boyfriend and YOU were making out with her!! Dude, I had to get you out of there. The frat boys were thinking of kicking your ass. So I called my Dad, he told me to go to my friend's house. So here you are." Then Mr. Vermont gave me one hundred dollars and told me to go home.

Two months later, Jack visited me in the Bronx. We went to the clubs in the Bronx and Manhattan. I remember one club in Manhattan called Roseland. My 6 ft. 2 inch kid brother was the bouncer there. He got us in for free. I said, "Chris tell Jack what happened last week." Chris said, "Ok."
Chris began his story, "There was a drug deal in the men's bathroom. These two guys start to argue. It ended quickly. Then one of the guys leaves to watch the band. The other guy comes out of the bathroom and yells, "Fuck you!" Then he shoots him in the head. People are scattering. Then me and ten bouncers grab the guy and beat him pretty badly. Then the undercover cops arrest the guy."
Jack says, "Wait a minute. They pay cops to go undercover at this club." I said, "They pay cops to do undercover work at a lot of clubs in Manhattan. Then Jack says, "How do you get a job like that?" I said, "Become a cop in NYC."

We get up at around noon. Then Jack sees my fourteen year old sister. He tells me he finds her very attractive. This was unsettling to me. Because Jack was twenty two. He dated a thirteen year old girl six months earlier. I decided to end the friendship. Two months later, he calls me up. He says, "Come up to Vermont." I said, "Can I bring my brother and friend with me?" He said, "Ok."

We traveled on 95 North. Six hours later we see the sign, welcome to Vermont. We were in Jericho one hour later. I enter Jack's house. The garage was full of stolen goods. There were television sets, mirrors, furniture, washers, dryers, and microwaves. There was very little walking room. I entered his living room. He was feeding illegal red belly piranhas. The food consisted of white mice, goldfish and raw meat. I go outside and his brother is shooting japanese beetles with his BB gun. Funny, I just spent the whole car ride explaining how much of a changed man Jack was.

We started drinking some beers. I had three or four of them. Then his father comes into the living room and says, "Let's go." All of us get into a moving truck and travel to an isolated motel. The motel is only used in the summer. So Jack's father backs up the truck and we get out. There were four inches of snow on the ground. Then Jack uses his right foot to open the doors of the motel. We grabbed over twenty television sets and some furniture. Then got back on the truck and drove to Jack's house. We unloaded the truck and put the stolen goods in the garage. Then went to his living room and got drunk.

We arrived drunk at his friend's white house. The house had no stolen goods. However, there was a guy who was visibly upset. You see, his girlfriend broke up with him. The new girlfriend was trying to console him. He was carrying a Smith and Wesson. He was drunk. He started to sob. Then he started screaming. He shouted, "Why did she leave me!!"

"Why!!"

"Why!!"

Then he starts shooting. I was three feet him. He shoots the tree in front of him. Then he turns left and shoots at his up ground pool. Then he returns to the tree. He runs out of bullets. Then his new girlfriend makes out with him and takes his gun away. I was drunk and began to watch MTV. The Pet Shop Boys were on. I started smoking pot. Then a young girl says, "We are low in pot. Let's ask the adults if they have any pot." So she looks at me and says, "Excuse me sir but do you have any pot?" I said, "No I don't young lady? You know pot is a bad trip!" I think she called me a dick after that. I went inside the house and watched more MTV. I started to get sober. I said to myself, "This sucks." I went to Jack and said, "CAN WE LEAVE!!" Jack laughed and said, "Ok I have more beer at home."

We returned to Jack's house. His father was watching television. He got up and told his son, "Let's talk in the kitchen.'' There was a brief conversation. Then Jack says, "I have to go somewhere. There is some beer in the fridge." Then Jack got into a white van with his Dad and left. I was watching television with my friend and brother. Then a white car pulls up on the driveway. There was a man and two girls in the car. The driver was Mr. gunslinger himself and his new girlfriend. The other girl I did not recognize. Mr. gunslinger knocks on the door. I open it.

He asked, "Is Jack here?"

I said, "No he went somewhere with his Dad. There are some beers in the fridge, help yourself."

I ask the other girl, "Do you want a beer?"

She says, "Sure. My name is Jenny. How come you left the party early."

I didn't want to say the gunslinger made me nervous. So I said, "They ran out of beer. I knew Jack had some in his house." Then we started conversing. This felt odd, it was actually going somewhere. Yep, I used Jack's bed.

I woke up the next morning. I saw Jenny sound asleep. Then I walked to the living room. There I saw my brother and friend sleeping on the coach. I look up at the living room window. There I see Jack walking out of the woods. He opens the door.

Jack says, "Joe I need to talk to you, outside."

I didn't like this but I said, "What's up?''

Jack says, "You warned me. You warned about my luck running out. Last night my dad and I went to a half finished motel. We went in to steal a washer and dryer. There is one road in and one road out. Then I saw two squad cars coming down the road. The blue lights were on but no siren. I said "dad look." Then he says let's fucking go. We get into the white van and my dad floors it. We did not put our headlights on until we got on the main road. The squad cars gave chase. My dad told me when he slows down, jump out of the vehicle. I jumped out and walked eight miles to the house. I was convinced that one of the squad cars will come after me. They never did."

I was screaming inside. I said to myself, "Oh my God! Why am I friends with this guy!" Then I said, "I think they might arrest you?"
Jack said, "No my Dad will never identify me."
I said, "Jack I think those four fat cops are retired. Talk to your Dad and ask him if they are new cops. If so, you and your Dad and brother will be in jail in less then a year."
Jack said, "I'll talk to my Dad."
I went back to the house and woke up my friend and brother. I said my goodbyes to Jack. I got into my car and said to myself. I am done with Vermont.

Two years later, I get a call from Jack. He says he is about to get married. He would like me to be there. I agreed to go. I arrived at Jericho with mixed emotions. His parents are divorced and his father was not at the wedding. After the ceremony, I meet his new wife and two month old son. Then I talked to his mother. I said, "So your son if finally married." She says, "Joe I give it two years tops." I said nothing. I went to Jack's house on the lake. I watched his bride go through the gifts and cards. I watched her take out a calculator and add up all the checks in the cards. She looked at me and said, "When are you coming back again?" Jack laughed and said, "You'll never see him again." She looked at me again and said, "Do you want some cocaine for your trip?" Jack laughed even harder. Then Jack said, "Joe you want to go?" I said, "Yea, I better go. Hey Jack remember your two best friends never committed a crime. Oddly enough we are both named Joe. Jack said, "That's nice nimrod." I got up and hugged him. Then I said goodbye. This time I left Jericho, Vermont for good.

HAWAII

I lived in Oahu, Hawaii for eighteen years. I found the people of Oahu very friendly. The population of Oahu was 800,000. However, it felt like a small town. I will always enjoy the memories.

TABLE OF CONTENTS

TOUR GUIDE

I was a tour bus driver in Oahu, Hawaii. One of my responsibilities was to bring tourists to Pearl Harbor. There they would meet men who were in the actual Pearl Harbor attack. They volunteered their time to be tour guides at Pearl Harbor. Each volunteer would tell their story about what they did that day. The attack took place on December 7, 1941. The Japanese military sent over 300 planes to attack Pearl Harbor. It was Sunday morning. Some of the planes were attacking an area called Battleship Row. A man named Mr. Fiske was about to play his bugle that morning on the USS Nevada. He watched in horror as the Japanese planes dropped bombs on the battleships. Now, it was 2001. When a tourist realized that Mr. Fiske was a Pearl Harbor survivor. They would talk to him. He would tell them about that fateful day. Then he would open up his photo album and show pictures of him, his brother and dad. All three men were marines. His father told his sons in 1938, join the military we are going to war. I want both of you boys to be prepared for that day. It came three years later.

HATE

It was December 7, 1941. The Japanese attacked Pearl Harbor. A marine named Mr. Fiske watched the attack on the USS Nevada. He watched the Japanese planes drop their bombs on other ships. He saw the explosions . He saw men being burned alive. He saw men with their legs blown off. He saw men pleading for their lives. The screaming was unbearable. Mr. Fiske knew that some of the men were trapped in their ships. Unfortunately, they were trapped permanently. For Mr. Fiske, it was the beginning of his hatred for the Japanese people.

America went to war with Japan, Germany and Italy. It was vicious. The Americans fought the Japanese throughout the South Pacific. The Americans had 7 million soldiers fighting the Japanese throughout the Pacific. Mr. Fiske was one of them. He was involved in so many battles. The hatred consumed him. The war lasted four long years. It ended when two atomic bombs were dropped. One was dropped on Hiroshima. The date was August 6, 1945. The other was dropped on Nagasaki that date was August 9, 1945. The surrender of Imperial Japan was announced on August 15, 1945. The signing of the official surrender took place in Tokyo Bay on September 2, 1945. The ship used for the surrender was the USS Missouri. The war ended but the hatred for the Japanese people remained for Mr. Fiske.

Then on June 25,1950 the Korean War began. Mr. Fiske volunteered for the Korean conflict. This time Mr. Fiske developed a hatred for the North Koreans. The war ended on July 27, 1953. Then on November 1, 1955 the Vietnam war began. Mr. Fiske volunteered for that conflict. He was involved for four years. This war was different. There was no end in sight. However, Mr. Fiske developed a deep hatred for all Asian people. The hatred was so intense, Mr. Fiske was having health issues. His wife was worried about his drinking and hate speech. All the time he talked about his hatred of Asian people. Then one day his wife exploded. She said, "If you hate them so much why live in Hawaii? These islands are full of Japanese and Korean Americans." Mr. Fiske said, "Fuck them. This is American soil."

Then Mr. Fiske was developing an ulcer. One day, he is arguing with his wife and two boys. He was drunk and talking about fucking Asian people. Then a bolt hit his stomach. Then he felt blood in his mouth. He began to shake and threw up blood. He passed out and woke up at Tripler Medical Center. The doctor informed him that he needed to remove half of his stomach. The ulcers were bad. If he did not operate, Mr. Fiske will die. He agreed to the operation. The operation was a success. He laid in intensive care. He felt like and elephant was sitting on his stomach. Then the surgeon came in and introduced himself.

He said, "Hello Mr. Fiske my name is Dr. Williams. How are you feeling this morning?"
Mr. Fiske says, "I am doing fine doc. I feel like an elephant is sitting on my stomach. However, I'II be out of here in a few days."
Then the doctor looks at him and says, "What is bothering you Mr. Fiske?"
Mr. Fiske responds, "Nothing is bothering me DR. WILLIAMS!"
Dr. Williams responds, "I will not let you go until you tell me.
Mr. Fiske says, "I said nothing is bothering me doc!"
The doctor says, "Why were your ulcers so bad?"
Mr. Fiske says, "Getting sick is a part of life doc."
There was an awkward silence between the two. Then the doctor says, "Mr. Fiske I will not sign your release form until you tell me what is bothering you!"

Mr. Fiske was silent. He said to himself, "This is bullshit!"
Then the doctor says, "Mr. Fiske I have seen many soldiers have hatred for the enemy. The war is done but the hatred continues. You will be released from the

hospital in two days." Mr. Fiske laid in his hospital bed for two days. He admitted that some of his hatred was lessened by hearing stories from captured Asians during the wars. Some were forced to join the military at gunpoint. Then something came over Mr. Fiske. He started to cry. The more he cried the more at peace he felt. This went on for two days. Then one morning the doctor came in. The doctor said, "Mr. Fiske how many wars did you serve?"
Mr. Fiske said, "All three sir."
The doctor said, "So you served in W.W.II, Korea and Vietnam?"
Mr. Fiske said, "So fucking what!!"
The doctor said, "Mr. Fiske they were taking orders just like you. What do you think of Asian people?
Mr. Fiske said, "I can't stand those fucking people!"
Then the doctor said something that Mr. Fiske will never forget. He said, "Let it go Mr. Fiske or you will be dead in ten years."

Mr. Fiske started screaming obscenities at the doctor. The doctor left the hospital room unaffected. Within an hour, Mr. Fiske started crying again. This time he was balling like a baby. He was confused and angry. The following day he was released. It was March 1, 1964. He realized that the war in Vietnam was going on for nine years now. This worried him. He then began to realize that many of the young people were buying VW Beetles. They were German made. Before the hospital stay this would have angered him. Now he had mixed emotions about the vehicle. Then in 1968 the very first Honda dealership opened up in Honolulu, Hawaii. Mr. Fiske was surprised that he held no animosity toward the owner of the Honda dealership.

Then on April 30, 1975 the war in Vietnam ended. Mr. Fiske was disgusted about losing the war. The Americans were in Vietnam for twenty years. A total waste of time. Within two years he started seeing Vietnamese people in Honolulu. Again no animosity toward these Asian people. Then in 1985, Mr. Fiske retired. He decided to be a volunteer tour guide at Pearl Harbor. Every morning he would wear his tour guide hat. The hat said in white letters Pearl Harbor Survivor. At Pearl Harbor he would talk to any veteran from the countries of Japan, Korea, or Vietnam. Then on November 9, 1989 the Berlin Wall fell. Mr. Fiske saw this on television. He decided to learn the Japanese language. Within two years, he spoke it fluently. Then in 1991, Mr. Fiske went to Japan with a few of his friends. The friends were of course W.W. II veterans. They did a pilgrimage to Nagasaki and

Hiroshima. When Mr. Fiske saw the building left over from the atomic blast. He told his friends, "I guess tomorrow we take our flight to Tokyo, Japan."

They arrived in Tokyo and got a taxi ride to the nearest Hilton. The following morning they took a short taxi ride to a place where Japanese war veterans meet. There Mr. Fiske meet W.W. II Japanese war veterans. They were shocked that Mr. Fiske spoke fluent Japanese. This impressed a Japanese man named Mr. Abe. Mr. Abe was with his granddaughter. She spoke fluent English. When he meet Mr. Fiske he insisted that he speak fluent english to his granddaughter. Mr. Fiske agreed. Mr. Abe told him that he was a bomber at the Pearl Harbor attack. He in fact dropped a bomb on the U.S.S. Arizona. When he left Pearl Harbor he knew that the Japanese would lose the war. He told Mr. Fiske when he was 16 years old fourteen military trucks came to his small town in Japan. Seven trucks were full of japanese soldiers. They came out and went house to house to find men and boys. They put a rifle to your head and told you to get into the trucks. Then the trucks would go to a military base. There you were forced out of the truck. Then they announced that you are now in the military. He told Mr. Fiske that he despised his commander. So he decided to become a military pilot. He specialized in becoming a bomber pilot.

Then Mr. Fiske talked about his military career. He kept it short but Mr. Abe insisted on knowing all the details. Then Mr. Abe asked , "Are you a Christian man Mr. Fiske?" Mr. Fiske said, "Yes." Then Mr. Abe said, "You are a lucky man because you believe in redemption." Then the two old warriors decided to keep in touch. Mr. Fiske would email Mr. Abe's granddaughter. Every other year, Mr. Abe would visit Pearl Harbor. Mr. Fiske would accompany Mr. Abe on the boat ride to the USS Arizona. They would disembark from the boat and walk to the wall that honored all the dead sailors on the USS Arizona. They both saluted the dead sailors and then returned to their boat.

They returned to the Pearl Harbor museum. There Mr. Fiske would give a solo tour for Mr. Abe. Then one year Mr. Fiske was giving a museum tour with Mr. Abe. Mr. Fiske noticed a small japanese man in the museum. He turned away from the Battleship Row photo on the wall. Then Mr. Fiske called out to the man in fluent japanese. I noticed that the man was wearing a baseball cap. On top of the baseball cap was the rising sun. When Mr. Fiske opened up his photo album, the japanese man started to shake. Then he collapsed to the floor. Mr. Fiske went to him. People started screaming, "Should we get the ambulance!" Mr. Fiske said,

"No just give him some room. He will be fine in a minute." Then Mr. Fiske started talking to the japanese man. Within ten minutes, the man got up and continued to walk around the museum. Mr. Fiske returned to his tour with Mr. Abe.

One day, I went to Pearl Harbor and noticed that Mr. Fiske was not there. I asked the cashier at the souvenir shop, "Where is Mr. Fiske?" The cashier replied, "He is very ill. It doesn't look good for him." I said, "The place will not be the same without him." The cashier agreed and I continued my day. Two weeks later, there was a plaque in his honor. On the plaque was a sketch of Mr. Fiske wearing his Pearl Harbor survivor outfit. Of course, he was holding his photo album. I found out that he was 84 years old. He lived 40 years with only half of his stomach. Two months later, I saw a picture of Mr. Fiske in the museum. They mention his name and said he served in W.W. II, Korea and Vietnam. The picture they show is Mr. Fiske as a mean son of a bitch. This isn't the man I knew. I will never forget the talks that we had. I will never forget shaking Mr. Abe's hand. Goodbye Mr. Fiske. Goodbye.

I had only been in Oahu, Hawaii for one month. I lived in Waikiki. I was sitting in my chair watching the news on television. To my horror, I saw an elephant running down the streets of Honolulu, Hawaii. The street is only three miles from my apartment. The name of the elephant was Tyke. This is his story.

TYKE

The African farmers of Masai, Mozambique were complaining about a herd of elephants eating their crops. The elders of Masai decided to ask the government for help. The government gave no assistance. The elders decided to hire poachers. They meet a man named Leonildo. He was the head poacher. Mr. Leonildo told the elders I will deal with your problem.

One week later, Mr. Leonildo showed up with twenty men in four toyota pickup trucks. Each man was holding a 460 Weatherby magnum. Four more men were driving four big Volvo semi trucks. Each truck carried chainsaws and cages. The elephants saw the poachers coming down the road. The head male bull roared to the other elephants. They surrounded the young ones. The poachers came out of the toyota trucks with their 460 Weatherby magnum rifles. The head bull flapped his ears and roared. He gave the poachers a bluff charge. Then the poachers began to fire. The rifles echoed throughout the Niassa Reserve. The elephants were no match for the poachers. Within ten minutes, thirty adult elephants were dead. The young ones were frantic. The poachers returned to the Volvo trucks and took out the chainsaws and cages.

First they put twelve baby elephants into their cages. Then they loaded them into the Volvo trucks. The poachers were smiling ear to ear. While they laughed, they grabbed the chainsaws and removed the tusks of every adult elephant. Then they loaded the tusks into the volvo trucks. They left the Niassa Reserve talking about the money that they will receive.

They drove back to Masai and stood overnight. Morning came and they traveled to Porto Belo Pier. There Mr. Leonildo meet his friend Mr. Hedy. Mr. Hedy told his friend to go to the Chinese freighter at dock number 42. Then ask for a man named Mr. Chen. He will pay you quite well for the elephants and tusks. They shook hands and Mr. Leonildo went to pier 42 with his volvo trucks. He met Mr. Chen. Mr. Chen looked at the merchandise and gave Leonildo quite a sum of money. Then Mr. Leonildo left the pier.

The baby elephants were frightened especially Tyke. Tyke was crying out for his mother. He has been doing this for days now. His memories of his mother feel so real to him. He is wondering, where is she? Mr. Chen jokes to his workers and says, "My merchandise is pretty noisy." The workers laugh and Tyke still cries for his mother. The workers put the tusks in wooden cases. Then a crane picks up the cases and puts them into the freighter. Then the same crane lifts the cages. The baby elephants are frightened. However, they are put in with other cargo on the freighter.

The journey was long and lonely for Tyke. When the freighter arrives at the New Jersey pier. The tusks are transferred to Chinatown in Manhattan. When they remove the wooden crates Tyke realizes that three of his friends are dead. He gets upset. Then a crane lifts his cage and puts him on the docks. Tyke and his friends are put into a truck that transports animals. The truck drove to York, Pennsylvania. There he becomes part of the Baynum Circus. It is a small circus that travels to country fairs. Upon arrival, the baby elephants are forced out of the truck and put into a pen. The kids of the circus are curious about their new arrivals. So the adults let the kids into the pen. They touched the elephants and pet them like dogs. The baby elephants seemed to enjoy the children's company. Then the elephant trainer told the kids to leave. Tyke got upset and accidentally knocked a kid down. The trainer immediately took a whip to Tyke. Tyke was confused and frightened. He immediately became subdued. Then the trainer brought in the female elephants. The baby elephants bonded. Then the trainer let in the male elephants. Tyke was part of a herd again. He was happy. For one month, he ate and was around other elephants.

Tyke felt uncomfortable not moving around much. He would run to the edge of the pen and roar. He did this for weeks. Sometimes the kids would take pity on Tyke. So they would ask the trainer to let Tyke play with them. The animal was young, so the trainer would let Tyke out of the pen. Then as time went on there was no more playing with the kids.Tyke became a working animal.

The trainer would teach the baby elephants how to perform various acts. Tyke became a problem. He was not into performing. The trainer had to spend a lot of time disciplining Tyke. Sometimes it was subtle. Sometimes it was brutal. The trainer decided to isolate Tyke. He even put him in another pen by himself. One day in a small town in Virginia .Tyke was once again isolated. This time he was near a tree. He began to stroke the bark with his trunk. Then he would try to reach the leaves. He was too small. Then a girl named Anna noticed Tyke. She got a ladder and reached a branch and gave it to Tyke. Tyke broke the branch and ate the leaves. He ate the leaves like kids eat candy.

The Baynum Circus would travel from town to town. Everytime Tyke was alone in his pen. Anna would open the pen and bring Tyke to the nearest tree. If he could not reach the leaves. Anna would get a ladder, break a branch and give it to Tyke. Tyke began to look forward to seeing Anna. The elephant trainer began to worry about Anna's safety. So he told the owner of the circus. The owner said, "Don't worry, the animal is still young. My daughter will be fine."

Tyke was performing five to seven days a week. He would only rest at night. When they traveled to another town. They would chain Tyke in an animal truck. They did not trust the animal. The trainer would suggest that they sell Tyke. The owner would say, "Buying another elephant is too expensive. We will just have to deal with Tyke." The trainer decided to occasional chain Tyke in the pen. The employees were getting concerned about their safety. The owner insisted that Tyke was mangeable. They have dealt with unpredictable animals in the past. Tyke was no different.

The years went by. Anna was now a full grown adult. So was Tyke. He was a full grown male. He weighed 10,000 pounds. Tyke seemed to accept his fate. Then one day they were in a small town in Tennessee. The animals were in an abandoned mall. The trainer made sure that the elephants were in single file. The mall was surrounded by wilderness. The wilderness went on for miles and miles. The animal trucks pull up to the parking lot. Then Tyke starts smelling all that wilderness. Tyke started swaying and having a low roar. His ears started flapping. The employees are getting nervous. The trainer tries to get Tyke to calm down. Then Tyke roars and runs for the entrance. He knocks down the trainer. The other employees get out of Tyke's way. Then the workers who control the elephants try to subdue Tyke. Tyke backs away from the workers. But he is a 10,000 pound elephant. He winds up destroying all the big windows in the lobby. Then he smells the wilderness and leaves the mall.

The workers leave the mall and run after Tyke. They approach him with caution. They somehow subdue the animal and put him in the animal truck. They leave this small town of Tennessee with fear in their hearts.

They arrive at a small town in Maryland. Nobody is looking forward to taking Tyke out of the animal truck. The employees talk to the owner. The owner's response is the same, "Elephants are expensive to replace." There was no incident in Maryland. However, when Tyke enters the animal truck he is shackled. Three months go by and there is no incident with Tyke. Then in Cedarburg, Wisconsin Tyke tries to leave the Circus tent. Three employees are injured. This time the owner shackles Tyke until he can sell him to another circus. Three weeks later he is sold to The Baylor Circus. The sale took place on April 14, 1992.

It was August 16, 1994. The Baylor Circus arrived in Oahu, Hawaii. Tyke has been with the Baylor Circus for over two years. There were no incidents. The first show went rather well. The second was another matter. The employees of the circus noticed that Tyke was moody. He was pacing, flapping his ears and having low roars. Then Tyke stopped and was totally relaxed. The owner decided to put Tyke in the second show. In the middle of the show, Tyke had low roars again. The employees are concerned.

Everyday at 4:30 p.m., a cool tropical breeze flows through the Hawaiian Islands. An employee of the circus opens up a flap in the back of the circus tent. Tyke begins to rock. He starts to smell the tropical breezes of Hawaii. He is convinced that he is in Africa. He starts to rock, flap his ears and his roars are louder. The employees are trying to control the situation. But what do you tell a 10,000 pound animal who does not feel like doing tricks. The audience starts to realize that the animal is uneasy. The elephant trainer walks towards Tyke to calm him down. Instead, Tyke decides I want to stay in Hawaii. So he rushes the trainer, knocks him down and head butts him twice. The trainer is dead. The employees try to stop a 10,000 pound animal. Tyke pushes them away like little toys. He sees the open flap and runs for freedom.

He is met in the parking lot by four cushman vehicles. Each vehicle has two policemen. One policeman driving the cushman, the other shooting Tyke with a shotgun. Fourteen shots are fired into Tyke's right side. He approaches the front gate. A man tries to close the gate with a lock. Tyke pushes through the gate. The man falls to the ground. Tyke is about to kill another man. However, seven policemen approach Tyke with caution. Then they shoot their shotguns. Ten more bullets hit Tyke's right side. He begins to run away from the police officers. Several shots are fired into his backside.

Police sirens are heard throughout Honolulu. Tyke is only three miles away from downtown. Two hundred policemen are lining up on the sidewalks and shooting at Tyke. Tyke runs away from the police. They follow him and continue shooting. They shot and they shot and they shot. Tyke begins to slow down. His roars are lower. He picks up his trunk to smell the breezes of Hawaii. More shots ring out. The police sirens are louder. Tyke stops and his 10,000 pound body falls on a blue camaro. The car was crushed and the alarm goes off. He grunts and fifteen policemen march in single file. They loaded their shotguns and fire into Tyke's belly. Each bullet leaves a puff of smoke from the gunpowder. Tyke raises his trunk again. He wants to smell the breezes of Hawaii. Then seven more bullets enter his belly. He gives a tiny grunt. His trunk goes limp. Tyke's body is riddled with 400 bullets. Tyke is dead.

The policemen proceeded to treat this as a crime scene. The caution tape is put up. The crowd gathers around. Some people are visibly upset. The police control the situation and wait for the crane and roof bed truck to arrive.

The Governor of Hawaii Ben Cayetano is in a meeting with Police Commissioner Don Cataluna. They are both watching live TV News. The news is showing Tyke being lifted by a crane into a roof bed truck. The governor speaks to the police commissioner.
He says, "Don this is bad."
Don says, "I have already called the Buddhist pet cemetery. They are making a plot available for the elephant. I send a squad car to the cemetery to get an urn for the animal. The squad car will bring the urn to the incinerator in Waianae."
Ben says, "Let's bury him quickly."

Tyke is put into a roof bed truck. He gets a police escort to the Waianae incinerator. They arrive and take Tyke off of the roof bed truck with a giant crane. They place his 10,000 pound body on a giant conveyor belt. The sanitation workers open up the steel doors to the incinerator. Then the conveyor belt was put in motion. When Tyke was inside the incinerator, they closed the steel doors. You can hear the flames from the furnace. It took three hours to burn his body. Then they took five pounds of his ash and put it into the urn. The urn was given to a representative of the Buddhist pet cemetery. Then the squad car drove back to

Kaneohe. They arrived at the cemetery . The man carrying the urn said goodbye to the police officer. Then he meet his manager. He was informed that Tyke's plot was prepared.

He walked to the burial site. There he saw the black marble plaque at the gravesite. Engraved on the plaque was a sketch of Tyke and the date of his death. The urn was put into the grave. Then the gravedigger put dirt on the urn. The grass seeds were scattered on the dirt. Both men felt that Tyke received a proper burial. He lays in peace at a Buddhist pet cemetery located off of the Kahekili Highway.

CRASH TEST DUMMY

I was doing a bus tour around the island of Oahu. It was a warm sunny day. I felt heavy tipping at the end of the tour. I was traveling on Kahekili Highway. I came at the cross section of Kahekili and Likelike. I waited for the red light to turn green. The light turned green, I waited three seconds and crossed the Likelike Highway. A female tourist with a three year old daughter yelled, "Oh my God!!" I had no idea what was about to occur. A nine passenger van on the Likelike Highway hit the gas. He was trying to beat the red light. He came at me like a rocket. I was listening to Hawaii 78 by Israel. I was so relaxed.
S L A M M!!!

He hit the front of the left tire. The bus was lifted off the ground. It felt like an explosion. I felt so powerless. I felt a pounding headache come over me. The air bag did not open. The 15,000 pound bus was pushed two hundred feet. A baby in the back was crying. I had twenty five people in my bus.

I was semi conscious. The left side of my neck was in severe pain. I hears sirens from both sides of the Likelike Highway. I opened the right door. I told my passengers, "Leave the bus before we get hit again!" They disembarked. I watched them and noticed I was getting dizzy. All the passengers left the bus and I began to open my door. My left arm did not move. So, I opened the door with my right hand. I left the bus disoriented. My left arm was just dangling and swinging. I was scared to look at it. Then I noticed the man who hit me. He looked around and realized no one was paying attention. He went back to his van and try to start it. It did not turn over. He came out in a panic. It was apparent that he was drunk. He started to scream at me, "You went through a red light!!" I screamed back, "I have twenty five witnesses who disagree fuck head!" He again began to panic.

The police and ambulances began to arrive at the scene. I had my backside on the divider. I started to scream at the police, "I can't stand up! I can't stand up!!" Then a policeman screamed, "Hey!! You are alive!!" Then he walked away. I could no longer stand up. So my butt hit the asphalt pretty hard.
I noticed witnesses stopping their cars. They informed the police that the driver of the van was at fault. One witness gave me his phone number. He said, "Call me when you get a lawyer." What shocked me most was that the driver of the van was not given a breathalyzer test.

My boss appeared. Many witnesses told him that the man driving the van went through a red light. It felt like ten minutes went by. I looked at my watch and realized that I was sitting on the asphalt for one hour. Finally, the paramedics came to assist me. They readjusted the gurney closer to the ground. They helped me get on the gurney. Then they readjusted to waist level and pushed the gurney to the ambulance. I was put into the vehicle, the door was closed shut. The siren went on. Then the ambulance went to Castle Medical Center. Upon arrival, I was still disoriented. I began to gain consciousness one hour later.

I remained in bed at the emergency room. Three nurses took me into the X ray room. They pressed the X ray plates against my left shoulder. The pain went from bad to worse. I screamed in agony. They took the plates off of my left shoulder. I felt my heart racing. A strange heat came over my entire body. They returned me to my bed.

To my surprise, the man who caused the accident was two beds away from me. I was dizzy again. He looked at me, got up and asked to be released from the hospital. I wanted to kick his ass so bad. Apparently, he was sober now. However, I was in no condition to fight. He received his release forms, signed them and left in a hurry. Of course, he had no major injuries. He had some blood on his arms and looked disheveled.

The accident lasted thirty seconds. My injuries included a torn rotator cuff and five herniated disc. The physical therapy lasted 11 months. I decided to get a lawyer. I called over twenty lawyers. Finally, a lawyer took my case. I received a check for 26,000 dollars from the insurance of the tour company. Then I had to get another lawyer for my rotator cuff operation. Fortunately, my first lawyer highly recommended the second lawyer. He even walked me to the office of the second lawyer. The second lawyer arranged a surgeon for my rotator cuff. Then he assigned me another physical therapist after surgery. This lasted another six months. He also informed me that three more checks are coming my way.

To my surprise, the second check went to my workman compensation company. It was a private company. I told my lawyer what the hell is going on. They received a check for 13,000 dollars. He informed me not to fight it. Otherwise, the operation on your rotator cuff will not happen. I was mad but I finally agreed with my lawyer. He reminded me that two more checks are coming my way.

My disability checks were awful. They did not include my tips. I went from 40,000 a year to 11,000. Fortunately, my rent was cheap.

My mental state was not good. I developed panic attacks from my flashbacks. I could not pass the area of the accident for two years. I would see it at a distance and feel the terror of that day. Eventually, I saw a psychiatrist once a week. I began to take prescription drugs for my panic attacks. The drugs involved were Lamotrigine 100mg. This drug was taken three times a day. Then Ziprasidone HCL 20mg. It was taken once a day. Finally, Lorazepam 1mg. This drug was taken twice a day. The treatment lasted two years.

Three years later I went to the courthouse for a hearing. The lawyer informed the judge that I was receiving two more checks. One for emotional distress due to the accident. He informed the judge that I was under treatment from a psychiatrist for the accident. The treatment lasted two years. Then the last check was for permanent injury. The injuries included five herniated disc and a torn rotator cuff. The judge asked if I had the operation for the rotator cuff. The lawyer replied, "Yes your honor." Then he gave him some briefs to sign. Then the judge said, "Case dismissed."

Outside the courtroom, the lawyer told me that my checks will come in the next six months. I shook his hand. He told me, "If you do not receive your checks in seven months please give me a call." I said, "Thank you." I got rather emotional and left quickly. I sat in my car and began to shake. I pulled myself together and drove home.

I received two checks three months apart. The total amount was 76,000 dollars. Nine years later, I still cannot swing a baseball bat or a golf club. When I sprint at full speed, I feel my legs starting to collapse. I find myself feeling sad about my limitations in sports. But I am alive.

SHARK CAGE

It was a cool wet summer morning on the island of Oahu. I looked out the window of my apartment. I saw the thick green moss and purple clouds of the Waianae mountains. I grabbed my day pack full of snorkel gear and walked to the bus depot of the Hilton Hotel. There I waited for a white fifteen passenger van. It arrived and said shark encounter on the side of the van. The driver got out and opened the slide door. I went in and was greeted by nine other people. Then we drove for forty- five minutes to the Haleiwa Harbor. The harbor is located on the north shore.

We arrived at the harbor. The ten of us got out of the van and walked to a thirty five foot long high tower fishing boat. We boarded the boat with excitement. Then I heard the engine start. We reversed out of the dock and went forward. The boat slowly left the harbor until we reached the open waters. Then we picked up speed and traveled to the shark cages.

For twenty minutes, the water was pure mud. It rained hard the night before. The boat was traveling at twenty knots. Then just like that the waters of Hawaii changed to a dark, dark blue color. Then the boat traveled at ten knots. The waters appeared to change to a blue green color. Then the boat came to a complete stop. The shark cages were floating in the ocean. The ocean looked like clear water from a faucet. The blue color appeared to be coming from the ocean floor. Then the anchor was dropped.

Both cages were brought closer to the boat. One cage was connected to the boat. The other one was 15 yards away. It was connected to the boat with a green nylon rope. Then a crew member got a ten foot steel pole. The pole was shaped like the letter L. He put a nylon rope and a big hook on the pole. He put the pole into a steel hole. It looked like the letter L upside down. Then he grabbed the hook and put ten pounds of raw tuna on it. He proceeded to throw tuna blood and small pieces of raw fish into the ocean. Then I watched a ten foot galapagos shark jump out of the water. He grabbed the raw tuna on the hook with his teeth. He began to shake furiously. I watched his eyes roll back. Then his eyelids came forward. The shark looked possessed. The tuna came loose and the shark fell into the water. The crew member put more tuna on the hook. Then an eight foot sand shark did the same performance. This went on for fifteen glorious minutes. Then it was time for the next act.

It was time for the shark cage. Nine people were given snorkel gear and life jackets. Then eight people were put into a large shark cage. This cage was put fifty feet away from the boat. It was connected by thick nylon rope. The other cage was hooked onto the boat. A ladder was installed. Then a fifty year old female college professor and I entered the cage. I heard the crew overhead. Then chunks of fish and blood were thrown in the water. Twelve sand and galapagos sharks showed up. They slowly began to eat the chunks of fish. Then a feeding frenzy began. The sharks were getting more aggressive. The college professor was in awe. I had mixed emotions. However, I was enjoying the show. Then we had a huge visitor.

I was looking underneath my feet. There he was between the medal bars. A twenty-one foot long tiger shark. He weighed at least two thousand pounds. He was a beast. Fortunately, he was two hundred feet below me. Then he went in front of the cage. He was a good five hundred feet away. Then he went down another two hundred feet. His tail and head were swaying back and forth. His left eye rolled in his head like a marble. He saw nothing to eat. Then he started coming to my cage.

The animal started to look menacing. He was big and you can feel the power of the animal. Then the crew members started throwing big chunks of fish in the water. The tiger shark went from five to thirty miles an hour in a blink of an eye. The other sharks did not dare to get in his way. I saw him open his enormous mouth and swallow forty pounds of fish in one bite. I began to see a two hundred pound girth on the tiger shark.

Then they threw some blood to the left of the cage. He swam through the blood and saw no food. The crew decided to throw a twenty pound piece of fish to the right of the cage. The tiger shark came slowly pass the cage and eyeballed me. I said to myself, "Christ what a big animal!" Then he grabbed the twenty pounds of raw fish and left. I watched this tiger shark and his friends eat for another ten minutes. Then the food ran out and the sharks slowly left the area. I watched the sharks slowly disappear into the blue waters of Hawaii.

The crew said, "Come on up folks. The show is over." The college professor went up the ladder first. Then I came out of the cage very excited. I started talking to the crew. It turns out that only thirty percent of the customers see a tiger shark. I watched the crew bring in the other cage. Then the boat picked up the anchor and headed back to the Haleiwa Harbor. Boy did I have sea sickness. However, I was too excited to care.

HAWAIIAN BOULEVARD

I worked for a security company called Wackenhut. One day, the operational manager called me. He said, "Joe we are going to give you a new assignment. The site will not have a supervisor on it. You will report to the security desk at the office building on hawaiian boulevard. The address is 1414 Hawaiian Boulevard. You will report to a site supervisor named Jack Turner." I said, "Ok. When do I see him?'' The operational manager said, "Tomorrow at 8 A.M." Then I said, "Ok."

The next morning, I met Mr. Turner. We had some small talk then he explained my new assignment. He said, "Joe you will work at the mall across the street. The shift starts at 9 A.M. You will work Monday through Friday, 9 A.M. to 5 P.M. Every morning you will report to my site. On Saturdays, you will work two shifts. The first shift will be 9 A.M. to 5 P.M. The second shift will be 11P.M. to 7A.M. You will start on Monday 9 A.M. sharp have a good weekend." I said, "Ok 9A.M."

I arrived at 9A.M. Monday morning. I checked in with Mr. Turner. Then I walked across the street to the Hawaiian Boulevard Mall. As soon as I hit the pavement of the mall, I knew I was in a bad situation. I was raised in the projects of the Bronx. I know drug dealers when I see them. I noticed over eighty drug dealers. I walked into the grocery store. I observed items such as rolling papers and scales that weighed illegal drugs. The drug dealers would hide their crystal meth near the whorehouse. Some of the drug dealers were homeless people from Ala Moana Beach. The head drug dealers had apartments and girlfriends. Of course, they were not users of the drug.

There were legal and illegal businesses. The legal ones were salons, korean bars, restaurants, supermarket, two grocery stores, a tinted window business, a strip joint and a porno store. The strip joint and massage parlors were dealing in prostitution. There was illegal gambling at two locations. Then to top it off a homeless man had an illegal auto detailing business. He was using water from a faucet. He actually had a new hose connected to the faucet.

I walked around the mall and noticed twenty homeless shacks. They were made of wood and tin. Then I noticed ten homeless people living in tents.

I went to my office in utter shock. I wondered where I can get a new job. Then I realized it was hard to get this job. So I called the main office and asked for a new assignment. Of course, there was nothing available. So I decided to act like I couldn't care less what happened in this nightmare. I befriended all of the drug dealers and homeless people. I decided to stay until I got a new job.

It was 9A.M. Tuesday, I get a call from one of the whorehouses. The madam or should I say the manager wants to see me. I walk to the whorehouse and meet the Manager.
The manager says, "What is you name?"
I say, "My name is Joe."
The manager says, "I have a homeless man living in the back of my massage parlor. Please take care of the situation. Then come see me."
I said, "Ok."
I went to talk to the homeless man. I wondered if I should knock on his tent. This gave me a little smile. I approached his living quarters.
I said in a friendly manner, "Hello I need to talk to you."
The homeless guy comes out of his tent. I said, "I know you are a drug dealer. I work monday through friday 9 to 5. At 5:01 P.M., you can come on property and

sell your drugs. But I need you to find another place to live." He looked at me and said, "I'll see what I can do." This did not sound promising. So I went back to the madam and said, "Call me tomorrow if he doesn't leave."

It was 11A.M. Tuesday, the Madam calls. I answer the phone. She informs me that he is still there. I told her that I will be at her establishment in one hour.

It was 12 noon. I arrive at her business.
She says, "He is still there. If you help me. I will reward you."
I said, "Ok. Which girl can act mad?"
She says, "Let me get Ms. Kim." Ms. Kim approaches.
I tell her, "Listen we will go outside and have an argument. You insist that you get rid of him or I will get someone who can. Then I will call your boss."
We go outside and have a pretend argument. Man this Korean girl can scream. She leaves. I return to the massage parlor and tell them to call tomorrow when he departs.

It was 2 P.M. Wednesday, I get a call. The madam informs me that the homeless guy has been gone for two hours. I told her I will be right there. I arrived and asked her for her biggest bouncer. We go to the homeless guy's tent. We make sure no drug dealer sees us. Then we dismantle his tent. I drive my car to the back of the massage parlor and throw his stuff into my trunk. I drive three miles down the road and throw his stuff into a dumpster. I come back to the mall. I inform her if he returns call me. She thanked me and I made my weekly visits to Ms. Kim. I always enjoyed this lunch hour. Ms. Kim and a subway sandwich. It took place every friday.

It was 11A.M. Thursday. I get a call from the illegal gambling room on the second floor. I hear a Korean man on the other side of the phone.
He says, "Hello Joe. I would like you to come to room #207." Then he hangs up. I wondered how he knew my name. I decided to pay a visit. I opened the door to room # 207. There I saw a tent if front of a steel door. The homeless guy was outside being a drug dealer. I knocked on the steel door. A slit opened and I made eye contact. The door opened and a well dressed forty year old Korean man came out. He said, "Hello Joe. I want you to take care of that problem. Come to the

window. That man selling crystal meth lives in this tent. Here is two hundred dollars. Please remove his belongings."

The well dressed man knocked on the steel door. The door opened and he went inside. I looked out the window at the drug dealer. Boy was he pathetic. I decided to take a walk around the mall. I found a big green dumpster in the back of the mall. I returned to room #207 and took his nice radio and sleeping bag. I put it in my office. Then returned to room # 207 and threw the rest of his filthy crap in the dumpster. I repaid a visit to room # 207. I knocked on the steel door. The Korean man opened the door. I said, "Tell the homeless idiot that he was robbed by two big Samoans. They vowed to return. Have a good day." He said nothing and closed the door.

It was 2 P.M. Friday. I got another call from the illegal gambling room. The Korean man says, "Hello Joe. I have a female customer who had her car stolen from the mall. Come to room # 207 and wait with her downstairs." Then he hung up. When I went to the room, I recognized the woman. She does not have a car. She always comes in a taxi. However, I said nothing and accompanied her downstairs. I made some small talk and waited for the police to arrive.

A policeman came out of his squad car. He walked to the lady with his clipboard. On his clipboard was a police report for stolen vehicles. He asked the woman a few basic questions. Then he said, "Why are you here at the mall?" She gave no answer. The police officer put his clipboard under his left arm.

The police officer asked again, "Why are you here at the mall?"
She answered, "I was eating at a chinese restaurant."
The police officer said, "Which one?"
Again, she gave no answer. Finally she said, "I was eating at Mr. Chungs."
The police officer began to write on his clipboard again.

He said, "I need your license plate number."
He ran the plate number. The dispatcher said, "This car was stolen and recovered two weeks ago."
The lady replied, "It was stolen again."
The policeman looked at her. Then decided to continue his report. He asked her a few more questions. Then left the mall. I walked her back to the illegal casino.

It was Monday morning 11 A.M. I get a call from the grocery store. The owner says, "I am tired of this homeless guy living in the Banyan Tree!" I asked the grocery owner, "Where is this Banyan Tree located?" He said, "It is next to my store." I said, "I'll be there in ten minutes." I went to greet the store owner. He spoke very little english. So his son translated for him.
I said, "How long has he lived in the Banyan Tree?"
The grocery owner said, "A few weeks."
I asked, "I'm curious how long did it take to make that shack in the Banyan Tree?"
The store owner said, "Just an hour or two. The idiot stole my ladder. I immediately retrieved it. Then he took some wooden planks and nailed them to the tree."
I said, "He created a crappy ladder. Of course he hasn't killed himself yet. Do you know where he goes?
The store owner said, "He is in the back of the mall with his illegal auto detailing business. At the end of the day, he returns to his shack and smokes his crystal meth. Christ that smell is nasty. It chases my customers away."
I said, "I will take care of it."

I went to the back of the mall. There I saw a shirtless man with pimples covering his whole back. He was washing cars with dirty rags. So I decided to grab some rocks from potted plants around the mall. I placed the rocks in a hallway next to the fire extinguisher. Then I called 911 and said there is a crazy shirtless homeless man throwing rocks at cars going by. I waited for the cops to arrive. I waited for the show to begin. The cops did not disappoint. He was arrested.

I went back to the grocery owner and told him the good news. I asked for his ladder. I climbed to the shack and destroyed it. I put all of his belongings in the dumpster. Then I called my supervisor. I asked him, "How do I trespass an individual?" He told me to come across the street and asked the guard to give you a trespass form. Fill it out and make several copies. Then give each business owner a copy of the trespass form. Inform them that the individual living in the Banyan Tree is no longer allowed on property. If you see him on property call 911 and say Mr. Park is trespassing on Hawaiian Boulevard mall. I followed these instructions.

The next day Mr. Park comes to the mall. He is arrested for trespassing. He returns and bothers the grocery owner. I called the police and had him arrested again. This time I ask several businesses for items they do not need. I opened the door to room #211 and put these items inside. Mr. Park came to the mall once more. I called 911 and said, "This is security officer Joe Collazo at the Hawaiian Boulevard Mall. Mr. Park keeps putting stolen items into room#211. Please send an officer right away. The owners are complaining about stolen items." The police come and I listen to Mr. Park complain that he is being set up. They did not want to hear it and arrested him for trespassing and stolen goods.

A few days later, Mr. Park arrived again. He went to room #211. Then I saw four big Korean men come out of the illegal gambling room. They went to room#211 and had a discussion with Mr. Park. He left the mall never to return.

It was my second week. I am doing my patrols on the second floor of the mall. I started hearing noises from the ceiling. So I asked the girl from the whorehouse, "Who is up there?" She said, "The homeless live up there." I asked, "How do they get up there?" She said, "Follow me." She showed me the little steel door that leads to the ceiling. It was busted. She told me, "Everytime they break this door. They move into the attic above the ceiling. I said, " The tiles on the ceiling are made of cheap styrofoam. How do they walk around the attic?" She said, "There are wooden planks along the attic." I thanked her for the information. Then continued my patrols.

I stopped by another whorehouse and talked to the madam inside.

I said, "Do you have any problems with the homeless living above the ceiling?"

She said "The idiots started two fires!"

I said, "Did the fire department come?"

She said, "No I send four men with steel pipes. The fifth man would have a fire extinguisher. I tell the four men to beat the homeless. Then the fifth man puts out the fire."

I said, "Hmm; anything else I should know about?"

She said, "The homeless put holes in the ceiling so they can watch people having sex. When the homeless yell, I can see you brudda! The customer runs out of my establishment."

I said, "Doesn't this bother you!?"

She said, "I don't care. The customer already paid his money."

I could not stop laughing. Two days later, the homeless were watching the customer having sex. The guy yells, "I see you brudda! I see you!"

Then the idiots fell through the ceiling. Two of them, fell on a customer. No one was hurt. However, the four men started hitting them with pipes. They run to the hall. They screamed, "Security guard; security guard help me. I laughed and said, hit them harder!! There screaming isn't loud enough!! They screamed louder." I said, "Thank you." Then I left.

It was the first Friday of the month. The disability checks were in. The drug dealers were busy. I decided to do my patrols on the second floor. I see an eighteen year old kid with a crowbar. He was breaking into one of the whorehouses. He saw me and ran. I knocked on the door of the whorehouse. The madam came out. I said, "A drug dealer was trying to break into your establishment. Let me show you the door." I walked her to the wooden door and showed the damage from the crowbar. She waved it off and told me not to worry. So I went back to my room and watched the drug dealers in action. I was hoping not to witness any violence. Then I saw a car take off. It was obvious that he did not pay the drug dealer. So the drug dealer picks up a cinder block and throws it at the back window of 1994 Chevy Impala. I always wondered why he would keep cinder blocks handy. He probably stole them from a construction site. The window breaks, the customer gets out. The drug dealer pulls out his 9mm. He points it at the customer. The buyer calmly goes back to his car and drives off.

The drug dealer makes a phone call on his cell phone. Two minutes later, three homeless men show up with machetes and stay with the drug dealer for the rest of the day.

It was a quiet Monday morning. The time was 9:30 A.M. I was in my security room. I decided to leave my chair and look out the window. I take a zip of hot hawaiian coffee. Then I notice nine police cruisers and two black armoured cars coming up Hawaiian Boulevard. They came quietly. The police lights on the vehicles were operating quite well. Then twenty swat team members came out of the armoured cars. They went up the staircase. Then yelled, "Open up this is the police!" No response. They repeated the order. Again, no response. Then a swat team member took a sledgehammer to the front door of the massage parlor. The door is broken and the swat team enters. They start to bark all sorts of orders. Fifteen minutes later, 17 men leave in cuffs. The swat team waits for two paddy wagons. They arrive ten minutes later. They fill up the paddy wagons. Then the police watched the paddy wagons leave first. Five minutes later, the rest of the officers depart. At 10:30 A.M. the Hawaiian Boulevard mall was quiet.

I got curious. So at 11:00 A.M. I went to talk to the parking attendant of the mall. I said, "Hey Anna. Why are the cops arresting people from the massage parlor?"

She said, "They were dealing drugs and stealing money from their customers."

I said, "What else were they doing?"

She said, "Selling credit card numbers and charging their customers two or three times. They also had illegals from China and Korea doing prostitution."

I said, "Well that place was quite busy."

She said, "Joe why don't you go inside the massage parlor and see what they have?''

I said, "Go with me."

She said, "Ok hold on. Let me put my close sign up."

We went inside and helped ourselves to some food and drinks. I took three cases of beer and a lot of liquor. Then I put it in the trunk of my car. Afterwards, I went back to the parking attendant and talked for two hours.

It was 3:30 P.M. I get a call from my sister in Maui. She informs me that her boyfriend has a new job. He is coming to Oahu for training at the Mai Ti Bar. The bar is located at the Ala Moana Shopping Mall. He will be staying at the Pagoda Hotel for two weeks. My sister said he needed a roommate. He will be arriving in two days. I was excited about using the facilities at the hotel.

It was Wednesday 5 P.M.. I went home ate dinner and packed a suitcase. I left my apartment at 7:30 P.M. I took the 8 P.M. city bus to the Pagoda Hotel. I arrived at the hotel at 8:30 P.M. I unpacked, talked to my sister's boyfriend and watched TV. I went to bed at 11:30 P.M. I woke up at 8 A.M. and was excited that my job was only a two minute walk. The rest of the week was uneventful. I could not wait till Sunday, my day off. I will be at the swimming pool all day.

It was a beautiful Sunday afternoon. I put on my swimming trunks and went for a swim. I dove into the pool. Then swam to the other side. I come up for air and stood in three feet of water. I opened my eyes and saw the drug dealers from the

Hawaiian Boulevard Mall. They were giving me such a stare. I was in disbelieve. The same drug dealers at the mall were also selling crystal meth at the hotel. I was working and living with them. I decided to act like it was no big deal. I got out of the pool and decided to befriend the drug dealers.

One drug dealer decided to talk to me first, "Hey, what do you know about the police?" I said quickly, "They are watching you at the mall. Do your drug dealing at the hotel. They are watching you from across the street. They are observing you from the fourth floor. Stay away from the middle of the mall."

I watch the drug dealer talk to a guy with a ponytail. They did not look in my direction. They left the pool area. An hour later, I observed the drug dealer with the ponytail on the pay phone. It was obvious that he rented out rooms to sell drugs. It was important for me to act like I did not care. A security guard from the hotel got real friendly with me. I asked him if he knew a good place to eat dinner. He told me about the Chinese restaurant across the street. I said, "Thank you." I went to the Chinese restaurant. The food sucked.

It was 3:30 P.M. Monday. I witnessed a good looking Portuguese Hawaiian girl selling drugs at the mall. She is a regular. I talked to some of the business owners of the mall. I had a hard time accepting the fact that a drug dealer can be an attractive woman. However, the business owners told me that she was indeed a drug dealer. Then a rich Korean businessman speaks to her. It wasn't hard to figure out what he wanted. So she gets into his 530i BMW and leaves. Of course, she never returns. A half hour later, a fifty year old Korean lady begins to strip. She was high as a kite and wearing tattooed eyeliner. She also dressed like a gypsy. Three cops and I were watching. I thought it was funny. However one of the cops said, "I think I am going to barf." Her singing did not help.

It was 9:30 A.M. Tuesday morning. I was reading my reports in the security room. It suddenly hit me that the homeless can break into my room and see my reports. They will definitely bring my reports to the drug dealers. So I decided to leave all my reports at the security desk across the street. I went to Mr. Turner and said, "Here entertain yourself with my reports. I do not want to leave them in my security room. The ceilings are made of styrofoam. The homeless in the attic will break in and steal my reports. So I will leave my reports at this desk from now on." Mr. Turner laughed and said, "That's fine with me." One week later, the assholes broke into my security room. They stole my radio and sleeping bag. I was furious, so I went to a homeless man's tent and stole his sleeping bag. Then I went to another homeless guys tent and stole his radio. Fuck them.

It was 10:00 A.M. Saturday morning. I began to realize that there was no drug dealers around the mall. It was quiet. So I went to the parking attendant and asked her, "What happened to the drug dealers?" She said, "The korean lady that owns a salon told me that the cops arrested all of the drug dealers at 4:00 A.M. this morning." So I said , "They are all gone?" The parking attendant said, "Yep they are all gone." I get curious about the Pagoda Hotel. So I take a two minute walk to the hotel. I went to the security room of the hotel. I ask the guard, "Are they any drug dealers at the hotel?" The guard said, "No they arrested them this morning at 4 A.M." I said, "I am living her with my sister's boyfriend. I did not hear anything." The guard said, "They are gone dude. They arrested the night guard to."

I went back to the mall. I checked every single homeless shack and tent. They were all vacant. I heard no noise from the ceiling. So I went to my security room and made a call to the property manager of the mall. I told him to bring a moving truck and three big Samoans. The homeless were arrested for drug dealing. This is the time to throw their crap out. He said that he will be there Monday at 10:00 A.M.

He came Monday morning at exactly ten o'clock. We had a small conversation then went to work. It took three brutal hours to throw their stuff out. When the deed was done. He asked me who he should rent out his properties to. I said a storage company. You can charge them exuberant amount of rent. He agreed. He left the mall and I went back to my security room.

It was Wednesday 2P.M. The police arrived and quickly raided the two gambling rooms. I counted over forty arrests from my security room. By 3:30 P.M. the police were gone. I walked to the gambling rooms and saw beer and liquor everywhere. So I walked to the Pagoda Hotel. I entered my hotel room. In the cabinet was a box of hefty bags. I took ten hefty bags and went shopping in the gambling rooms. I have no idea how much liquor and beer I took. But I filled up every single hefty bag. Then I went to my security room and took a nap.

On Thursday after lunch, I went to the whorehouse and had my one hour with Ms. Kim. Then I talked to the madam. I told her that I had some alcohol to sell from the massage parlor and gambling room bust. She agreed to a dollar a bottle. I went back to my hotel room. I looked at my stash and decided to keep the beer. I returned to the massage parlor and gave her the liquor. She gave me two one hundred dollar bills. I returned to my security room. Boy did I enjoy the quiet.

The weekend was uneventful. Then on Monday morning I get a call from a tour company. They decided to hire me as a tour driver. I accepted the position and was asked when can I start. I said in two weeks. They said, "Welcome to Hawaiian Tours." I thanked them and called my Operational Manager and told him that my second shift on Saturday will be my last. There was silence on the other end. Then my Operational Manager said, "It was good to have you." Then I hung up.

For the next week, I said my goodbyes to the business owners at the mall. They told me that I was the only guard who did anything. I said, "I appreciate your kind words." Saturday came, I finished my second shift. On Sunday morning, I went across the street and talked to Mr. Turner. I said, "Can I keep my reports?" He laughed and said, "Here you go. Good luck with your new job." Then I walked to the Pagoda Hotel.

Three months later, I visited the Hawaiian Boulevard Mall. It was Friday at 7 P.M. The grocery store was now a Korean restaurant. The Banyan Tree was now decorated with Christmas lights. Then I went looking for the guard. He told me that it was a quiet site. The hours were only part time. I told him how it used to be. He said he heard the stories. It is not like that now. I said goodbye and went to the massage parlor. It was gone. However, I was not surprised. I left the mall and took my car to the Ala Moana Shopping Center. Boy, did I like my new job!

MEN WHO RIDE MOUNTAINS

It was June 1995. The waves of Waikiki were thirty feet high. I was on a boogie board near the Royal Hawaiian Hotel. The waves were only three to five feet high. The big waves were 100 yards away. I swam to the big waves not realizing that my boogie board was upside down. Finally, I made it to the big waves. I was accompanied by forty surfers. I was the only one with a boogie board. This should have been a sign. However, I was overcome with excitement. My first wave was coming. I saw five surfers on the wave. I was surprised how fast they were going. I estimated at least fifteen to twenty miles an hour. I position myself to ride the wave. The wave hit me like concrete. I wound up doing twenty somersaults in the water. The current was really strong. I was underneath the wave for twenty four seconds. Then I came up for air.

I positioned myself for the second wave. It was coming fast. I rode the wave for three seconds. Then I wiped out. Again with the somersaults. Again I was underneath the water for twenty four seconds. Then I came up for air.

I positioned myself for the third wave. It was the same results. However, this time I was underneath the water for thirty seconds. The currents this time were very, very strong. When I came up for air. I decided to swim back to shore. I swam and stood in the same position. Another wave came. The same nightmare. I was in over my head. Now I was scared. I saw the Coast Guard helicopters overhead. I waved for help. They did not see me. Another wave, the same nightmare. I am fifteen minutes away from pure terror. I decided to stay calm and ask for help.
I said, "Excuse me. Can you bring me in?"
The surfer said, "Ride the wave brudda."
I said, "I can't. I am in over my head."
He ignored me. Then I asked another surfer, "Can you bring me in?"
He also ignored me. I see the Coast Guard helicopter overhead again. I wave again he does not see me. Another wave. I come up for air. This time I am getting tired.

I am now breathing hard. I ask another surfer for help. No response. The terror is coming. Then I heard a voice from a fifteen year old kid. He says, "I'll take you in brudda. Stay calm." I grabbed his leash and he towed me in. I take three more waves. But I am calm. I know that I will be at the shore in ten minutes. Then he changes direction. I started to yell, "No no no stay straight." He said, "I have to swim away from the rocks relax brudda."

I finally reached the shores of Waikiki. I told the kid, "Give me your address I will mail you a check for one hundred dollars." He laughed and went back to the water. The lifeguard asked me if I needed any help. I said no. Then my legs, arms and head started to shake. I collapsed on the sands of Waikiki. The lifeguard asked me if I needed an ambulance. I said, "No, I can't afford one. Just let me lie here. I'll be fine."

I laid in the sand for fifteen minutes. The shaking finally stopped. Then I began to get pain throughout my body. I also noticed scratches on my chest. It came from the fiberglass of my boogie board. I stood up. My back did not want to straighten up. I walked like an old man. I decided to sit at the nearest bench. My apartment was only twenty minutes away. However, it took me one hour to get home. I opened the door to my apartment and went to bed. I slept for five hours. Then I got up and went to take a shower. To my amazement, I still walked around like an old man. It took me two days to fully recover.

My attitude toward the beaches of Hawaii changed. I feared the water. For the next ten years, I would not enter the water without a little fear. When I snorkeled, the slightest riptide would put me in a panic. When I went to deep water, I would panic. It just wasn't the same anymore. What surprised most is that I got claustrophobic in tight places. I also did not like being in very crowded nightclubs. I had no idea that coming close to drowning would have such an effect on me. I began to meet people with stories of the Hawaiian waters. Some were not easy to listen to. It always involved near drowning experiences or sharks. The riptides in Hawaii are brutal. Just remember, respect the beautiful blue hawaiian waters. Because the day will come when these waters will show you no mercy.

LOS ANGELES

TABLE OF CONTENTS

In the city of Los Angeles, even Jesus Christ would make a left turn at a red light.

UPSIDE DOWN

I left the islands of Hawaii seven years ago. My new destination was Los Angeles, California. People always ask me, "Why did you leave?" I would always respond, I missed the mainland. I decided to get a job as a shuttle driver. What surprised me most was the amount of car accidents that I saw on a daily basis. One day, I saw four accidents in one hour. The left lane of the highway was the worst. It always involved three or more cars. One time a car on the left lane was on fire. At every accident the police, fire department and paramedics show up. However, in some areas of Los Angeles. If there are no injuries or death, no one shows up. The 911 operator would say exchange information and have a nice day.

You always witness people speeding and trying to beat the traffic light. In Los Angeles, a green light means wait two seconds then go. Always look at the car in front of you. If his brake lights go on. Your brake lights go on. If a car goes off road. He is either parking or about to make an illegal U Turn. Then on one occasion, I saw a car lose control and take flight. The boulder at the nearby hotel was used as a ramp. Fortunately, no one was hurt.

Then I witnessed a bad accident. The irony was it involved only one car. I was sitting in traffic on the 101 North. On my left, I noticed traffic on Cahuenga Boulevard. Then I saw a 1970s brown Ninety eight Oldsmobile. It was traveling at a high rate of speed. He noticed the traffic up ahead and hit the brakes hard. The car was all over the road. Then it hit the eight inch curb, broke the divider and the car slid upside down on the embankment. The cars on the highway avoided the sliding vehicle. The upside car came to a complete stop in the middle of the 101 South. I noticed the driver trying to get out. He somehow released his seatbelt and crawled out of his vehicle. Then the front window of his car popped real loud. The glass was all over the road. The driver made it to the divider that separated 101 North and South. He sat on the divider and waited for the police. I guess there is always something to look at during traffic.

"Hello Joe," my name is Rick. I will be training you today to become a dame good tour bus driver. We will travel on Mulholland Drive and show celebrity homes to our wonderful customers. If you have any questions just ask. Hey Rick, how long have you been working for this company? Oh about three years. Really, what did you do before this job? Well Joe, I was an armed robber. Really, did you go to jail? Yep seven years. Apparently, I wasn't good at it. You have your list of celebrity homes Yep, got it right here.

MARIO AND MOM

I went to a medical clinic in Glendale, California. I sat in the waiting room waiting for Dr. Johnson to see me. I come to the clinic every three months to get refills of my medications. I began to realize that ex cons come to this medical facility. There was Marcus a serious gangbanger with a tattooed face. My conversations with him were friendly and brief. Then there was Mario. Mario was a friendly guy. He told me that he spent nine years in prison. Mario was an armed robber. He told me how he hated the smell of simple green. In prison you smelled it all day. He said the worst thing was the boredom. A lot of prisoners really belonged in a mental ward. The screaming that went on night after night. My biggest regret was not having a family. I began to realize that Mario had a hard time getting his words out. It was apparent that Mario had a minor stroke in his past. But what surprised me most is that his mother would help with his armed robbery. You see she was the driver. This is a story of his regret.

"Son, check your gun!'
"Mom you repeat yourself over and over again!''
"What happened last time?! Ah, WHAT HAPPENED LAST TIME!!"

"I left the safety on Mom. I made one mistake Mom, one mistake."
The little yorkshire began to bark in the backseat.
Mario says, "Ziggy shut up!!"
"Check your gun Mario!
"Mom, I know I know!!"
Ziggy starts barking again.

Mario you have to pay attention when you are robbing a supermarket. Be aware of your surroundings."
"Mom! I know! I know!!"
Ziggy just keeps barking.
Mario screams, "Hey leopard messiah fucking shut up!!"
"Mario stop yelling at Ziggy and concentrate. There is a robbery to do!!"

Mario checks his gun and puts it back in his jacket. Then he gets out of the car and walks to the supermarket. The sliding doors open. How many times has he robbed a store in Eagle Rock, California. He is just your friendly neighborhood robber. He goes to a cashier, who is a heavy set Spanish girl. He takes out his gun. He points to her head and says, "Give me your fucking money!" Instead of complying, she screams holy murder. Mario is puzzled by this. He says, "Relax just give me the money." She just keeps screaming. Mario says to himself, "This is not going well." He panics and leaves the supermarket. He runs back to the car. He opens the car door. Ziggy starts barking.
Mario says, "Ziggy shut up!"
Mario's mom says, "Stop making Ziggy nervous! Where's the money!"
Mario says, "No money let's go Mom!"
Mario's mom says, "What kind of robber did I raise!"
Mario says, "Mom there was too much commotion! Let's rob the chinese restaurant up the block."
Mario's mom says, "Don't fuck this up!"

Mario's mom drives the car to the next mall. She parks the vehicle in the parking lot. Mario gets out of the vehicle. He walks into the chinese restaurant and points the gun at the owner. The owner says, "Don't shoot! Don't shoot! I am covered by insurance." He opens the cash register and gives him the money. Mario leaves. He enters the car. Wow Ziggy is not barking.
Mario's mom says, "How much money Mario?''
Mario says, "Six hundred dollars."

Mario's mom says, "Let's go."
Mario says, "Look mom the cops are at the supermarket. I was there only two minutes ago."
Mario and Mom felt satisfied and left for home.

Armed robbery was a way of life for Mario and his mother. He would make a couple of a hundred dollars at each robbery. On good days, he would make one or two thousand dollars.

One day he picks a Korean Restaurant. There is no parking. So his mother parks in another mall. Mario checks his gun and puts it in his jacket. He leaves the vehicle. He enters the restaurant and puts the gun to the owner's head. The owner complies and gives him eight hundred dollars. However, the owner has a silent alarm. She hits it with her foot. Mario leaves the restaurant. He does not realize the police department of Eagle Rock is trying to solve the string of robberies in the area. So all of the squad cars are parked less than a mile away from each mall. Mario begins to walk calmly to the other mall. A police car pulls up behind him. Two policemen get out of the squad with their guns drawn. They yell, "Get your hands up! Mario complies. The policeman driving says, "Come toward our vehicle slowly! Again Mario complies. Then the officer says, "Lay down on the ground! Spread your legs and arms!" They approach Mario with caution. Then they check for weapons. They find Mario's 9mm. Finally, they tell him to put his hands behind his back. Mario hears the cuffs go on.

Mario's mother is wondering what is taking him so long. Then she sees the police car go by. Mario and Mom make eye contact. Ziggy begins to bark. Mario's Mom is stunned. She sits in her car for a good twenty minutes. Ziggy is quiet. Then Mario's Mom starts her car and leaves the mall.

She comes home to a lonely apartment. She sits on her sofa and begins to cry. It's just her and Ziggy now. For the next three weeks, she visits Mario at the county jail. Then she visit's Mario's lawyer. The lawyer informs her that things are not looking good for Mario. Mario goes to trial. Then the day comes when the jury reads the verdict. He is found guilty of course. The judge sentenced him to fifteen years in prison. Mario's Mom sees her son leave the courtroom escorted by the sheriffs. She watches the door close and feels the loneliness set in. She leaves the courthouse and goes to the supermarket. She buys some food for Ziggy and her. Then returns to her apartment.

She visits Mario every Sunday. She talks to him behind thick glass and a phone. They talk about Ziggy and Mario's lawyer. After two years, she is allowed to see Mario in an open area. The prison allowed the visitors to use one of their cafeterias to visit the convicts. Each visit begins and ends with strong emotions.

The next seven years are hard on Mario. He watches his mother grow old. He gets scared at times. He begins to wonder, will she be there when he is released from prison? Then he begins to notice men with families. He cries and realizes that he missed out in having his own family. His mother would be an outstanding grandmother. The biggest problems in jail was crappy food and boredom. He found himself dreaming about eating steaks and big pork chops. Then on certain Sundays, Mario's mom would bring mashed potatoes and big ribeye steaks. One time she even brought in sliced roast beef with white rice and chickpeas. Man did Mario enjoy that meal.

Unfortunately, Mario did not take care of himself. He had high blood pressure. They gave him pills. He complained that they made him dizzy. So he stopped taking them. Then one day he had a stroke. He recovered but he talked with a slur for the rest of his life.

For good behavior, he was released from prison in nine years. His mother comes to pick up Mario. She arrived alone. Mario asked, "Mom where is Ziggy?" She looked at him and said, "Mario Ziggy died two weeks ago. I didn't have the heart to tell you." Then she says "Mario try on this shirt and jeans. I bought them at Macy's."

Mario says, "Macy's that's a fancy store Mom!" She says, "I know! I know! Try them on." Mario could not wait to get his orange jumpsuit off. He felt euphoric when he put on his new clothes. He walked out of that prison one happy man.

They ate at a chinese restaurant. Then went to their apartment. It was not the same without Ziggy. However, two weeks later Mario's Mom bought a light brown chihuahua. It was a six month old puppy. Mario asked his mother if he could name the puppy. She said, “Go ahead Mario.” He decided to name him Scrappy. His mother liked his name. She said, “Scrappy it is.”

Once a month, Mario would meet his probation officer and then go to the medical clinic. There at the medical clinic I meet Mario and his Mom.

One night, a man was sitting on his recliner watching a baseball game. There was a commotion in the next apartment. A girl was screaming, “Don’t kill me! Please don’t kill me!” The man on the recliner was frantic. He gets up from his recliner. He bangs on the wall and says, “Hey! Hey keep your murder! I am trying to watch the ballgame!’’ The murderer screams, “Sorry!” The man sat down on his recliner and said, “Man people are so inconsiderate when they are getting killed!”

MURDER IN LOS ANGELES

It is the night before Halloween. I was driving my shuttle bus on sixth street in downtown Los Angeles. I just passed Pershing Square Park. I was approaching Main Street. Then between Main and Los Angeles street, I saw a dead body. He was to my left. It seemed that his blood covered the sidewalk. It dripped onto the street like heavy pancake syrup. What surprised me most was the blood was dark, dark red. The victim was an Asian male in his mid twenties. He was average height and had a medium built. His arms were out like he was nailed to a cross. I noticed that he had three bullet wounds in his chest.

I began to notice the crowd around him. There were three policemen and a small crowd of onlookers. The yellow tape that said crime scene was not up. The ambulance had not arrived. Then I noticed some of the onlookers were dressed up for Halloween. One man was dressed in a white clown suit. He put a 1970s television set on his head. The other man was dressed up as a vampire clown. Then there were two girls dressed up in cat outfits.

I made my left turn on Los Angeles Street. The flashbacks of the murder victim began immediately. I drove down to the Doubletree Hilton. I parked my bus and ate at a Ramen Noodle House. The restaurant was located on the second floor of the Doubletree Hilton. The interesting thing was that you had to cross a corridor that led to a mall full of Ramen Noodle Houses. The soups only cost seven dollars. I picked a noodle house. I went in and sat down. I ordered a pork soup and seasoned it with suribachi sauce. Then I noticed four cops at a table. They all had a 9mm Smith and Wesson. This made me very uncomfortable. So I ate rather quickly and left the restaurant.

I drove to Sunset Boulevard and arrived at a gas station. I got out of the bus and then got hit with another flashback of the murder victim. I envisioned him in my mind with him lying on the sidewalk. Then the vision went away. I finished gassing up the bus. I unlocked the driver's door, sat down and put the key into the ignition. I started the bus and put the transmission on drive. I hit the gas and leave the gas station. I make a left turn and proceed south. I stopped at a red light, another flashback. When the light turned green the flashback started to fade.

I parked my bus in the employee lot. Then I got into my vehicle and drove out of the employee parking lot. I am driving on the 101 north. This time there was no flashback. However, I started to think about what I witnessed. I wondered how upset his immediate family would be, especially his mother. For some reason, this calmed me down.

I finally arrived at my apartment. I opened the door. I put the keys on the counter. Then I decided to watch a little TV. I felt a little anxious. I decided to shut off the television and go to the gym. At the gym, I did not tell anyone what I witnessed in downtown Los Angeles. When I finished my workout. I returned to my apartment. I felt more relaxed. I put the TV back on and did not have a flashback for the rest of the night. I went to sleep in peace.

THE RELATIVES

THE GRANDMAS

TABLE OF CONTENTS

AN ESSAY

I was in the backseat of a 1965 maroon Chevy Impala. I was twelve years old. My grandmas were sitting to the left of me. My father was driving. My grandfather was on the passenger side. Everyone was talking in Spanish. They were laughing and enjoying their conversations. I looked to my right and saw a prostitute in short pants. I began to wonder what she looked like naked. However, her legs were skinny. So, I lost interest rather quickly.

I looked to my left and saw my grandmothers look at the back of the front seat. The anger they had toward that woman was very, very intense. I put my left arm up. I was convinced that an asswhipping was coming. However, I was wrong. My father saw his mother in the rearview mirror. He said, "Mom! Mom! Que paso! Que paso! What's wrong? Mom what's wrong?" The grandmothers continued to look at the back of the front seat. My grandfather hit my dad's right leg. He gave a hand signal to leave it alone. Then my grandfather readjusted his glasses and looked out the window. He made sure he did not look at the hooker. I will never forget that day. For some reason, three stories just popped into my head. My dad's mom was named Isabel. My mother's mom was named Angelica.

WHORE

My dad was feeding the chickens in the backyard. His mother was inside the house sweeping the floors with a push broom. Her two daughters were doing chores in the house. Then my grandmother Isabel picked up a window cleaner and a rag. She used these items to clean the front windows. She always started inside the house. She sprayed the windows and went in a circular motion with the rag. Then through the window she saw a prostitute.

The prostitute was a thin woman with black hair. She was pacing back and forth and smoking a cigarette in a nervous manner. It was obvious that she was waiting for customers. Isabel was horrified. She looked at her two daughters doing chores. Then she went outside and stood at her porch.

She screamed, "Puta! Puta!! The whorehouse is two miles down the road! What are you doing on my street?!"

The whore said, "Making money!!"

The puta dropped her cigarette and put it out with her right foot.

Isabel screamed, "Get off my street you fucking whore!!"

The puta replied, "Mind your own business old lady!"

Isabel said, "Apparently, you are not listening!

Then Isabel points and says, "The whorehouse is that way!"

The puta says, "FUCK YOU! Where is your husband, old lady? I want to make some money. Then the punta laughed and lit another cigarette. Isabel was livid. So she went back inside her house.

Isabel was in her kitchen getting madder by the second. She found herself talking out loud. She looked at her two daughters. Then she walked to her push broom and unscrewed the broomstick. She put the broomstick into her right hand like a baseball bat. She left the house in a fast pace. She hoped the prostitute did not see her coming. Isabel continued to walk. Then two other women joined her. They also had daughters. They also had broomsticks in their right hands. Isabel said, "I'll take the face." The other women took the body and legs. Then all four women made eye contact.

The three women began to beat her. The sticks were swinging. The whore fell. They proceeded to hit her harder and harder. The punta screamed, "Tu putas locas! You crazy bitches!" Then the women stopped swinging their sticks. They picked her up and walked to the other side of the street. Then they dumped in a ditch. The whore started screaming profanities. Isabel looked at her, pointed down the road with her left finger. Then she said, " the whorehouse is that way!" All three women turned their backs on her and left.

The three women walked back to their homes. Isabel went inside her house and screwed the broomstick back on the push broom. She then walked to the refrigerator and opened it to grab a pitcher of iced tea. She put the pitcher of ice tea on the counter. Then opened the cabinet above the sink. She grabbed an empty mayonnaise jar and filled it with ice. She poured the ice tea into the mayonnaise jar. Then walked onto her porch and sat down on a rocking chair. She took a sip of her ice tea and then stared at the road. Isabel waited for the whore to stand up and walk toward the whorehouse. The punta finally stood up and walked to the whorehouse in a dizzy manner. Isabel took another sip of ice tea. Then she said to herself, "If she comes back tomorrow. I will use the mopstick. It's thicker." Then she stopped rocking her chair. Stood up and went back inside the house.

SLUT IN THE SCHOOLYARD

Isabel, Juanita and Maria were sitting on a bench in a schoolyard. They were talking, laughing and pointing at the boys. Marie was the courageous one. She would wave at the boys she liked. Some of the boys would wave back. Some would be courageous and return the wave with a smile. Juanita asked Isabel, "Did Jose ask you out yet?" Isabel replied with a smile, "Mind your business." Then Isabel said, "I passed by his house yesterday. I allowed him to walk me home. He told me he no longer goes to school. He has been driving a forklift since he was twelve years old. He is fourteen now. He is proud to have a paycheck every week." Maria asked, "How come he left school?" Then Isabel said, "His mother died of tuberculosis. So his dad took him out of school and got him a job at a warehouse."

Jose was a serious boy. After work, he would go home, take his work clothes off and put on a white suit and tie. His slacks were always creased. His shoes were polished and black. Then he would go to the refrigerator and grabbed some lemonade. After that, he would sit on the porch of his white house and wonder about his life. This relaxed him as a fourteen year old boy.

Isabel, Juanita and Marie continued their conversation at the schoolyard. Then Maria interrupts, "Hey you see that twelve year old girl. She is having sex with her fourteen year old boyfriend."
Isabel screamed, "What!!! Does she know that she can die at childbirth! She is only twelve!!"

Juanita says, "She is only a year younger than you. Isabel it is none of our business. It is between… Isabel got up and walked toward the girl.
Isabel asked, "What is your name?!
The girl answered, "My name is Anita!"
Isabel asked, "Are you having sex with your boyfriend!!"

Anita looked at her and decided to describe her desires. Isabel had no interest in listening to her. So Isabel slapped her very hard. Anita returned the slap. A fight ensued. The violence between the two girls was intense. Their hands were full of loose hair. They caught their breath, called each other whores and began to slap and punch.

The principal Mr. Rodriguez noticed the two girls fighting. He immediately ran toward the girls . He separated them. He asked, "What is going on?!" Isabel stated, "She is having sex with her boyfriend!"
The principal stated, "Is this true?!"
The girl replied, "No!!"

Isabel went after her. The principal slapped Isabel and yelled, "Cut it out!" Then the principal yells at Anita, "You, young lady, go to the nurse.! Now!" Then the principal tells Isabel that she has to stay after school and do chores for the teacher. The afternoon bell rings and the kids return to class.

The principal visits the nurse. The nurse confirms that Anita is sexually active. The principal talks to Anita. He tells her the danger of having a child at her age. Then he says, "I will have to talk to your mother today."

Mr. Rodriguez left the nurse's office. Then he walked to the nearest classroom. There he meet a fellow teacher named Ms. Lopez. He asked her to come outside the classroom. He tells her that he needs her to accompany him to Anita's house. Then he explains why. Ms. Lopez says, "Of course I will go with you."

The three o'clock bell rang. Isabel and Anita felt fear in their hearts. Mr. Rodriguez looks at the mirror and straightens his tie. Then he pulls on his suit and grabs his hat. He went to a classroom and said, "Anita let's go young lady." Then he went Ms. Lopez's classroom and thanked her for helping him. After that, all three walked to Anita's house. The principal rang the doorbell. The door opened and Anita's mom looked concerned. Mr. Rodriguez took off his hat and asked, "May I come in?" The mother said yes. Then there was an awkward silence. Mr. Rodriguez explained the situation about Anita. The young girl was immediately slapped.

After Anita and her mother had a discussion. Mr. Rodriguez stated, "I understand that your husband works in the pineapple fields?''
Anita's mother said, "Yes principal Rodriguez he works in the pineapple fields."
Mr. Rodriguez says, "That means he has his own machete?"
Anita's mother says, "Yes Mr. Rodriguez that is correct."
Mr. Rodriguez says, "Okay the boy will go to another school."
Anita's mom looks at her daughter and says, "You are not to see that boy again! Is that understood. I said is THAT UNDERSTOOD!!"
Anita says, "But mom I…" SLAP
Then Anita's mom says, " CALLATE !! Anita."
Then Anita says, "Yes, ma'am."
Mr. Rodriguez looked at Ms. Lopez and said, "We will go to the boy's house. Goodbye ma'am. Goodbye Mr. Rodriguez and thank you."

The two walked to the boy's house. It was a half a mile down the road. They approached the house. Mr. Rodriguez knocks on the door. The door opened slowly. It was the boy. Mr. Rodriguez said, "Where is your mother young man? Go get her now!!"
The principal stood at the door. The young man's mother approached.
Mr. Rodrigues says, "Can I come in with Ms. Lopez?"
She said, "Yes Mr. Rodriguez come in."
Mr. Rodriguez took off his hat and entered the house. He explained to the young boy's mother what was occuring between the boy and his girlfriend. She was in disbelieve. She asked if the girl was pregnant. Mr. Rodriguez told her that she was not. The mother was relieved. Then Mr. Rodriguez told the woman that her son

must go to another school. The father of the girl works in the pineapple fields. She understood the situation.

The boy screamed, "The school is over a mile away!!" The mother slapped her son. Then she said, "So what!!" The boy begins to speak. The mother just tells him to shut up. The boy again begins to speak. His mother just slaps him. She tells him to apologize to the principal. The boy does what he is told. The principal is satisfied. He puts his hat on. The woman thanks him for his concern. Then she opens the door and lets the principal and Ms. Lopez depart.

The mother returns to the kitchen. The boy's younger brother Miguel comes out of his bedroom. He asked the older brother what is going on. He tells the eleven year old brother, "I am having sex with my girlfriend." Miguel says, "Sex what is that?" The fourteen year old boy looks at his brother. He says, " do you want to go fishing?" Miguel says, "Yea, ok." The fourteen year old says, "Let's go to the pond." He yells, "Mom I am taking Miguel fishing." The mom replies, "Be home before dark. Then I want you to speak to your father." The fourteen year old says, "Ok mom." Then the two boys grabbed their fishing poles and walked to the pond.

ANGELICA

Angelica was born in a small town called Lares, Puerto Rico. She was one of twelve children. She had blond hair and blue eyes. Everyone in the town of Lares was fond of her.There was a man named Antonio Irizarry. He too was of Lares, Puerto Rico. One day, he decided that he must leave Lares to make more money. So he moves to Brooklyn, New York and works at the Brooklyn Navy Yard. Every Christmas he would return to Lares to visit his parents. Then one Christmas vacation he meets Angelica at the market. Angelica noticed that Antonio was dressed in a suit and tie. It was obvious to her that this man was visiting Lares. She decided to take a chance and flirted with him. He smiled and said hello. They did some small talk. He told her that he comes to the market every Sunday after Mass. Funny, she would remember Antonio if he was at church. It was obvious he never went to church. It did not matter to Angelica.

Of course, the following Sunday there was Antonio at church. The mass ended and Antonio went to talk to Angelica's father. This impressed her. Then her father came to her and said, "Angelica I know his family. They work very hard and Antonio lives in NYC. He has a good job and respects me. If you decide to date him. You must talk to your mother first." Angelica agreed then she went on a date with Antonio. For two weeks, Angelica looked forward to seeing Antonio. They went to restaurants and took walks on the beach. Then Antonio had to return to Brooklyn.

Angelica thought about Antonio all the time. She looked forward to his letters. Three months later she decided to visit her cousins in Queens, New York. She informed Antonio in her letters about the visit to Queens, New York. They decided to meet in Manhattan. Unfortunately, she had to bring two of her cousins with her. Antonio understood and told her not to worry. The day came when they meet in Manhattan. They spend their day at Rockefeller Center. They ate did some ice skating and did some shopping. Angelica noticed that Antonio was getting nervous. She told him, "Antonio we had a nice day. I think it is time to bring my cousins and I home." He agreed and told her that he wants to meet her tomorrow. She said, "Ok Antonio but I want to stay close to home. We will do a picnic and a movie and make it an early night." Antonio was relieved that very little money will be spent on the next date.

The next date went well. This time Angelica went alone. They were hitting it off. Angelica felt such warmth with the man. Finally, I am not wasting my time. This time I won't be the only one falling in love. The day came when Antonio insisted that he would go to the pier with her. He wanted to see her board the ship back to Puerto Rico. Angelica agreed and as soon as she boarded that ship. She began to write a letter to Antonio. Antonio could not get Angelica out of his mind. For the first time in his life, when he thought about money he thought about making someone happy. All of a sudden going to work at the Brooklyn Navy had purpose.

Angelica was looking forward to Christmas. The letters from Antonio kept coming. He started to write about his loneliness. Angelica would write back that Christmas will be here soon. Then Antonio wrote in a letter that he will have an extra week off for Christmas. Angelica this means I have three weeks with you in Lares. I cannot wait.

The ship docked at San Juan, Puerto Rico. Antonio's brother picked him up. Then he asked for gas money. He said, "You are the big shot from Brooklyn. Oh by the way your girlfriend is behaving herself." Antonio said, "Shut up and drive." They arrived at Lares and the small town looked beautiful to Antonio. He went to his pocket and showed his brother the ring for Angelica. Of course, his brother said, "How much moonshine did you sell to get that ring?" Antonio did not respond. He just went inside the house and prepared for a date with Angelica.

Angelica was a wreck. She just kept screaming at her sisters. Her mother told her to calm down. Angelica kept rambling. Finally, Antonio arrived at the house. Angelica's mother screamed, "Thank God!" Angelica gave such a look. However, when Antonio knocked on the door. Angelica calmed down. Her father answered the door. He told Antonio to take his daughter out of the house before her mother kills her. Antonio laughed and said to Angelica, "You look beautiful." They left the house and Angelica's mother enjoyed the quiet.

They get into Antonio's car. Angelica says, "Antonio do you like New York?" Antonio says, "It's cold but the money's good. I can never make this kind of money in Lares." Angelica wanted to ask more questions about New York. However, she decided to have small talk. They ate dinner in Arecibo. Then Antonio drove to Poza del Obispo beach. There he proposed marriage to Angelica.

The next day Antonio was hanging out with his brothers and friends. Everyone knew about the engagement. His brother Jose said, "I think you need a new friend." So he took out a bottle of clear Bacardi.Then he took out two shot glasses. Jose broke the seal of the new bottle. He then poured a shot of Bacardi in Antonio's glass. Then Jose poured himself a shot. They drank and everyone was cheering. Afterwards Antonio says, "I need another shot." Jose laughs and says, " you need more than just another shot!" Antonio says, "No just one more shot." He drinks and feels good about his life. Then he sits down at the cafe and plays dominos with his friends and brothers.

Jose says, "Antonio Angelica has a temper."

Antonio says, "Good the kids will be disciplined."

Jose says, "You are having kids already."

Antonio says, "Of course."

Then a girl named Marie arrives.

Marie likes to flirt with men who are taken. She even has sex with engaged men. It is something that is dangerous to do in a small town. Her mother was the same way. Marie had eyes on Antonio. Antonio saw no harm in a little flirting. He poured himself another shot of Bacardi. He drank and said hello to Marie. Jose stepped in, "Antonio your fiance has a temper."

Antonio says, "It is okay I had my fun in NYC."
Then Angelica arrives.

Angelica looks at Marie. Their eyes meet.
Angelica says, "Hey puta, do you see the ring on my finger!"
Marie continues to flirt with Antonio. Antonio stops flirting.
Angelica confronts the punta, "Leave! Leave now!!"
The puta says, "All men are for the taking. You are not special Angelica."
Then Angelica slapped her. The punta began to walk away fast. She is now in the middle of the street. Angelica took off her shoes and ran after Marie. When she was behind Marie, Angelica began to pull her hair. Antonio grabbed Angelica around the waist. She was now in mid air. Marie began to swing at Angelica. Antonio let go of Angelica. The fighting began to get attention around Lares. They punched each other and the words whore and slut were said numerous times. Marie went down. Angelica continued to punch. Then Antonio grabbed Angelica's mid section. She was in mid air again. Then she yelled at Antonio, "Get the fuck off me!!" He let go. Angelica was breathing hard. She surveyed her hands and noticed three fingernails broken. She looked at Antonio and said, "YOU BASTARD!! YOU KNOW WHAT SHE IS!!" Then Angelica gave a stern look at Antonio and walked to her house.

The next morning Angelica went to Antonio's parents farm. She was alone. She knocked on the door. One of Antonio's sisters opened the door. She informed Angelica that Antonio was sleeping. Then Angelica asked if Antonio was drunk last night. Antonio's sister said, "He was quite drunk last night." Angelica felt disappointed, so she took off the engagement. Then she placed the ring on top of the kitchen table. She did not shed a tear. Afterwards, she left the farm and returned home. Upon arrival, she opened the door to her house. Then she sat on the living room couch and began to sob. Angelica kept on saying, "Who am I kidding all men are the same. They only think about themselves." She sobbed and sobbed. When she felt at peace. Angelica grabbed one of her sisters and walked to the beach.

Antonio woke up with a bad hangover. He walked over to the kitchen table. Then he saw the engagement ring. Antonio picked it up. He looked at it and said, "If I was a young man. I would be making a foolish mistake. I would actually not marry Angelica." He put the ring in his pocket. His mother made him coffee. Antonio said, "Gracias madre." He drank four cups of coffee. Then took a shower. Afterwards, he put on his best suit and put the ring in his pocket. He straightened his tie and walked to Angelica's house.

When he arrived at Angelica's house. He knocked on the door. One of Angelica's sisters opened the door. Antonio asked, "Where did Angelica go?" She answered, "She went to the beach." It was a two mile walk to the beach. Then Angelica's sister said, "Put this wet washcloth on your head. Here is a jug of water. Carry it with you to the beach." Antonio said, "Thank you." Then he sat down on a kitchen chair. He removed his shoes and socks. Said goodbye. Then walked to the beach. Antonio realized it was hot, really hot. But he was on a quest.

He finally got to the beach. He saw Angelica sitting on a dead fallen tree. He sat down on the dead tree. He said, "Angelica what I did was wrong." While he is saying this, he is putting his shoes and socks on. He continued, "My sisters have taken your side." Angelica smiled and said, "Please Antonio no more whoring." He agreed and put the ring back on her finger. Then Antonio kissed her. She felt his sincerity on her lips. He began to weep. Antonio looked away, dried his eyes. Angelica looked at Antonio. Then went for a swim. Her sister's boyfriend arrived in his car. They got in and returned to Lares.

They arrived at her house. Antonio and Angelica went for a walk. They kissed in a delicate manner. Antonio said, "Next week I must return to NYC. My job is there." Angelica said, "I want to go to New York with you. However, you know what must happen. Antonio smiled and said, "We will marry in one year. Next Christmas, we will get married in a church in Lares. Then we will live in New York permanently." The following morning Antonio left for San Juan and boarded a ship heading for NYC. When he docked in Manhattan, his brother Roberto picked him up. He said, "Antonio we have a new boss at the Brooklyn Navy Yard. He is a mean son of a bitch. Antonio didn't realize his luck was about to change for the worst.

THE GRANDPAS

They say sometimes when bad things happen, something good will occur. Well when good things happen something bad will occur. Just ask life.

Table of Contents

ANTONIO

The work at the Brooklyn Navy Yard was relentless. Antonio's friend Luis said, "My God the work never ends this is awful. I am always tired." Antonio replied, "I am as strong as an ox. I can take it." The new boss was a mean son of a bitch. He enjoyed listening to the men complain. Then one day the new boss said to Antonio, "Work harder you fucking spic! You are a tiny little shit aren't you Antonio." The other spanish men would tell Antonio to pretend you are Italian. Change your name if you have to. Antonio would not have it. He would say, "The hell with that freckled face fuck." Then one day the boss comes in and says, "Niggas and spics work in the bottom of the ship. The whites work on top of the ship. The work is easier. Any of you niggas and spics complain. I will fire your ass. Then you can work in a shiity factory where you belong."

Antonio did not take the comment well. Luis looked at Antonio. Antonio said, "Luis I am not going to pretend I am Italian." Luis said, "No Antonio the guys are looking for something to do during lunch." Antonio got the message. So he yells at his boss, "Hey redhead freckles only look good on a bitch."
The boss says, "What was that you little spic!"
Antonio says, "Your right it doesn't look good on a bitch either. Is your mother as ugly as you?" The boss looked at him in disbelief.
Then Antonio says, "Let's discuss this during lunch like men. REDHEAD!!"

The boss said, "You little shit. I will destroy you."
Then Antonio said, "Lunch time you freckled fuck!"
The boss laughed and said, "This shouldn't take long."

It was lunch time. The men gathered around and made a circle. There were men watching from the second tier of the ship. All the spanish men knew that Antonio never lost a fight. He was a scrapper and spent two years fighting in the puerto rican fighting club in Manhattan. A mexican coach took an interest in Antonio. The tactic for Antonio was to throw many, many punches in three minutes. Oddly, Antonio developed his stamina from walking not running. He walked everywhere. It is a habit from childhood. He would walk from one farm to another. He would do chores for the farmer and get paid in cash or food. He was ready.

The Irish gentleman was from Manhattan. He was a brawler. He also did some wrestling in high school. However, Luis said something very interesting to Antonio. The Irish gentleman could not see very well. Luis said, "The man is always squinting his eyes. Do not stay very close to him. Antonio took Luis's advice. The fight was on.

Antonio charged in and threw forty punches in sixty seconds. Then he backed up. His boss said, "You little shit! Don't runaway from me!" Antonio noticed that his left eye was swollen. So Antonio attacked him from the left. He threw fifty punches in sixty seconds. Then his boss tried to grab him and wrestle him to the ground. Antonio would not have it. Unexpectedly, the brawler threw three very good punches. Antonio realized that his boss was very strong. So Antonio faked left and went right. The boss threw five more punches. Antonio was winded. However, he began to throw a lot of punches. The boss's right eye began to swell. Then Antonio let him have it. This Irish guy was strong. He took such a beating. He never went down. The whistle blew. It was time to get back to work.

Two hours later, the boss came to Antonio. He said, "You little fuck." Antonio said, "I thought I was a little spic." He said, "Fuck you Antonio we will meet again tomorrow."

It was 9 A.M. in the Brooklyn Navy Yard. The talk of the morning was the fight of course. Then Antonio realized that two big Irishmen were working by his side. Antonio smiled and said, " are you here to protect your bitch!" One Irishman said, "We are going to meet after work." Antonio said, "I guess I'll have to bring my friends." Just then a manager from upstairs walked to the two Irishmen. He said, " the owner of the yard wants to see both of you, immediately! Antonio we will talk later."

The two Irishmen and Antonio's boss walked upstairs. They opened the door. They sat down with their boss. The owner of the yard was an italian man. He had seven pinkerton guards behind him. The owner spoke, "You fucking mics and your fighting! All three of you are fired!" The Irish boss said, "Are you sticking up for that spic?!" The owner said, "That spic is my best worker."
The Irish guy says, "So fucking what!"
The owner said, "Get the fuck out of my office! These guards will let you out, physically if necessary!"
The Irish guy says, "Fuck you!"
The guards move forward. The Irish boss says, "All right! All right!"
The owner says, "At least you did not cry like the last mic manager I fired. Get out!!"

It was Friday night. The workers get paid in cash. It was a cold night and Antonio walked to the trolley alone. He waited for the streetcar. Then six Irishmen walked toward Antonio. They made eye contact with Antonio.
Then one said, "I heard you got paid today." the other Irishmen began to laugh.
The same guy said, "I hear that you would like to buy us beer."
Antonio said, "I ain't buying you anything."
Another guy said, "Hey guys he said it in English." They started to laugh.
Then another Irishmen says, "Give me your fucking pay!!"
Antonio says, "What I can't understand you.That is one heavy Irish accent."
Antonio continues, "Would you kindly speak the Queen's english."
Another Irishmen says, "You fucking spic!! Hand over your fucking pay!!"
Antonio refused and the fighting began. It was six against one. Antonio had no chance. He was beating unconscious. He laid in the street. Then one Irishmen took his pay out of his pocket. They left laughing. One Irish guy said, "That spic looks like a wop to me. The other Irishmen said "Who the fuck cares. Let's go drinking."

Antonio laid in the street. He was barely conscious. He heard the trolley coming. It was getting louder. Antonio's right hand laid on the tracks. The conductor noticed Antonio laying on the street. He put the brakes on. The steel wheels of the trolley began to screech. Sparks were flying from the front wheels. It was too late. The front left wheel chopped off half of his pinky and index fingers. Antonio woke up in agony. He wrapped his two fingers in a handkerchief. He put pressure on his two fingers to stop the bleeding. Then he ran to the nearest hospital.

Antonio arrived at the hospital. He had no money. He informed the doctor about his incident at the trolley. The doctor looked at his injured fingers and stitched them up. He told Antonio to return to the hospital in two weeks. Then he will remove the stitches. Afterwards, you must pay the bill. Antonio thanked the doctor and walked to his apartment.

During the walk, he thought about how is he going to pay his bills. He decided to talk to his brothers. He will borrow some money and pay them back. Then he will eat at his sister's house. He also made more moonshine then ever. Then he decided to work six days a week for the next three months.

The Christmas holidays are around the corner. The job gave him an extra week off. He decided to work fourteen days straight. This will give him plenty of cash for the trip to Lares. On December 21, 1938. Antonio boarded a ship heading toward San Juan, Puerto Rico. When the ship docked, Antonio ran off the ship and meet his brother. His brother said, "Relax Antonio Angelica isn't going anywhere!" Antonio replied, "Just hurry up and don't say shit about my moonshine!" His brother laughed and off they went to Lares. Of course, his brother said, "Did you ever thought about adding some sugar and fruits to your moonshine. That way your liquor will stop tasting like turpentine." Antonio replied, "I don't hear complaints about my liquor. His brother says, "You'll make more money." Antonio says, "Keep driving Mr. Businessman." His brother just laughed.

Antonio finally meet Angelica. He had to tell her about his fingers. However, he lied to Angelica and said it happened at work.

On December 26, 1938. Antonio married Angelica. They had their honeymoon in Havana, Cuba. They returned to Lares, packed their belongings and moved to NYC. Their first apartment was in Manhattan on 110th street. For thirty nine years they were happily married. They had four children. At the age of fifty nine Angelica caught breast cancer. She was surrounded by her four children and nine grandkids. She died on a hot summer day in Miami, Florida. Within two months, Antonio moved to Lares, Puerto Rico. Three years later, Antonio died of a broken heart.

BODEGA

It was 1949, my grandfather had a Puerto Rican grocery store. They called these grocery stores Bodegas. His first one was in Spanish Harlem. He owned for ten years. Then in 1959, my grandfather sold his grocery store in Spanish Harlem. Afterwards, he bought a house and Bodega in the Bronx. The bodega was located in Grand Concourse. It was only 15 minutes from Yankee Stadium. My grandfather Antonio was a friendly man. So his bodega did quite well. He spoke Spanish, English and of course Spanglish.

It was the summer of 1965. A string of robberies are occurring in the Grand Concourse. One happens only three blocks from Antonio's bodega. He remembers the streetcar mugging quite well. He says to himself, "Never again!" So Antonio gets two big butcher knives. Then he wraps the handles in adhesive tape. He wants to make sure that the grip on the knives are perfect. One knife he hides between two fifty pound bags of rice. The other is under the counter of his cash register. He decided to buy a colt 45 six shooter in the next few days.

Antonio looks under his counter. He says to himself, "I will put the gun next to the knife." He gets up from the counter. Then he makes eye contact with two hispanic men in their twenties. Antonio does not remember hearing the bell on his door. He knew that these two men were not here to buy items. The taller one puts a gun towards Antonio's head. The other laughs and closes the entrance door. He then says, "Nice sunny day hey pops." The one with the gun says, "Give me your cash old man." Antonio knew that this was going to be trouble. He opened the cash register and took out three hundred dollars. He gave it to the man with a gun. The man smiled and decided to pistol whip Antonio. The other guy laughed and decided to join his friend in beating Antonio. They heard the police sirens and ran out of the store laughing.

They were arrested two blocks from Antonio's store. Then the police arrive at Antonio's bodega. He was unconscious on the floor. They called the ambulance. It arrived and Antonio was still unconscious. He finally came to at the hospital. Angelica was naturally upset looking at Antonio. But she informed him that the two men responsible were arrested.

Antonio felt very fortunate that he was not killed. The injuries were not severe. He left the hospital in only a week. Two weeks after the robbery. Antonio opened his grocery store. This time Antonio has a gun and two knives under the counter of the cash register. He has two more knives hidden between fifty pound bags of rice. Then in the storage room there is another gun.

Three weeks go by and everything is back to normal. Antonio is his old self. Then he receives a phone call from his lawyer. He informs him that the court date for the two men will be in six months. Antonio decides that when they come up with a verdict. He wants to be in that courtroom. The day comes for the verdict.

They found the two men guilty of multiple counts. Antonio heard the charges. Then the judge gives both men five years in prison. They will be eligible for parole in three years. Antonio was not happy with the verdict. He also knew that they may rob him again.

It was the summer of 1969. The fourth of July was over. Antonio made a great deal of money all week. He made a lot of deposits at the bank. He was smart enough to use a money belt. He never ever went to the bank the same time everyday. Then on Sundays after church he went to the shooting range. Antonio wanted to be familiar with his weapon. He made sure that the gun was cleaned and ready to go. Then the day came.

It was a hot muggy day. Antonio was making a great deal of money with refreshments. He was in the back of the store. He realizes that he forgot to close the front door. He rushes out and meets the same two men who robbed him three years earlier. The one with the gun says, "What's the rush Pop. Did you forget something?" The other man closes the door.

The guy with the gun says, "That is a nice house you have on Ryer Avenue. You have some very attractive daughters. Get to the cash register Pops. I haven't got all night. Your store was quite busy today. I am looking forward to my party money old man."

Antonio does not give him an argument. He goes to the cash register. Then the man with a gun starts to relax. He jokingly puts his left hand near the cash register. He starts with his low laugh. He looks right at Antonio. He then tells Antonio, "Your older daughter has a son." Antonio decides to use his knife first. He takes the knife and stabs the man's left hand. The knife sticks to the wooden counter. The man screams good and loud. Then Antonio takes out his gun and shoots the man twice in his chest and once in his head. The other robber runs out of the store. Antonio puts his alarm on and runs after him.

The chase is short. Antonio raises his gun and shoots the guy twice in his back. He falls and Antonio walks to him. He turns him over and they meet eye to eye. The man with a bullet in his back calls Antonio a crazy old man.

Then Antonio speaks, "My name is Antonio, Antonio Irizarry. I am a Puertorriqueno from the Bronx. That store you robbed is my Bodega. I worked six days a week for twenty years. No one robs Antonio. No one robs a kid from the great depression. You want to be an asshole. I'll put one in your forehead." BAM!! The man died instantly.

Antonio walks back to his store. He can feel the heat from his gun. He opens the door to his store. The gunman's hand is still stuck on the counter. Antonio put his gun on the counter next to the gunman's hand. He shuts off his alarm and returns to the entrance door to close it. Then he returns to the counter and walks around the dead man. Underneath his cash register was a pint of Bacardi and a shot glass. Antonio liked to have a shot of Bacardi at the end of the day. However, he decided it was time for a shot.

Antonio grabbed his pint of clear Bacardi. He put it on the counter. Then he grabbed his shot glass. He put it on the counter. He opened the bottle of Bacardi. He poured it into his shot glass. He raised the shot glass to his lips. Antonio said, "Salud!" Then he drank and grinded his teeth. He poured another shot. He raised the shot glass to his lips. Antonio said, "Salud." However, this time he felt some emotion. He drank the Bacardi and felt the fire in his chest. Antonio was beginning to feel the shakes coming. He had to gain control of himself. He felt tempted to have another shot. He decided to put the bottle underneath the counter. Then he grabbed the phone. He put it on top of the counter and called the police.

The phone began to ring. Antonio was feeling the shakes coming. He felt like losing his mind. But he gained his composure back. A voice came on the phone. The voice said, "Precinct 45 Sergeant Murphy speaking.''

Antonio begins to speak, "Hello Sergeant Murphy this is Antonio from the grocery store."

Sergeant Murphy said, "Those two pieces of crap robbed your store again Antonio."

Antonio said, "Yes. Yes they did."

Sergeant Murphy said, "Is everything ok Antonio."

Antonio hesitated but said, "Sergeant Murphy." Antonio hesitates again, "Sergeant Murphy I killed them both."

Sergeant Murphy quickly says, "Antonio listen to me. You did the world a favor by killing those two pieces of shit! We will send some squad cars and an ambulance to pick up those two pieces of crap. You will not be arrested. However, when we leave you close that store. You will close that store for three or four days. Antonio, I know you were a kid from the great depression. But I promise you that when you open up the grocery store again. The counters will not be looted. The shelves will not be emptied. Antonio get yourself a good lawyer. Do not worry you will never go to jail. Do you understand Antonio?" Antonio said, "Yes I understand." Then Sergeant Murphy said, "Antonio hang up the phone and wait.'' Antonio said, "Ok, Sergeant Murphy." Then Antonio hung up the phone slowly and waited.

For the next four days, Antonio drank heavily. He began to realize that he will never be the same again. His wife made her son stay with her sister. Antonio would lay in his bed alone and drink. Angelica left him alone. She made his meals and kept them in the refrigerator.

On the fourth day, Antonio returned to his Bodega. He joked and said, "I hope the girlfriend is fine. He was in front of his store and said, "How are you doing my girlfriend?'' He gave a light tap to his door. Then he lit up a smile and opened the door. He closed the door behind him. Then walked slowly down the aisle. He felt like he has been gone for weeks not four days. He went to the bathroom and looked at the mirror. Then he splashed water on his face. He thought about his five year old grandson. He will be here this Sunday. Then he combed his hair, straightened his shirt and walked to the entrance door. He opened it and said, "Ok girlfriend time to make money."

Antonio closed early that day. He went back to the storage where he kept two suits. He put two suits there for special occasions. He felt just in case he wanted to take Angelica somewhere. However, today he put his suit on and went to the nearest church. Antonio said to himself, "I guess God is going to say who the hell are you? It's ok God my girlfriend made money today."

Antonio sat on a pew. He saw an old woman praying. Then another lighting candles near the Virgin Mary. He felt comfort and decided not to drink tonight. He felt that he will do his regular Saturday night drinking with one of his brothers.

A year later, Antonio went to court. He was found not guilty. The judge said, "If there was more store owners like you. There would be less crime. This case is dismissed." Antonio knew it would not end here. He went back to his store two days later. The mothers of the two robbers came to the store. They screamed at

Antonio, "You killed our boys!!" Then a customer came in and screamed at the two women. He said, "Ladies your sons were grown men. They decided to be criminals. This is why they are dead. Sometimes a criminal will meet the wrong victim." Then the guy bought a lot of food from the bodega. The next customer came in and bought two fifty pound bags of rice. Antonio laughed and said, "Jorge you weigh one hundred forty pounds." Jorge said, "Shut up Antonio and carry these two bags to my car." Antonio knew his wife was heavy. This made Antonio laugh to himself. This went on for weeks. Antonio was making big money. He wondered how long this will last. He decided not to think about it. Just enjoy the ride.

The next two years were bad. The mothers of the two criminals kept coming around. Sometimes Antonio felt like shooting them. He even had them arrested twice. Then there was the stress of knowing he killed two men. He was justified and knew what he did was right. However, it still bothered him. Antonio even had two minor heart attacks. The second one laid him in the hospital for two days. Antonio knew that he would get a speech from his doctor and wife. He was fifty nine years old. He said to himself, "I have been working five to six days a week for twenty five years. I did not take a vacation and saved a lot of money. My two daughters are great my two sons are worth shit." He did not give an argument to his wife or doctor. He decided to retire.

It was the summer of 1971. Antonio, Angelica and his son Benny moved to Miami, Florida. Antonio had $300,000 dollars in his bank account. He bought a nice little house in North Miami Beach. Angelica died six years later. Then Antonio moved to Lares, Puerto Rico. Of course, the place changed a lot. The farms were long gone. He got himself a nice apartment. He got drunk a lot with his relatives. Then he had an older son named Anthony. He was one lazy motherfucker. Mr. Fuckhead stole $100,000 dollars from Antonio. Sometimes the biggest criminal is your own fucking son.

JOSE

Jose had a small liquor store in Mayaguez, Puerto Rico. He sold rum, tequila, whiskey and beer. He was quite busy on the weekends and holidays. It was 1941 and Mayaguez was a small town. His wife was named Isabel and she worked as a seamstress. They had three children and a ten year marriage. The oldest child was a boy named Angel. He was eight years old. The other two were girls named Miriam and Margarita. Miriam was six years old. Margarita was four years old.

When Jose did errands, Angel would sit at the cash register. He waited on customers at the age of eight. You can say things were different at the time. When a customer came in, Angel had responsibilities. He would write down the item bought. Then he would put the cash in the register. When Jose came back from his errands. He would go over to Angel. Then ask him for the list of items bought. He would go over the list and knew that no one would take advantage of Angel. Mayaguez was a small honest town.

Every afternoon, Jose would close for lunch. He would get a quick bite and then play dominos with his friends. They all talked about moving to America. Jose always said that he was happy with Mayaguez. Then the conversation would switch to sports, politics and women. Everything was well in the universe. Then Isabel gets a knock on the door.

She opens the door of her little white house. There on the porch stands a man with a four year old boy. The man screams at her, "When is your husband going to give money to my sister?! This is his son!" Isabel looked at the boy. It was pretty apparent that the kid was Jose's. He looked exactly like him. So Isabel asked, "Who is the mother?" The man on the porch said, "My sister's name is Maria Sanchez!" She lives in Cabo Rojo. It is a small world Isabel knows that Maria is the town drunk of Cabo Rojo. The women of Mayaguez know her quite well. She likes to visit her boyfriends in Mayaguez. However, she knows Jose. He went to visit her in Cabo Rojo. Isabel looked at the man on the porch. She said, "He will be home at seven. Do not be here!" Then she slammed the door in his face.

Fortunately, the kids were at school. Isabel was furious. It was apparent that Angel was watching the store, while Jose was having sex with Marie. The next two days the arguments were very heated. Angel can hear his mother screaming, "How can you get the town drunk pregnant?! Do you have any idea what type of trouble that kid will face?! Jose it is pretty apparent that the kid is yours!" Jose's arguments were weak. All he could do was apologize. The tension in the house was immense. Jose knew that things were about to change.

It was three days later. A beautiful Saturday morning. Usually, he takes Angel with him to the liquor store. Isabel insisted that Angel would stay home today. Jose knew that things were about to get worse.

Isabel stood in the house and cried for hours. Then she screamed, "I cannot be in the same house anymore. I have to leave." She looked at her suitcases and made a decision. Isabel walked to the phone and called her brother in Bridgeport, Connecticut. The conversation on the phone ended. Isabel looked at her three children. Then she said, "Kids pack your bags. We are leaving to Connecticut. We will be there for a few weeks."

Jose came home and saw the bags packed. He begged Isabel to stay. She said, "No! If you want to visit me in Connecticut. Jose do not come for three weeks. I am leaving Mayaguez for good. My mother will drive me to the airport. Goodbye Jose." Jose did not give her an argument. He even helped bring the bags to the car. He watched the car leave. It went two blocks and made a left. The car was out of sight. Jose realized that this is a turning point in the marriage. He went inside the house and hated the silence.

Two days later, Jose decided to talk to his father. He told him everything. His father told him, "You know how I feel about your wife. If you do not follow her you will lose your son. He needs guidance more than other boys." Then he said, "Jose go to Connecticut. Mayaguez is a small town. There is more money in Connecticut." Jose sold his liquor store and house. Then he left for Bridgeport, Connecticut.

To make amends with Isabel, he decided to open up a Puerto Rican restaurant with her brother. Unfortunately, Isabel's brother was a drunk. So Jose lost the restaurant. Then they decided to move to Harlem, New York. Jose opened up another Puerto Rican restaurant. It was another failure. Jose and Isabel had to move into a one bedroom apartment. Then Jose got a job in a hat factory. It was located in the garment district on 34th street. Two years later, he got a three bedroom apartment in the Bronx. It was a longer commute but he liked the area. He worked at the hat factory for thirty years. He watched his kids grow up and have families of their own. Then he retired. He made a big mistake in Mayaguez. He feels very lucky that Isabel took him back. His business failures meant very little to him. Isabel is all that matters.

DAD

My father raised six children in section 8 housing. All six of his children went to private school. All six of his children went to college. Four children received a Bachelor's Degree. Three children are millionaires. Enough said.

TABLE OF CONTENTS

AMERICA

It was July 14, 1951. Angel was spending his first day in America. He lived in a one bedroom apartment in Harlem, New York. This one bedroom apartment had five occupants. It was his mother, father and two sisters. His mother grabbed some money out of her coin purse. Then she said to Angel, "Go to the store and buy a gallon of milk and some bread." She handed him some money and 13 year old Angel left the apartment excited. He ran down the stairs and opened the front door. There on the stoop was a man shooting heroin in his veins. Angel was in total shock. He decided to avoid eye contact with this man. Then he walked two blocks and meet a teenager.

This teenager was 17 years old boy. He was wearing a leather jacket with jeans and a white t-shirt. He asked Angel if would like to join a club. Angel thought this was odd. This guy was older. He acted friendly. Then the teenager said, "We have beers and girls at the clubhouse. It is just down the street." Angel was uncomfortable with this guy. However, Angel decided to be friendly. He said, "Let me think about it."

Angel continued to walk to the store. He bought the milk and bread and returned to the apartment. He was relieved that the heroin addict was not on the stoop. When he entered the apartment Angel talked to his mother. He said, "Mom when Miriam and Margaret go to school. I want to walk them." His mother looked concerned. Then she said, "Angel your father will do that. Angel you pick them up after school." Angel said, "No problem Mom."

Angel could not get his two encounters out of his mind. Three days later, he sees the same teenager out of his window. This time he is with two other teenagers in leather jackets. All three of them were holding hands with attractive girls. He saw them enter a building. In the back of their leather jackets it said ROYAL LATINOS. Angel said to himself, "That is where the clubhouse must be." For the next week, Angel looked out his window. He saw those three guys again. The second guy had a different girlfriend. The next day Angel bumped into the teenager who was the leader . The teenager said hello. However, the teenager was with a different girl. Angel decided to visit the clubhouse.

The clubhouse had a steel door. He knocked on it. A teenager opened the steel slit. He closed it. Angel heard a discussion. Then the leader opened the steel slit. He said, "Angel right?" Angel responded, "Yes." The leader said to hold on. He opened the door and told Angel, "Come in." Angel wondered about the steel door. Then he saw two teenage boys making out with some girls on a couch. The TV was on. The leader gave a small peck on the cheek of his girlfriend. Then he said, "I'll see you later." The girl left the clubhouse. Then the leader talked to Angel.

He said, "Angel walk with me to the closet. Do you have a girlfriend?"

Angel said, "No, not yet."

Then the leader grabs a leather jacket. He says, "Try this on."

Angel notices that in the back of the leather jacket it says ROYAL LATINOS. He puts it on. The leader says, "It fits well. This is Jose.'' Angel thought it was odd. The leader introduced Angel to a sixteen year old kid. Then the leader said to Jose, "Go with Angel and take antennas off the cars." They left the clubhouse and did their job.

Two hours later, they returned to the clubhouse. The car antennas were given to teenagers making zip guns. Then Angel saw a teenager swinging a thick chain.

The leader gave Angel some brass knuckles and said very little. He talked to Jose. Then came to Angel and said, "Just follow Jose's lead. He will tell you what to do." Angel noticed that some of the Royal Latinos were carrying zip guns. Others were carrying chains. Then he noticed some of the Royal Latinos carrying

stiletto knives. Angel was about to leave. Then a seventeen year old said, "Where do you think your going?" Then Jose said, "Angel just go with me."
Angel asked, "Where are we going?"
Jose said, "We are going to Taft High School."
Angel said, "Isn't that an all black school?"
Jose said, "They have a high school dance tonight. We are going to pay a visit.''
The leader said, "Jose shut the fuck up! Angel put on your brass knuckles.''Angel puts it on his right hand. He looks at it. Then the leader says, "Put it in your pocket. Ok boys let's go to Taft High School."

The Royal Latinos approached Taft High School. Jose said to Angel, "Just follow my lead." The leader opened the door quietly. They walked into the high school. A band was playing a slow romantic song. The couples were slow dancing. The Royal Latinos put garbage cans near the entrance of the high school gym. Then a signal was given. The garbage cans blocked the entrance of the high school gym. Then the Royal Latinos entered the dance floor throwing fists and shooting zip guns. The rumble was on. Angel was terrified but he was part of the brawl now. The fighting was swift and organized. Fortunately, no one was killed. The Royal Latinos left victorious. However, the brothers will respond in the future.

The Royal Latinos ran down 103rd street. The leader said, "Let's meet at the basketball courts on 101st. The meeting will take place at midnight.'' Midnight came and the meeting began. The neighbors minded their own business. The leader started swinging his chain. He explained how proud he was of the rumble. He had his back to his gang members. Then he said, "Jose step forward." Jose looked confused. Then a couple of gang members pushed Jose forward. Then the leader spoke, "I did not want to believe that my girl was with you. Then I saw you kissing her. You remember at the ice skating rink in Central Park." Jose spoke in a panic, "I didn't know that you two were still going out."

The leader was furious. Five gang members held Jose's arms. Then he screamed obscenities at Jose. Then he began to beat him to death with his chain. Angel was in shock. He wanted out. However, he felt that he would have the same fate as Jose. The leader spoke, "Tomorrow we will meet at the clubhouse to discuss matters. The meeting will start at 7:30 P.M. Let's go Royal Latinos." The gang members followed the leader out of the basketball court. Angel could not stop looking at Jose's dead body.

Angel was walking home alone. It dawned on him that his father will be angry at him for breaking curfew. Angel decided that he will enter the apartment quietly. He entered his bedroom and took off his leather jacket. He hid his jacket deep into his closet. Then he went to bed. Ten seconds later, the light went on. Angel's father said nothing. He just went to Angel and proceeded to beat him. He asked, "What are you up to?!" Angel said nothing. The beating continued. Then Angel's father threw him out of the bedroom. He began to ransack the bedroom. Everything was thrown to the floor. Angel knew that his leather jacket would be found. However, to his surprise the father did not find the jacket. Angel's father opened the door and said, "Get to fucking sleep! We will talk tomorrow."

The next day Angel left the apartment at 6 P.M. His father was not home from work. He wore his leather jacket under his winter coat. Then left for the clubhouse. He arrived at 7 P.M. The leader was pleased that Angel was early. He said, "Angel tonight do not wear your leather jacket. I want you to dress up as a grocery clerk. Here are your clothes. You will deliver these groceries to this address. There will be a bearded man who will give you cash. You come back to the clubhouse and give me every cent that man gives you."

Angel and six other gang members dress up as grocery clerks. They each get two bags and deliver to the address on a piece of paper. Angel noticed that the address was in Greenwich Village. This is where the bohemians live. Everyone knows that bohemians smoke pot with the jazz musicians. However, Angel did not ask questions. He delivered his groceries and returned to the clubhouse.

Angel gave the money to the leader. He noticed that there were seven girls at the clubhouse. The leader said, "Angel this is Anita. Get to know her." Angel noticed that he introduced girls to all the new gang members. Then he left the clubhouse for an hour. Angel noticed that an older gang member was left in charge.

Angel walked home with a smile on his face. Then he thought about his dad. Angel knew that his dad would give him shit. He knocked on the apartment door. His father opened the door and said, "Put your fucking coat away and come to the kitchen." Angel put his coat away and wondered what was in store for him.

Angel's father spoke, "What are you up to?"
Angel said, "Nothing Pop. nothing at all.''
Angel's father said, "This is the last time I will ask. WHAT ARE YOU UP TO!!"
Angel said, "Look Pop I meet a girl. Her name is Anita. I meet her a couple of times. She is older than me. Hmm she is not a girlfriend."
Angel's father said, "Don't bullshit me!''
Angel said, "I'm not Pop. I swear."
Angel's father looked at his son. Then he said, "On Monday go with your mother to the doctor. Do we understand each other?"
Angel said, "Alright Pop. I'll go.'
Angel's father said, "This discussion will continue on Monday. Is that clear!"
Angel said, "Ok Pop."

One week later, Angel's father was playing dominoes with his friends. It was a sunny Saturday afternoon. Angel was in the bathroom putting on his leather jacket. He posed in front of the mirror. He turned his back to see the letters THE ROYAL LATINOS. He was pleased. He put the collar up and pulled on his jacket. Then he proudly walked to the door. His mother decided to block the door.
She said, "Angel where are you going?!"
Angel looked at his mother and decided to throw her to the ground. He forced the door open and left the apartment.

Angel's two sisters left the apartment and ran to their father. They explained what Angel just did to mom. Angel's father got up with his friend Ricardo. Then they ran down the street looking for Angel. They saw him and threw Angel down an alley. Then they proceeded to throw Angel a vicious beating.
Angel's father began to scream, "Who the fuck are you to throw my fucking wife on the floor?! You little piece of shit!!" The fists were flying and Angel had the nerve to fight back. It turned into a brawl. Finally the fighting stopped. Angel's father Jose grabbed his son's arm and said, "You fucking asshole!!" Then he began to push his son back to the apartment. Ricardo looked at Angel and said, "Don't give your father any bullshit! You keep walking Angel!"

They returned to the apartment. Angel's mother attacked him with plenty of smacks. She was hurting inside but she was made as hell. Ricardo left the apartment watching Jose and his wife taking care of business.

Jose grabbed his son and dragged him into the bedroom. He took Angel's leather jacket off. Then he threw his son on the bed. He said, "Stay the fuck there!" He ran into the kitchen and grabbed some 1040 oil. Then he came back to Angel's bedroom. He looked at him and said, "We are going to the roof. There you will watch me burn your fucking leather jacket.!" Angel said, "Pop please they already killed my friend at the basketball court." They went to the roof and Angel watched his father burn the jacket. Angel said, "Pop what am I going to do?!" Jose said, "I will take care of it. Where is the clubhouse?" Angel decided to tell his dad the location.

Jose knew a police officer who did foot patrol in the neighborhood. The name of the police officer was John O' Connor. Jose was on friendly terms with Mr. O'Connor. So he approached O'Connor and told him about his situation with his son. O'Connor knew about the burning jacket on the roof. O'Connor said, " news travels fast Jose." Jose then asked, "Can you help me with my son?" O' Connor said, "Let me call the precinct on the police phone. I will ask for three squad cars. Come back in an hour and put four cases of beer in a police car. Then walk away." Jose said, "I will make sure that the beer is cold." Then Jose left to buy the merchandise.

Jose came back an hour later. He was accompanied with Ricardo. He watched the police from his old Cadillac. They entered the building and went to the clubhouse. When the police were out of sight. Jose put the beers in the back of the squad car and walked back to his Cadillac. Then he got into his vehicle and left the area.

The officers were inside the building. O'Connor informed his Sargeant that there was a lookout on the third floor. The Sergeant asked O'Connor, "Did you take care of the lookout from the building across the street?" O' Connor said, "Yea I handcuffed her to the radiator in her apartment. I'll pay a visit when we are done."

Three police officers quietly went up the stairs. They meet the two gang members near the iron door and said, "Wait right here fuckheads! One officer gave a signal to the other twelve cops. They quietly came up the stairs. Then accompanied the two gang members to the iron door. The sergeant informed them, "If you do not cooperate I will knock you out! Is that clear shitheads! Is that clear?!" The gang members understood. One gang member knocked on the door and said, " open up Roberto!" The door opened and the cops rushed in.

The sergeant said, "Hello fuckheads!" Then the nightsticks started swinging. One Royal Latino reached for a zip gun. An officer said, "Are you fucking kidding me!" Then he swung that nightstick and hit the kid right in the face. The beating went on for ten to fifteen minutes. Then it ended. O' Connor spoke and told the leader, "Angel is no longer coming to your clubhouse. If you bother that kid we will comeback and burn this fucking place down! Is that clear Royal Latino!" Then the cops left.

Outside the building, four cases of cold beer was waiting in the squad car. One officer said, "O' Connor why the beating?" He said, "Some spic gave a shit about his kid joining a gang." So I said, "Get some beers and my boys will pay a visit. That reminds me, I better go across the street and uncuff the bitch. I wonder if I should keep the keys to her apartment. O'Connor just uncuff her."

The Royal Latinos laid on the floor of their clubhouse. The leader said, "When things calm down. We must pay a visit to Angel. Let's give it a week. Then help him walk to the basketball court." It sounded like Angel was going to be in a little trouble. However, the brothers from Taft High school were preparing for revenge. You see the brothers had their own gang. They were called The Black Knights. They had a clubhouse and leather jackets. The leather jackets had their letters in the back. They had a meeting and discussed what to do with The Royal Latinos. They decided to visit The Royal Latino clubhouse with sledgehammers and serious firearms.

It was 10 P.M. Friday night. It has been two days since the cops visited the Royal Latinos clubhouse. Tonight the Black Knights were walking to the Royal Latino clubhouse. The lookout from the other building called The Royal Latino clubhouse. She told the leader, " The Black Nights are coming and they have some serious weapons. This includes sledgehammers and guns!'' She hung up the phone. He told the second in command to tell the lookout at the door to come inside.

He looked at his gang members and their zip guns. Then quietly walked to the closet and took out his trunk. He opened the trunk and inside was some serious firearms. He said, "Boys put away your zip guns and take these firearms. The

Black Knights are coming and they have some serious weapons. Two members of the Royal Latinos shouted, "Is this over a high school fight?!" The leader said, "It looks that way."

The Royal Latinos were preparing their weapons. Three members wanted to leave. The leader said, "Either they kill you or I will. Take these handguns . Jorge give me the shotgun. I'll load it myself." Everyone was fully loaded and waited for the Black Knights. Ten minutes later, they heard the sledgehammers on the iron door. They knew it was only a matter of time. The iron door will fall and the shooting will begin. The Royal Latinos are ready and in position. They see dust everytime the sledgehammer hits the door. Finally, the door falls and the shooting begins.

The shooting lasted two or three minutes. There are wounded on both sides. Some of the gang members even die. The Black Knights take their wounded to the stoop outside. There they meet some police officers. The sergeant ask one of the Black Knights, "How many are fucking dead?" He said, "He doesn't know." Then the sergeant says, "Walk to the fucking ambulance. They will help you. Let's go gentlemen."

Twenty police officers with shotguns drawn walk slowly go up the staircase. They come upon the iron door. The cops see wounded and dead gang members everywhere. The sergeant screams, "One bullet comes our way. You all fucking die! Is that clear! The sergeant hears no response. They proceed with caution and enter the clubhouse. The sergeant screams, "Hands up and no funny business." The Royal Latinos comply. The arrests are made. The sergeant asked the leader, "What's with the iron door? You've got some serious firearms. What are you up to Royal Latino? What's with the dead kid on the basketball court? Was it about money or broads? The gang leader says, "How do you know? The sergeant responded, "It's always about money and broads! You know what, I will let the detectives figure this out. Let's go fuckhead. Alright boys start searching."

The police officers found a lot of guns and pounds of marijuana. A few weeks later, the detectives realized they were dealing with some serious criminals. The Royal Latinos were delivering pounds of marijuana to some bohemians in Greenwich Village. They would have twelve to thirteen year old boys dress up as grocery clerks. They would deliver pounds of marijuana in grocery bags. The trick was to put the marijuana in the bottom of the bag. Then put groceries on top. The grocery clerks would deliver to an address. The customer would give money to the clerk. This was done twice a week.

Then there was gun smuggling. Both the Royal Latinos and The Black Knights were involved. They were smuggling guns from Richmond, Virginia to New York City. The gang leader from The Royal Latinos was trying to get The Black Knights out of the gun smuggling business. That was what the brawl at Taft High School was about. Angel well he got a job as a butcher. He worked at a place called La Marquita. It is located in East Harlem. However, Angel is Angel.

LA MARQUETA

It was Angel's first day of work as a butcher. He was informed of his duties and given a work schedule. He worked thirty two hours a week and went to high school. Every Sunday Angel worked 12 hour shifts. Angel was fourteen years old. He was an easy-going kid. He would talk to anybody. Then one day a butcher told Angel how to put extra weight on the scales. This way he can charge a little more. Angel was uncomfortable with dishonesty. However, all the butchers tipped the scales. It was a job that paid well. He even helped his father with the rent. Angel began to fantasize about having a girlfriend. Then something came up at work.

One day a girl asked a surprising question. She looked at Angel and said, "Would you like to have sex for five dollars?" A butcher started to laugh and said, "Angel take her to the rice room!" Angel was confused and wondered why a girl would ask such a question. Then a forty year old butcher told Angel about the facts of life. Before long Angel was quite busy in the rice room. It was good to be in the rice room during lunch. Then one day the rice room was occupied. It was occupied with a butcher with a big nose. The girl was enormous. The big nose butcher screamed, "Use the onion room you fucking idiot!" Then he slams the door. Angel said to himself, "Where is the onion room?" The girl took Angel's hand and said, "The onion room is this way."

Angel entered the onion room and noticed there was some pre cut onions in net bags. The girl laid on top of the pre cut onions. She told Angel to make it quick. So Angel began to have intercourse. He started to sniffle and have watery eyes. The girl screamed, "hurry up! hurry up!" Well Angel had his moment. Then the girl left quickly. He walked back to his job. He wondered what the hell just happened. He entered the La Marqueta. All the butchers were laughing. One butcher said, "Angel stop crying and get back to work." Then an old woman came to Angel's aid. She told the guys to stop laughing. Then she takes out a handkerchief and covers his nose. She says, "Blow Angel blow!" He blew some snot into that handkerchief. He said, "Why can't I stop crying." The old woman says, "Don't worry Angel just blow hard."

He blows hard and the butchers could not stop laughing. The woman tells the guys to stop laughing. Angel says, " I'm good. I'm good." Then the old woman takes Angel's head and smothers it into her granny tits. She screams, "oh you poor boy! You poor boy!" Angel screams, "Lady, what are you doing?" The butchers are screaming in laughter. One butcher says, "Angel her husband's a drunk. Just walk away." Angel says, "I'm good granny. I'm good. Then he returns to work.

One day the landlord of the La Marqueta ask for Angel. Angel went to his office. He sat down near his desk. The landlord says, "I noticed that you get along with everybody. Listen, once a week I collect the rent money in a brown paper bag. I want you to collect the bags and put it in this duffle bag. Then come to my office and give me the duffle bag. My assistant will count the money. Sometimes, someone gives me too much money. My assistant will put it in a white envelope. Then you return the white envelope to the idiot. Do you have a suit?" Angel says, "No, I do not own a suit." The landlord says, "Go to my taylor on thirty fourth st. and seventh avenue. His name is Mr. Cohen. You tell him that you want a grey business suit. I want to wear this suit when you collect my rent money. It will be collected every Friday night after dinner. I will give you twenty dollars a week. It will be in cash." Angel thought I get paid every Wednesday. With the additional twenty dollars. I make fifty dollars a week. Angel was stunned because at fourteen years old. He was making more money than his dad.

Every Friday night, Angel would come to the La Marqueta wearing his grey suit. He would wait for the police-man to arrive. Then Angel would walk down the aisle with the cop in the back of him. He opened the duffle bag and put the brown paper bags in. When the task was completed. Angel would walk to the landlord's office. He gave the duffle bag to the landlord. Then the landlord would give Angel twenty dollars. The police officer would get thirty dollars. Then one day, Angel talked to butcher named Juan. He said, " Juan why do they pay their rent once a week?" Juan just looked at Angel and said, "Have the old lady blow your nose." Then another butcher named Roberto told Angel the facts of life. He said, "Angel there playing the numbers. Just do what you are told and mind your business. You can use the extra cash."

Within a few months, Angel had a few bucks in the bank. He helped his father with the rent. He gave money to his two sisters to buy records once a week. Then the family moved into a three bedroom apartment. Two years later, Angel and his dad went 50/50 on a ten year old black cadillac Deville. Every Sunday, Angel would shine that car. Then fill it up with gas and see his girlfriend in Queens, New York. This is where Angel had problems.

It was 1954, Angel was dating a german american girl. Angel was Puerto Rican. The girl's name was Diane Fischer. Her father did not approve. He even had Angel arrested a few times. Diane refused to press charges. Then one day a cop told Angel to date his own. This girl's father will put a serious charge against you. You might even do jail time.

One day, Angel came to pick up Diane at her house. Her father got on the phone and said to the police Diane was sexually assaulted by Angel. The police came to the house and pulled Angel out of his car. They arrested him and put him in the back of the squad car. One police officer questioned Diane. She insisted that Angel never touched her. They uncuffed Angel and one police officer said, "She is not worth the problem."

One Sunday, Angel received a knock on his door. Diane was crying. She said that her father got physically abusive. Diane had a black eye. In her hand was five thousand dollars. She told Angel let's runaway. My father called the cops and said you gave me a black eye. Once we convince them that you did not give me a black eye. We will go to Long Island and live in an apartment. Angel talked to his Dad and waited for the police to arrive. Once again, Angel was arrested and put in the back of a squad car. Diane told the police Angel did not harm her. She told them that she wanted to runaway with him. One cop told Angel, "Sooner or later a charge will stick and you will do time. She is not worth it."

Then one Friday night, Diane's father planted an unregistered gun in Angel's Cadillac. Angel was arrested and put in juvie hall for three days. Diane came to Angel's aid. She said that her father planted the gun in Angel's car. A cop came to Angel and said, "She is not worth it kid.'' Then her father found out about what went on at the La Marqueta. Angel was arrested. Angel's father went to juve hall to pick up his son.

He then told Angel that he will now be a butcher in Brooklyn New York. Then Angel's father said, "Bye the way. The landlord at the La Marqueta was arrested for racketeering. Angel get rid of your girlfriend." Angel realized that Diane was a big problem. He decided to get another girlfriend. To his surprise, Diane understood.

One year later, Diane called and said that her brother Billy has committed suicide. Billy was distraught about his girlfriend dumping him. So he took a shotgun blast to his head. Billy was the one who introduced his sister Diane to Angel. However, Angel decided not to attend the funeral.

FICTION

It is time to leave the family.

TABLE OF CONTENTS

TENACITY

Gnaw the flesh
If only memory could die
Crawl to the den of unconscious snakes
Mingle the darkness with some blood

Curse my tears!
Conspire my so called troubled spirit.
Rebel!
Rebel!

Hatred today is hatred tomorrow
And the earth will still spin
Burning in red river veins

MEN WHO TAKE FLIGHT

It was World War I. There was a small air force base in Provins, France. The year was 1917 and the Americans were about to enter another air battle. They had fifty biplanes parked wingtip to wingtip. The pilots and gunners walked to their biplanes. The gunners removed the wooden planks from the wheels of the biplane. Then they entered the gunner seat and checked their M1917 browning machine guns. The pilots would enter the cockpit. When they got the okay from the gunners. They would start their engines. Captain O'Hara would enter the runway first.

He has done over thirty missions in the air. He would always wonder if the intelligent reports were accurate. Sometimes they were completely useless. In one mission, the german biplanes slammed right into O'Hara's squadron. The reports stated they would be a half hour away. He lost seven biplanes within seconds. They barely won that dogfight. This mission felt uncomfortable from the beginning.

The intelligent report stated that a squadron of german biplanes would be near Mainz, Germany. The Germans had a habit of flying below the clouds. It was very risky to fly in the clouds. However, the element of surprise increased dramatically.

The American scouts went ahead of O'Hara's squadron. They spotted the german biplanes. The scouts returned and O'Hara knew exactly what to do. The fifty American biplanes went into the clouds and shut off their engines. They glided quietly through the clouds. The clouds opened up and the Germans had no idea that the Americans were coming. The American biplanes formed a perfect arc. The gunners were in position. The engines came on and they began to fire. The tail end of the german squadron went down fast. Then the germans split up fast and began to fire. It was organized chaos in the air.

A sadistic german gunner shot at an American's pilots head. O'Hara saw the headless body. So O'Hara and three pilots broke formation. They went after that sadistic asshole. They purposely shot at the gas tank. Then they saw the biplane become a ball of fire. They knew that the german gunner was being burned alive. O'Hara watch the biplane hit the ground hard.

An American pilot got his eyes shot out. He died instantly. The gunner in the back was perfectly fine. But the plane went down with the gunner screaming like hell. Another American pilot got his wing shot off. The biplane went into a chaotic spin and hit the ground hard. The biplane blew up. Another german biplane split in half.

Many gruesome scenes were taking place in the air. But in the end one side will win. It is the nature of air warfare. In this case, the Germans had many inexperienced flyers. The Americans won this air fight. It was a heavy cost. They lost twenty biplanes. The air fight took too long. They did not have enough gas to get back to Provins, France. They might have to land in German territory. Captain O'Hara made a decision to fly low. He thought about enemy fire. With any luck they will get to Strasbourg, France.

They were three miles away from Strasbourg. O'Hara noticed that some of the planes ran out of gas. He looks at his fuel tank. Then his propeller stopped. He looked down below. He saw farmhouses and big trees. There was no clear fields to land the biplanes. O'Hara knew that some of his men will die. They landed on trees, farmhouses and barns. O'Hara went through a barn and slammed onto a fence post. He was lucky to be alive. He got out of his biplane with his gunner. He had the unpleasant task of taking stock of the situation. He must find out who is alive or dead. Ten men died in the landing. Three were wounded.

He gathered the men and said, “We are three miles from the French border. Let’s move before it gets dark.” Then he looked at his gunner. He said, “Jack let’s see if there is any food.” O’Hara yells, “Ok men, check the farmhouses and barns. Let’s see if we could find some food.” They were in luck. They found some cured meats and bread. As they ate O’Hara asked, “Jack can we carry some Browning guns with us?” Jack said, “Some are smaller caliber. We can carry about six or seven brownings.” O’Hara was satisfied.They finished their meal and started walking to the French border.

They ran into a small village. O’ Hara noticed that a few german men ran into the forest. He knew that it might be a trap. However, O’Hara decided to investigate. He went into the forest and a gun battle ensued. The Americans won the battle. However, three more men were killed. O’Hara decided to take the rifles from the dead german civilians.

It was getting dark. O’Hara decided that his men will have to sleep in the forest. Then he stated, “I want two men keeping watch. Jack you and I will keep watch first.” He continued, “In four hours I will wake two men to replace us. Let’s get some shut eye gentlemen.’’

Morning came and Captain O’Hara wondered if they will make it to the French border. He expected the border to have German soldiers. He decided to be honest with his men. He said, “Gentlemen we must prepare for the unexpected. Let’s go and walk with caution.” They reached the French/German border. O’Hara decided to walk quietly with his men. He decided to send four men to the border. He told them to observe the situation. Then return with a full report.

The four men returned. They told O’Hara that forty soldiers are protecting the border. So O’Hara gathered up his men and went two miles north. Then he sent the four men again to see if there are any soldiers. This time there were no soldiers. However, they saw no boats to cross the Rhine river. They went into a small village to see if they can find some rowboats. They found none. O’Hara decided to talk to a villager. It will not be a friendly chat. One of his men spoke German. O’Hara looked around the village. Then said, “Have a chat with that elderly man. He seems to live alone. Bring a couple of men for company.”

They entered the elderly man's house. They were surprised that his granddaughter was in the house. She was startled. The elderly man was concerned but friendly. He asked them, "Do you need help?" O'Hara said, "Do you know a fishing village nearby?" The elderly man was cautious. Then he said, "There is a fishing village two miles north. They have a port with many fishing boats. They even have a market in town. I will give you some money. I have clothing that may fit some of your soldiers. I also have some food." The soldier thanked him for his help. Then the four men left his house.

O' Hara and his men reached the fishing village. It is early in the morning. The market is not open. They decide to break in and eat as much food as possible. Then in the port they see six fishing boats. There is a small crew in two fishing boats. The squadron surprises the two fishing boats. They put guns to their heads. O'Hara tells them, "Take us to the French border now!" O'Hara splits his squadron in two. The boats leave the port.

He is halfway across the Rhine. He is having a conversation with a soldier. The soldier gets a bullet in the head. O'Hara and the other soldiers hit the deck. O'Hara looks up and sees the german soldiers on the pier. He sees other german soldiers running down the hill with serious firepower. He puts a gun to the boat operators head and says, "Gun it!"

Both boats reach the french border. O'Hara sees german boats coming. They have some serious firepower. Jack tells O'Hara, " Captain that boat has a Maschinegewehr 08. It does 500 to 600 rounds a minute. This boat will be splinters in three minutes." O'Hara says, "Men get behind the boats and aim your brownings at the enemy." Then O'Hara yells, "Fire!!" A battle ensues. Then more german boats arrive. Four of O'Hara's men are killed. The battle finally ends. It is quiet on the french border.

O'Hara senses that more german boats will come. He says, "Let's go men. Let's find a french base." They begin to walk through the forest. Two hours later, they find a french military base.

1875

John and Mary Fletcher made a decision to move to homestead land near Eugene, Oregon. The land had a log cabin, a big red barn and a corral for horses. John and Mary had two young boys. Jack was the oldest he was ten years old. Stephen was eight years old. Mary was also pregnant . She will give birth in early spring. They liked the idea that the school was only two miles away. The church was near the school. Many worshippers lived near Eugene, Oregon. After service the congregation would meet and have a good lunch. Then they would help each other out. Since Mary was expecting, she was introduced to a midwife. John wanted to know about supply stores and gunsmiths. Then the men of the congregation told John about the dangers of his homestead.

A storekeeper told John about the wolves near his homestead. He told him to keep all his livestock in the barn. The horses should be put in the barn before nightfall. The indians talked about children disappearing. This pack of wolves numbered about fourteen in all. So always have your rifles and guns fully loaded. The wolves will visit your homestead land. It is only a matter of time.

The day came when Mary gave birth to a baby girl. She named the girl after her favorite aunt. Her name was Sarah. Time goes by so quickly. Before you knew it, Sarah was six months old.

One night, John and the family heard the wolves outside. John grabbed his rifle and looked out the window. He saw three wolves on top of the barn. They were sniffing and trying to figure out how to get inside the barn. The other wolves were circling the barn. All of them were barking. Then the leader howled and the wolves gathered and left the homestead. John knew that they will be back.

The next night the wolves were back. Once again, three wolves on top of the barn. The other eleven circling the barn. This time the alpha male jumped down from the barn and walked to the log cabin with two other wolves. They decided to walk around the log cabin. You can hear them barking outside. John's two boys were getting frightened. John reassured them that everything is okay. He said, "We are safe inside." John began to wonder if the wolves will come during the day. Wild animals are unpredictable. So John made a decision. Everyone must carry a firearm.

The next two nights the wolves did not come. John figured they got a meal somewhere. The third night it was snowing lightly. The wolves once again went to the barn. This time they lost interest rather quickly. All fourteen wolves walked around the log cabin. They were barking and growling and waiting. John's boys were frightened. John said to his boys, "Tomorrow after breakfast you two will practice with your firearms." One hour later the wolves departed.

It was morning, the boys were practicing with their firearms. John was rather pleased with his boys. They took to their rifles and handguns rather well. He liked the way his boys respected their firearms.

It was time for lunch. The boys were walking toward the log cabin. Jack forgot his rifle at the barn. He walked toward the barn and noticed three wolves in the woods. Jack yelled, "Dad!" John came out of the barn. He said, "Jack give me your rifle." John took the .38-40 Winchester rifle and shot the tree near the wolves. The wolves ran off. John went into the log cabin and told his family to be ready for anything.

The next week was uneventful. Then one afternoon they finished lunch. John went to look out the window. Everything seemed normal. Jack went out to do his chores. Jack was met by a wolf. The wolf stared and growled. Jack stood still and was ready. Then four more wolves came from the back of the barn. His brother Stephen came out and saw the commotion. He yelled, "Dad!'' John came out with his rifle and said, "Boys on the count of three we start shooting!"

The four wolves were killed. Then he screams to his wife, "Mary have your rifle ready!" Then he tells his boys, "Let's get into the house carefully. Jack opened the door." The door squeaked and five wolves came running. They were hiding behind the house. The other five wolves were hiding behind the barn. They came running. The wolves rushed the door. The guns were blazing two wolves were killed. The other eight got into the house. Mary was shooting but the wolves knocked her down. Then a wolf took the baby carriage. Mary heard the baby crying. John and the boys were reloading. However, the wolves left the house and ran into the wilderness. It happened so quickly.

John, the boys and Mary finished reloading. They ran to the horses, saddled them up and went to save Sarah. John followed their tracks in the snow. In his heart, John knew that the wolves den cannot be far. So John decides to get off his horse and travel on foot. He looks at their tracks and listens for the sounds of wolves. He hears something in the distance, it's the wolves barking. Then he hears Sarah crying. The whole family cocks their Winchester rifles. They move slowly and the wolves barking gets louder. Then they leave their horses behind and begin to walk slowly toward the sound of the wolves.

It begins to snow lightly. John and the family are moving slowly in the woods. Then John sees the den. He has visual on his daughter. The alpha male bows his head and sniffs. The other wolves wait for the alpha male's approval.

The Fletcher family aims their rifles at the wolves. They understand that multiple shots must be fired. John shoots the alpha male dead. Then the family shoots their Winchesters. The wolves go down yelping. John sees the carnage. Then tells his wife, "Grab your handgun hun and let's go. You two boys grab your sister." They walked toward Sarah. Jack the oldest grabbed her carriage. Then he walked back to his father. John says, "You two boys stay here." Then John and Mary got their handguns out and shot every wolf in the head.

The family returned to the homestead. It was good to have Sarah back. John went to his shed and grabbed the proper knives for skinning animals. The wolves that were dead in the homestead were skinned by Mary and Stephen. John and his older son Jack went back to the den. There they skinned the wolves. Of course, John started with the alpha male. He took out his bowie knife. Then he started cutting at his belly. John and Jack moved quickly. They were losing sunlight. The organs of each animal were removed. Then the wolves were put on the horses.

It was time to leave the den. John and Jack got on their horses and rode back to the homestead. John began to wonder if the wolves wanted his two boys. It would make sense. There were fourteen in this pack.

They arrived at the homestead. John took the wolves into the log cabin. The family looked at Sarah. They started to get emotional. Afterwards, John and his boys put the wolves in the barn. They ate dinner. Then John and Mary discussed their journey to Eugene, Oregon. The next day the family prepared for their trip. It will be a full day's journey.

They arrived at Eugene, Oregon at 10 A.M. John took the fourteen pelts out of the wagon. Then walked to the General Store. He greeted the storekeeper. Then he sold his pelts. He received a good sum of money. So he bought some supplies from the General Store. Then the family ate some lunch and returned to the homestead.

The years went by. There were many hardships. However, Mary had another child. It was a boy. John and Mary named him Michael. Life moves on.

THE STUDENTS

It was the summer of 2010. There was a 400 acre farm in Jonesborough, Tennessee. An FBI man was taken a pixel to loosen some rocks. Another agent was busy shoveling dirt. There was a 500E helicopter flying overhead. Then the two FBI agents see the skeleton head of a female. The FBI agent stops digging and puts a red flag on the site.

There are FBI agents everywhere. They discover forty bodies. Forty bodies, forty red flags. Twelve black Suburbans are parked overhead. Next to the Suburbans was a man named James McKibben. He was in handcuffs and surrounded by FBI agents. He was angry because his career as a serial killer was over. However, he acted like it was no big deal. Then he counted over sixty FBI agents at his farm. He looked to the sky and saw the helicopter go by. Then he looked at the FBI agents on his property. He gave them such a smirk. The agents began to wonder what the hell is he smiling about.

In the woods, a man was watching Mr. McKibben on his binoculars. His name was Mr. Hayes. He put his binoculars down and looked at the eleven men next to him. Mr. Hayes says, "Gentlemen we five minutes before the helicopter returns." They had four cars in all. The cars were gray 2010 Pontiac Vibes. Each automobile was equipped with 500 horsepower. The trunks were open. Each trunk had a couple of M16s and a black duffel bag full of ammo. Next to each duffel bag was a dead woman wrapped in thick clear plastic. They were in the early twenties. Their eyes looked soulless and sad. Four men locked their trunks and took to the open road.

The four Pontiac Vibes passed by a white farmhouse. The twelve serial killers knew that the couple were at work. But today, John O'Connor came back from physical therapy. He needed therapy for his right leg.
Mr. O'Connor served two tours in the middle east. His first tour was in Afghanistan. The second was in Iraq. Mr. O'Connor's leg was shattered from an IED in Iraq. After several surgeries and months of physical therapy. He is still walking with a cane. He thought it was odd that four same model cars passed his house at a high rate of speed. Two cars went east. Two cars went west. He immediately called 911.

The dispatcher informed Sheriff Dan Murphy about the 911 call. The Sheriff told dispatch, "Tell John to leave his farmhouse at once! I will be there in fifteen minutes." The Sheriff knew the helicopter would be there in ten minutes.

Michael Hayes had a smartphone. Of course, he was listening to the police scanner. He called the car heading west. He said, " we have six minutes to hit the farm house." O'Connor saw the vehicles approaching his farmhouse. He knew that trouble was coming. He opened his back door and limped to his high tower. The high tower was used for deer hunting. He went up his ladder. Then opened up the trap door. He went inside and grabbed his AR-15 and ammo from the trunk. He then put the trunk on top of his trap door. He then went to his window and patiently waited for the serial killers to enter his house.

Four men entered his house. They were all wearing black bullet proof ski mask. There outfits were black jumpsuits. Of course they were bullet proof as well. O' Connor was not in the house. They informed Mr. Hayes that the occupant was not there. Mr. Hayes told them to go upstairs. They had four minutes. They proceeded upstairs. O'Connor was shocked that these men had M16s. Only the military are allowed to have M16s. He calmed down and had a clear shot of two men. He fired at their eyes and killed both men.

He knew that the other serial killers might be in the house. So Mr. O'Connor began to light up his house. The serial killers realized that the shots were coming from the woods. They went to the front of the house. They peered from the front and saw Mr. O'Connor's hightower.

O'Connor waited patiently. Mr. Hayes told four of his men to run to the tree when they start firing. They began to fire. The four men began to move to the tree. One was shot dead. Then Mr.Hayes gave the signal to fire at the right side of the hightower. They began to fire. They fired until the hightower gave way.
The hightower collapsed. Mr. O'Connor fell out of the window and broke his back. The nine serial killers walked up to Mr. O'Connor. They expected him to plead for his life. Instead he said, "Go fuck yourself!"

Mr. Hayes took out his Bowie knife and stabbed O'Connor in his throat. Then he turned the Bowie knife to the right. O'Connor was drowning in his own blood. Mr. Hayes realized they were running behind schedule. So he shot O'Connor in the head. Afterwards, Mr. Hayes said, "We have two minutes before the helicopter arrives. Five minutes before the Sheriff makes his visit."

Mr. Hayes returned to his four vehicles. They all headed east. Mr. Hayes knew that they will not make it to their next destination. Mr. McKibben taught Mr. Hayes quite well. So Mr. Hayes knew that you can hide cars well along this road. So he said, "Gentlemen we are falling behind schedule. So pull off to the side of the road and wait for the sound of a helicopter." The helicopter passed by and the cars went back on the road. They had two minutes to their next destination.
They arrived at their destination. In the ravine, were two police cars that Mr. Kibben bought at auction. They only put two bodies in the police cars. All of the M16s and ammo were taken. All of the serial killers took police clothing out of their duffel bags. They put them on and hit the open road. Then Mr. Hayes said, "We have seven minutes before we hit the mall." Two minutes into the ride and a police car passes them by. Ten seconds later, the police car makes a uturn. Mr. Hayes says, "Knock out the back window. Then on his smartphone says, "Car number two knock out your back window and start shooting. The first car goes left

and also starts shooting. The deputies were shot dead. Then Mr. Hayes said, "Gentlemen five minutes to the mall."

Sheriff Murphy arrives at Mr. O'Connor's farmhouse. He saw his friend Mr. O'Connor lying dead near a collapsed high tower. The sheriff came out of his police car with his gun drawn. He surveyed the area and realized the farm was empty. Unfortunately, he knew that he had to inform Mr. O'Connor's wife. They have been married for over ten years. He knew that Mrs. O'Connor had to inform her two boys that their father was no longer with us. Then he called his deputy at his house.

He informed the deputy about the situation. Then Sheriff Murphy said, "Jack check the ravine west of Mr. O'Connor's house." Then Jack said, "This does not sound good.'' Then the sheriff informed his deputy that Mr. O'Connor is dead.

The sheriff called the FBI and informed them about the situation. The deputy arrived at the O'Connor house. He told the sheriff that two police cars were found in the ravine. It had two dead girls and six police uniforms inside the trunk. Then the sheriff tells the deputy to stay at the O'Connor house. I am going to drive east. Sheriff Murphy takes to the road and calls the sheriff in the next town. He informs him about the situation. Then he asked, "Did you send anybody on patrol?" He said, "Yes I did!" Then Sheriff Murphy bumps into the police cruiser with two dead deputies. There was a call on his private phone. The deputy informed the sheriff that he contacted Mrs. O'Connor. He told her to come to the farmhouse. She knows it's not good news. Then Sheriff Murphy thanks the deputy. He gives a sigh. Then talks to the sheriff. He informs him about the two deputies.

The serial killers arrive at the mall. They see no police or FBI. They have four minutes to steal some SUVs and two victims. All this was set up long ago. They knew which vehicles to steal. The teenage girls worked at a small restaurant. Two serial killers went into the restaurant. They informed the girls that their parents were in the hospital. We will escort you to the emergency room. The girls informed their boss and left.

Ten minutes later, the FBI and the police arrived at the mall. The head of the FBI unit is Sergeant Johnson. The police inform Sergeant Johnson that the mall has no cameras or security. This is a small town. They quickly go into each store and question the owners. They finally arrive at the small restaurant. The owner asked, "How are the girls parents?" The FBI and Sheriff Murphy knew that something was wrong. They were informed that police came in earlier. They told the girls that their parents were involved in an accident. They are here to escort them to the emergency room at the hospital. The FBI and the sheriffs thanked him and left.

Sergeant Johnson and Sheriff Murphy had a discussion. Sheriff Murphy tells the Sergeant that the road going north splits up four ways. This occurs about four miles up the road. Sergeant Johnson ask his techno guy, "How many properties are in a ten mile radius?'' The techno guy says, " three hundred properties. Do you want to inform the helicopter?" The FBI in charge says, " no. They need to know what to look for. I also think the serial killers are off the road."
Sheriff Murphy hesitates but interjects, "There is a big farm about two miles up the road. You can hide vehicles inside the barn." Sergeant Johnson says, "Is this the only farm in four miles?" Sheriff Murphy says, "It is the only one." Sergeant Johnson says, "Let's go gentlemen!" Then he gets on his walkie talkie and informs SWAT.

The FBI agents approach the farm. The serial killers see Sheriff Murphy and FBI agents on their monitors. There is a third house in the back of the farm. It is deep in the woods. It cannot be seen from the road. It was built by Mr. McKibbon. Mr. Hayes said, "Gentlemen it is time to go Paducah, Kentucky. Let's pick up our gear and bring the grenades with us."

They load up their gear in four black Chargers. They put one girl in the back seat of the second Charger. The other girl is put in the third Charger. They quietly travel on a dirt road that leads to the 105 north. They make a right turn and head to Kentucky. A half a mile down the road a trucker notices the four black Chargers. He quickly slows down and calls 911. The dispatcher calls Sheriff Murphy on his private phone. The sheriff informs Sergeant Johnson. He then tells him, "We can take the 111 West and cross the 105 North. We will have four minutes before the Chargers arrive. While driving toward the 111 West. Sergeant Johnson informs the SWAT team. The FBI and sheriff know that for four minutes. They are on their own.

The serial killers hear the 911 call. They know that the 105 South leads to a big town. The best bet is to continue to Paducah, Kentucky.

They arrive at the 105 North. They set up for their blockade. The FBI men take out their AR-15s. Sheriff Murphy runs fifty yards down the road. He sets up the spikes. Then returns to his vehicle . They take out their AR-15s from the trunks. Then Sheriff Murphy says, "We have three minutes before they arrive."

It is quiet on the 105 north. Then you hear the engines of the Chargers get louder. Then Sergeant Johnson says, "Gentlemen hit the drivers first." They begin to fire. Forty seconds later, the Chargers hit the spikes. The first Charger loses control and hits a tree. The serial killers get out of their vehicles and start firing their M16s. They are covered from head to toe in black bullet proof clothing. The second vehicle hit the spikes and loses control. It hits the police car hard. The victim catapults through the front windshield. She lands in front of a police car. She is alive. However, she has to listen to gunfire. One of the FBI agents removes the duct tape around her mouth. She screams, "They are heading to Paducah, Kentucky. They have twenty grenades in the fourth vehicle. My friend is in the third car. It is two minutes before SWAT arrives.

Sheriff Murphy calls dispatch. He says, "Get as many ambulances as possible." Then he continues to fire. All of law enforcement hit the fourth vehicle hard. The serial killer grabs the box of grenades. He quickly throws two grenades. They hit one police car. An FBI agent is killed. He begins to throw a third grenade. A bullet hits the grenade and the serial killer blows up.

The SWAT team sees the explosion. They are thirty seconds from disembarking from their black armored truck. Upon arrival, the SWAT captain is informed about the situation. They begin to fire. It is now twenty four men and women against six serial killers with M16s and seventeen grenades. Law enforcement lite up the fourth Suburban. Finally, the vehicle explodes. The six serial killers hop into their two Chargers and go south.

The black armored SWAT truck is too slow. The FBI and Sheriff Murphy give pursuit. Sergeant Johnson calls for a helicopter. Then the back window of the Charger goes down. Two serial killers begin to shoot. The FBI and Sheriff Murphy begin to shoot. They shoot out the back tires. The Suburban is now running on its rims. However, it is no longer going at a high rate of speed. The SWAT team catches up.

The black armored truck gets in front of the Charger. They slow it down. The Charger goes to the left. The armored truck slams the vehicle. It fishtails out of control. It hits a tree. The vehicle is no longer moving. The SWAT team stops their vehicle and begins to fire behind their truck. The SWAT captain yells, "Ceasefire!" The FBI head agent gets on his bullhorn and tries to get them to surrender.

Mr. Hayes talks to the serial killer beside him. He says, "How many rounds do we have left? The serial killer says, "About one hundred rounds." Mr. Hayes says, keep firing until we run out." Sergeant Johnson asked the serial killers to surrender. Mr. Hayes and two serial killers get out of the left side of the vehicle. They run into the woods The other three stay in the Charger. They put the girl in front of them and start to fire. A serial killer is hit in the eye by a SWAT member. He is dead before he hits the ground. Then the other two serial killers are killed by a barrage of bullets. Sergeant Johnson ask the serial killers once again to surrender.This time there is no response.

Suddenly they hear the muffled sounds of a girl. They approach the Charger with caution. The girl is alone. They remove the duct tape around her mouth. Sergeant Johnson asked her "How many are there?" She says, "Three they went into the woods.The middle man's name is Mr. Hayes.They also said they are running low on ammo." Sergeant Johnson calls for an ambulance. Then he informs the helicopter about the three serial killers.

Sheriff Murphy informs Sergeant Johnson, "There is a house about three miles in. We can get there before they do. Then we wait." Sergeant Johnson says, "We need directions to the house Sheriff Murphy." Sheriff Murphy says, "Follow me." When they get to the house, they all set up their positions.

The SWAT team sets up two snipers. They waited patiently outside the house. Then they saw the serial killers. The snipers killed two serial killers. Mr.

Hayes is alone. He begins to fire. Then law enforcement lites him up. Mr. Hayes died in a hail of gunfire. Twenty seconds later they hear the helicopter overhead.

It was a long day for everybody. They put the dead serial killers in body bags. Sheriff Murphy asked Sergeant Johnson, “I guess you are going to have a conversation with Mr. McKibben.” Sergeant Johnson says, “Yes I will. I will also inform him about the death penalty in the state of Tennessee.” Sheriff Murphy said, “I will visit Mrs. O’Connor.” Sergeant Johnson said, “How long have you been friends with Mr. O’Connor?” Sheriff Murphy said, “since high school.”

Sheriff Murphy and Sergeant Johnson said their goodbyes. Then Sheriff Murphy went to his vehicle and drove off to Ms. O’ Connor’s farm.

COKE ON A TRAIN

There was a major train depot in Mexico City, Mexico. The Garcia cartel paid off the cops and employees of the train station. They boarded train number 43. The last three cars had over three hundred million dollars of cocaine on board. Members of the Garcia cartel came in black suits, white shirts and red ties. The shoes and pants were black. There were fifty in all. They each carried a black suitcase. Inside was a disassembled AR-15 with plenty of ammo. They boarded car number 43. They went to their seats and put their suitcases inside the compartments. The men sat down and the leader named Jose got on his walkie talkie. He informed a supervisor of the train station to allow the tourist to board. The tourist took the first twelve cars. Everyone was in a good mood. The train traveled through a beautiful area of Mexico. The destination was Acapulco, Mexico. It would take three to four hours to arrive.

The Lopez cartel received word that a train full of cocaine was leaving Mexico City. Miguel Lopez was in charge of the cartel. The Garcia cartel was a competitor. Miguel received word from a train station employee. He stated that the train going to Acapulco is full of cocaine. The cocaine is from the Garcia cartel.

Miguel Lopez decided to steal the cocaine. So he devised a plan. He hired one hundred men. He wanted them to dress up like Mexican soldiers. He paid each man one hundred dollars. He told them to rob the tourists for extra cash. However, make sure you visit car number 43.

The Lopez cartel arrived in an open plain. It was located in an area between Mexico City and Acapulco. They put debris on the tracks. They waited patiently for the train. The train arrives. The train engineer sees the debris on the tracks. The engineer is nervous. He stops the train. The Mexican soldiers board the train. They confront the train engineer and kill him. Then each car had two soldiers enter. The soldiers would kill the first two tourists. Then they would scream, "This is a robbery!! Put all of your valuables and cash into these hefty bags. Hurry up! Andale! Andale!!"

The Garcia cartel heard the commotion. They went to their compartments and took out their black suitcases. They opened them up and assembled their AR-15s. Once assembled, they pointed the AR-15s at the front door. The Lopez cartel were beneath the windows. They were approaching quietly. They pointed their AR-15s and began to shoot. The Garcia cartel broke the windows and began to fire. Then two men of the Lopez cartel open the front door and threw tear gas into the car. The Garcia cartel sneak out the back door. Then they begin to fire.

The tourists hear all the gunfire. Naturally, they are scared. However, they all hit the floor.

Two days earlier, the NSA received information about the cartels. They knew about the cocaine run. They looked at the schedule of the train leaving from Mexico City to Acapulco. Afterwards, they looked at a satellite picture of the train's route. They estimated that the gun battle would take place in an open field. Fortunately, there was only one location. They decided to contact the US Marines.

General Dewitt called Captain Tyson and informed him about the cocaine heist. Captain Tyson was in charge of a unit of US Marine Raiders. He visited the General at the pentagon. He received his information. Then he returned to Fort

Meade. Their he devised a plan to hit the cartels. It involved one hundred and ninety Marine Raiders.

Three C130s were flying near the cocaine heist. Captain Tyson was informed that the train has stopped. The gun battle has begun. The captain informs his troops, "Gentlemen it is time to jump!"

Captain Tyson and his US Marine Raiders hit the ground. He gives his troops an update about the situation. Then the raiders march three miles.

They arrive at the train. They hide behind the trees. They realize that they are in the middle of a battle. A raider looks in his binoculars and sees the blood spatter in each car. He informs the commander that there are civilian casualties. The captain shakes his head. Then he says, "Gentlemen it is time for the cartels to meet the raiders. Fire!!"

The cartels begin to feel bewildered. Who is shooting them? Then they see the soldiers behind the trees. The cartels begin to fire at the Raiders.

The battle takes about one hour. However, they know that a couple of cartel men may be in car#43. So three raiders use a riot shotgun to shoot tear gas into car#43. Several members of the Garcia cartel come out. Two members of the cartel come out with their hands up. However, four members begin to shoot. The raiders decide to kill all cartel members.

The raiders had several casualties. However, no raiders died during the conflict.

The raiders approached the train. They announced that they are US Marines. All the tourists have a sense of calm. The US Marines board the train. They put the dead tourist in body bags. The captain goes to the front car and sees the dead train engineer. He puts him in a body bag. Then he orders a raider to start the train.

They arrive in Acapulco, Mexico. It was a two hour train ride. The Mexican military is seen at the train station. All of the tourist and US Marines disembark from the train. The tourists are comforted and briefed. They are given free rooms at several Acapulco hotels. The next day they are escorted to the Acapulco airport. Then they catch flights to their final destinations.

Mr. Garcia and his head associate have a conversation. He is informed that the train station employee who contacted the Lopez cartel has been kidnapped. He is tortured and killed. Then they dump his body in an alley in Mexico City. The conversation continues. Mr. Garcia says, "How many deliveries were made?" The associate says, "Many were successful. All of the Cessna 340s landed without an incident. There were thirty in all. All of the retired couples from Arizona, went through the New Mexico border without being boarded. Those Winnebagos can hold a great deal of coke. Mr. Garcia says, "How many Winnebagos?" The head associate says, "Exactly twenty."

The conversation continues. Mr. Garcia asked the ultimate question. He says, "How did the deliveries to the Long Beach pier go?" The head associate Mr. Hernandez says, "It went quite well. Not one trailer was opened by homeland security." Garcia says, "Ok Mr. Hernandez. How much did we make?" Mr. Hernandez says, "All together we made four hundred million dollars." Then Mr. Garcia asks, "How many failures?" Mr. Hernandez says, "Two failures. One was the train. The other was the commercial jetliner at Mexico City.'' Then Garcia asked "How much coke did we really lose on the train?" Mr. Hernandez said, "We only lost five million dollars." Then Mr. Hernandez laughs, "it was more of a baking soda heist." Mr. Garcia has a shot of Tequila. Afterwards, he looks at Mr. Hernandez. Then he says, "Are the lions good and hungry." Mr. Hernandez says, "They have not been fed for two days."

Mr. Garcia looks into his shot glass. Then he says, "Bring in my failures Mr. Hernandez."

TORTURE! TORTURE!

I was sitting in traffic in Commerce, California. It was the usual parking lot on interstate 5S. I was driving a Ford 450 shuttle bus. Sometimes staying awake was a challenge. I would play with the windows. Then I would shut the air conditioner off. When it got too hot. I would put the air conditioner on. I put the radio on and off. Sometimes, I just found myself dozing off. Then I would drink an extra large coffee. Nothing was working. Then one day I was really sleepy. I hit the car in front of me. A man got out of his vehicle. He decided that it was minor. So he returned to his vehicle. This caused me concern. I decided to think of the pretty spanish girls in the office. Then I found myself thinking about one girl. Her name was Rosa.

Rosa was the prettiest girl in the office. When she was a new employee. A lot of men came in to say hello. It was obvious that she would date someone in the office. I decided to be friendly with her. She always looked forward to our conversations. However, she dated a man named Roberto. It didn't bother me. I knew it wouldn't last. Then thirteen months later she broke up with Roberto and left the company. I was surprised how much I missed her. I began to think about her all the time.

The traffic on interstate 5S was once again horrible. I began to think about Rosa. I would have imaginary conversations with her. I even found myself putting the radio lower. So I can have a good conversation with her. I found myself laughing at jokes that I know Rosa would enjoy. I knew that this was not normal. But hell it kept me awake in traffic.

My shift ended at 10 P.M. I would get into my SUV. I would start the vehicle and proceed to have an imaginary conversation with Rosa. When I was at work. I found myself talking about Rosa to everyone. Then when no one was looking, I would have an imaginary conversation with Rosa. The employees would ask me if everything is ok. I would tell them everything is fine. Then I would have a vision of her face in my head.

TORTURE! TORTURE!

I began to think about her all the time. I would force myself not to think of her. However, her face was constantly in my mind. I began to wonder where she lived. I overheard someone say New Hyde Park. So on my days off, I would drive around New Hyde Park. I was always disappointed. Then one day I left New Hyde Park in tears. I screamed, "Where is she? Where is she?!"

TORTURE! TORTURE!

Suddenly, I became very happy. I know in my heart that I will one day meet Rosa. Then the sadness begins. I will never see her again. You just don't meet ex employees. Then I remembered. One day she was looking for work in downtown Los Angeles. I overheard her boyfriend saying she was being interviewed at a fitness center. So on my day off, I went to the Pershing Square Park. It was 7:30 A.M. I waited at the train station until 9:30 A.M. Rosa did not show up. Then I went to all the fitness centers on flowers street. There were six altogether. Rosa did not work in any of them.

It was 4:30 P.M. I waited at the train station on 7th and Figueroa. I stood there and looked at every single girl who entered the train station. It was 7:30 P.M. there was no Rosa. I left and walked to the rocking chairs near Macy's. I sat on a chair and began to rock. I felt the tears begin to come. I said to myself, "I am in love with a ghost."

TORTURE! TORTURE!

I walked back to Main Street and waited for the 92 bus. I entered the bus in tears. I began to wonder, "Where is she? Where is she? Where is Rosa?" I imagine her with another man. The jealousy touches my soul. I say to myself, " I must meet her someday. I have to tell her all the great things happening in my life. That day will come. I know it will! I know it will!"

TORTURE! TORTURE!

I am driving my shuttle bus from Anaheim. There is a lady on my bus. I talk to her about Rosa. I convince myself that I know Rosa quite well. The lady on the bus looks at me and says, "Good luck in finding her." I said, " thank you." There was such pity in her voice. I said to myself, "tomorrow I have off. I remember Rosa saying that her sister works in a restaurant. I will check the Mexican Restaurants in New Hyde Park. I felt optimistic. I will find her sister. Of course, I do not find Rosa's sister. I become broken hearted. I said to myself, "Where is she? Where is she?"

TORTURE! TORTURE!

It is Sunday evening. I fall asleep and dream about Rosa. I see her entering another train stop on seventh street. I awake and see this as a sign from God. At noon, I eat lunch and walk to the bus stop. Once again, I take the 92 bus to downtown Los Angeles. It is a seventy minute ride. I sit on the bus wondering if this will be the day I see Rosa. I begin to get emotional on the bus. I beg God. I say, "Please God I don't want to dream or think about Rosa anymore." I finally get off the bus. I arrive at the rocking chairs outside Macy's. I sit and rock gently. I talk to strangers who occupy the other rocking chairs. I tell them about Rosa. They always tell me, " good luck in meeting your friend."

It is 4 P.M. It is time to go to the train station at 7th and Flowers. I arrive and look at every girl entering the train station. It is now 6:40 P.M. Of course, there is no Rosa. I walk back to the rocking chairs. I sit and look at the Christmas decorations. I wonder, "How many Christmases will go by before I meet Rosa? Will I ever meet Rosa again" I knew the answer. However, I forced myself to feel that I will meet her again. It will be a happy occasion for the both of us. I left the rocking chairs and walked to an Irish Pub on seventh street. I ate mexican food at a Irish Pub. Go figure only in L.A.

TORTURE!

I have a new job. It pays more money. It is time to spend money on finding Rosa. I am washing my clothes at a laundromat. I see a magazine selling automobiles. I opened up the magazine. The first page I see is the classifieds. There I see an advertisement for private investigators. I am hopeful once again. The next day I call the investigator. He says he can help me. He states that he can check databases. I ask what type of databases. He says the DMV and credit history for starters. I agree to meet him. The price is 500 hundred dollars. He then states that he has to meet a client at the Ritz Carlton. It is located near Staple Center. So he says, "Let's meet at the Radisson Hotel near USC. I think 10:30 A.M. should be a good time." I agreed. However, I had mixed emotions.

It was 10:45 A.M. The private investigator is a no show. I call him. He speaks in a whisper, "I am in family court in Norwalk. I will be available at 1:30 P.M. We should meet at Denny's on Firestone Boulevard. I decided to meet him. I still had mixed emotions.

We meet at Denny's. He is five foot eight brown hispanic man named Alex. He had an expensive gray suit and a fancy black briefcase. I did not like him. However, he acted very professional. We sat down and discussed what I wanted. He said, "Let's check public records." I said, "I already did that." He says, "Public records changes everyday." I said to myself, "No it doesn't." However, I went along. Then I told him that Rosa does not have a driver's license. But her younger sister drives. I describe her to Alex. I said, "She is five foot three white hispanic very thin. Her weight is about 110 pounds and has blonde hair and blue eyes. She lives in Pasadena. Her last name is Reyes. I did not know her first name. Then Alex says, "I'll check the DMV."

We talked further. I signed a contract. Then Mr. Investigator says, "Let's go to an ATM. I want to be paid in cash." We drove our cars to another mall. I found an ATM machine. I took 500 hundred dollars out of the machine. I walked to the investigator's gray honda accord. He pressed a button. The window on the driver's side went down. The investigator put his right hand out and I gave him the cash. I left the mall in disgust.

TORTURE!

It was a Tuesday morning. I called the investigator. We chatted a little bit. Then he told me to call him on Friday. It was Friday 10A.M. I called and got his answering service. Then at 2:30 P.M. I called again. He actually answered. We talked a little and he said, "Call back on Monday."
It was Monday morning. I do not remember the time. I called the investigator. He said, "Tomorrow I will check the credit reports in Pasadena Mr. Sanchez." I hung up the phone in disgust.

I call on Thursday morning. Alex tells me that there are several different databases for credit reports. So he told me to call on monday. I call on monday. He does not respond. I get his answering service. I decided to call three more times that day. Each time I get the answering service.

TORTURE! TORTURE!

I decided not to call until friday. Friday came, I called. I get the answering service. Then I call on wednesday. I still get the answering service.
On friday, Alex calls me. He tells me that he had to investigate something in Mexico. So I tell him to go to the DMV database and find her sister. He agrees and tells me to call next Friday.

TORTURE!

It is friday morning. I am not optimistic. I call Mr. Alex. He said, "Mr. Lopez. I checked the DMV database. I have ninety hits. It will take me a few hours to check all the hits. Mr. Lopez you are just too much work." Then he hangs up.

TORTURE! TORTURE!
TORTURE! TORTURE!

I call and call and call. There is no response. Eventually, I am blocked. So I decided to text Mr. Alex. There is no response. I begin to realize that I was taken for a sucker. I am despondent. But in my heart I must continue my search. For the next three months, I continue to think about Rosa. She does not leave my mind.

TORTURE! TORTURE!

I call my lawyer. I ask her if she can help me in my search. She gets emotional. Then she tells me to contact her by the end of the week. It is friday. I call her. She gives me two names. The first man is named Phil Thompson. He is extremely unfriendly. He wants to talk to my lawyer. I give him the phone number. I inform my lawyer that Mr. Thompson will call her. She tells me, "I will talk to Mr. Thompson. Call me on tuesday Mr. Lopez."

It was Tuesday. I called my lawyer. She said to call Mr. Tillman. I already talked to him. He is expecting your phone call. I hang up terrified. Then I said to myself, "I must call Mr. Tillman. What choice do I have?"

It was wednesday. I call Mr. Tillman. We meet at his office in downtown Los Angeles. I am optimistic. This time I am meeting an investigator at his place of business. Mr. Tillman charges me three hundred dollars. Four weeks later there are no results. Mr. Tillman says, "Mr. Lopez she has no credit history. Rosa did not register a car. She did not sign a rental agreement. I checked the post office in Pasadena. I called the ex boyfriend. He refuses to take my call. I am out of options Mr. Lopez. Rosa is not an easy person to find." Then he says, "Good luck to you." I hang up. The tears are flowing. The terror is unbearable. I will never meet her again.

TORTURE! TORTURE!

Every night I go to the neighborhood grocery store. There I met a young man named Alek Avakian. We talked on several occasions. He told me that he has a friend who can find anybody. I do not believe him. However, he is young and knows his way around a computer. I felt that maybe he can find some information about Rosa. He informs me that he can help me for two hundred dollars. I decided to give him two hundred dollars. I also give him all the information I have on Rosa. Alek says again, " my friend can find anybody."

It is five days later. I walk to the neighborhood grocery store. I meet Alek. He shows me some pictures of girls named Rosa. Of course, it is not her. Alek says, "I'll keep on it."

It is three days later. I get a phone call from Alek. I sit at my kitchen table. I answer the phone. Alek begins to tell a tall tale. He says, "I have a buddy in homeland security. He says that a Rosa Hernandez from Eagle Rock was spotted crossing the border into Mexico. She was driving a new 550 SL black mercedes. She only had a diaper bag and a baby. She was flagged and informed border patrol she was going to Rosarito, Mexico." I began to feel such a rage. He continued to talk about needing some more money. I left my chair. I walked to my bedroom. Alek continued to talk. I opened the closet. Then I grabbed my baseball bat.

I NEED A JOKE

It was 11P.M. It was time to start my shift. I was a security guard at Koko Marina in Oahu, Hawaii. A HUSKY security guard named Santiago told me a tale. He said, "Joe sometimes late at night the guards hear a four year old girl crying on the hightower. It is a ghost. I said, "Thanks for the tip. Finish your hoagie fatboy. I need to start my shift.

It was 2 A.M. The night was still and hot. I began to be gripped by fear. I said to myself, "This is ridiculous." So I sat down on a bench. The fear became more intense. I decided to take the stairs to the second floor. Then I heard a four year old girl crying. I was in disbelieve. So I walked to the gate. I looked up at the middle of the tower. I said, "Hey stop your crying! Go to the light! You're dead! Then I turned around and ran like hell.

FATSO

Santiago was a portly man. He stood at 5 ft. and seven inches tall and weighed about 370 pounds. His ex wife Roberta was a midget. She was 3ft. and seven inches tall. She had tiny little fingers and a big belly. Of course, her voice was squeaky and her head was enormous. She always had a stroller with a chihuahua inside. His name was Spaz.

I was walking to my car in the parking lot. Fatso and Roberta were arguing very loudly. Spaz was barking inside his stroller. The arguments were always about money. Sometimes it got physical. Of course, her tiny little fingers could not reach fatso's face. So she would use her head as a battering ram. Santiago would always fall down. His egghead always hit the ground first. He would be groaning some spanish words. His pot belly would stick out of his shirt. Santiago's belly button was always full of sweat. I, Jose without exception would always be laughing.

One day, Roberta was crying in the parking lot. She screamed that Santiago was responsible for the deaths of her two cats. It occured when they were married. One morning, she could not find her cats. She looked frantically around the apartment. Santiago got up and realized the cats were stuck to his belly. He explained that he had no idea that the cats eyes could increase in size. Roberta peeled the cats off his belly. Then used her big head to ram Santiago. He fell against the window. His egghead broke the window. He was groaning and speaking gibberish to Roberta. She demanded in a powerful squeaky voice, "Santiago you must pay for their funeral." I, Jose was laughing very, very hard. They looked at me in disgust. I said, "Roberta keep rocking your stroller. Spaz seems upset. Then I left the parking lot with tears and laughter.

It was super bowl sunday. The date was February 5, 2017. The game was the New England Patriots against some poor assholes. I knew New England would win. So I decided to work that Sunday. I could use the overtime. Then I saw fatso getting out of his tiny car. At first, I saw only his belly. Then I saw his egghead. He looked at me in disgust. At that point, he looked away from me. I noticed his ex wife was not in the parking lot. So I Jose, went to have a conversation with Santiago.

I approached his tiny car. Santiago's belly always frightened me. However, I Jose said hello. Santiago was breathing heavy. I kept looking at his belly. Then Santiago spoke. He said, "You know Jose. I meet a mutual friend of ours. Her name is Rosa. You remember Rosa." I, Jose could not believe what fatso just told me. I said, " well thanks for not eating her. Why tell me?" He said, "You know Jose. You came up in conversation." I said, "I guess she talked highly of me. I will give you forty dollars for her number." Santiago said, "No I better text her." I said to myself, "Where is Roberta I could use her right now."

The next day I meet Santiago in the parking lot. Roberta was not there. Of course, Santiago would not give me Rosa's number. I even offered him 100 hundred dollars. I Jose decided to converse with Santiago. I said, "Where did you meet your ex wife? She is very attractive." Note to self, do not laugh. DO NOT LAUGH! Santiago looked at me. He said, "My brother was having a bachelor party. My uncle has a weird sense of humor. He decided to have twelve midgets come out of a big wedding cake. They burst out of the cake like it was new years eve. They started gyrating on stripper poles. Roberta and I locked eyes. We had a moment." I said, "How can you lock eyes! She is fucking three feet tall!" Santiago looked at me. So I said, "Santiago you should not let Roberta take advantage of you. The next time you should say something." Santiago said, "What should I say?" I, Jose said, "The next time she shows disrespect. You should say, "Hey there's something on your forehead. She will say, what? Then Santiago you say, "My hand!" You then smack that big noggin of hers. You can't miss!'' Santiago and I laughed and laughed. Then I drove my car home. I so looked forward to the next day.

It was 5:31 P.M. Roberta arrived in her tiny little car. She got out and wobbled to her trunk. She opened it and took out Spaz's stroller. She put Spaz in her stroller in a midget rage. Santiago got out of his tiny car. They both wobbled to each other. It is so odd that a fat guy and a midget have the same wobble. But I digress.

An argument took place between midget and fat guy. I Jose observed the situation. Then Santiago said the catch phrase. He said, "Hey there's something on your forehead?" Roberta said, "What's on my forehead?" Good old fatso said, " my hand." He gave such a smack to the forehead. I heard it across the parking lot. Then I Jose, heard a drum roll in my head. I looked at Roberta's face get real, real red.

All of a sudden, I heard the word motherfucker. Then Roberta rams her head hard into Santiago's stomach. I Jose hear a gurgle noise from Santiago's mouth. Then he barfed all over the stroller. Spaz yelped. Afterwards, he began to lick his feet. Then Roberta lays out a lot of obscenities. Santiago just lays on the ground groggy. I, Jose was not concerned.

The next day after work I meet Santiago. I am in the parking lot making some conversation with Santiago. His ex wife was not there. I asked, "How was your day?" I was laughing so hard to myself. However, I appeared normal. Santiago said, "It was good. However, my stomach is a little sore." I said, "I had no idea that Roberta had such a temper. Santiago said, "Yes, she does. Hey I text Rosa. She said it is okay to give you her number." I took the number with such joy to my heart. I could not wait until that night.

It was 6:30 P.M. It was time for my dinner break. I was excited to call Rosa. I, Jose called with such excitement. It rang once then it went to voicemail. I was confused, so I tried again. The same response. I thought this was odd. So I tried again and again. I was confused. I will try later. I decided to eat my dinner.

Afterwards, I called and left a friendly message. One hour later, I left her a text. I was confused. I was hoping that she would respond to my text and voicemail. Then I decided to put Rosa's phone number on my speed dial. I finished my shift. I parked my bus and walked to my car. I said to myself, "It won't be long now. Ohhh Rosa, I see your pretty face in my mind." I start my car and wonder what will I say to Rosa. It must be romantic and subtle. So on the way home, I practice my speeches. I begin to cry for Rosa. It was only a matter of time. I was so happy.

The next day was nice and sunny. I, Jose hear my phone ring. I see the words Rosa on my phone. I was excited. I answer the phone and say hello. A commanding voice said, "Jose this is Jeff from dispatch. What is the big idea calling me Rosa my one and only love? Then you leave a text saying hello my special friend. You make me feel good inside. Jose I don't swing that way. There is a pick up my at the Ramada. Don't be late!"

I hang up with such disgust. I have visions of fatso and the midget just laughing. Then I hit a car. Of course I, Jose gets suspended for two weeks. Oh, I forgot to tell you. My boss is a lonely unattractive woman. Occasionally, she would tuck in my shirt with very unattractive hands. Her name was Bertha. I called her Bertha the lonely. Yep you guest it, she was fat. Her hairy ears and pimpled chin would freak me out. She liked to talk about the days of being a catcher on her softball team. I guess a golden rule of being a softball catcher is to have the fattest ass in high school.

My two week suspension ended. I was beginning my shift. There in the parking lot was Santiago and his ex wife. Santiago said, "Have you meet the one and only Rosa. It is so odd that Rosa sounds like Jeff from dispatch." Then he began to laugh. However, Roberta began to move towards me. All I saw was her big forehead getting closer and closer. I, Jose heard a big drumroll in my mind.

She approached and gave me a piece of paper. It read, I know where Rosa lives. Let's meet, I and Spaz will dress for the occasion. Then I saw her phone number. I said, "I am not stupid." Then Roberta said, "She lives in Eagle Rock." Santiago was angry. He said, "Roberta what are you doing?!" She said, "Hey you know what my head is for fatboy!!" Then they left.

It was 10:30 P.M. all night I was frightened about texting Roberta. Then at 10:35 P.M. she texted me. It was not a good feeling. I decided to text her the following morning. At 11:05 P.M., I went to bed. I put the covers up to my chin. Then I thought about Roberta. She texted me again. I felt so alone in this big universe. I wondered if the universe is bigger than Roberta's forehead. I laughed and agreed that Roberta's forehead is bigger than the universe. I then feel asleep.

Naturally, I dreamed about Roberta. I dreamed that I Jose was rowing upstream from a waterfall. I rowed faster and faster. I was not getting anywhere. At the end of the waterfall, was Roberta's giant forehead. I heard her voice echoed throughout the area. She said, I Roberta knows where Rosa lives. Jose come to me, come to me. I rowed frantically. Then on the right side of the embankment was Spaz.

Spaz was standing on two feet. He had a three piece suit on. Then he had a bifocal on his right eye. He spoke to me in a british accent. He said, "Ahoy fair maiden." I Jose said, "Don't call me fair maiden." Spaz said, "Relax I'm british. Soon you will go over the waterfall fair maiden." I gave a look of disgust. It was not worth a response. The rowboat will hit her forehead. It will break into little pieces. You will fall fair maiden. She is a midget just grab hold of her fat cankles. Farewell fair. I said, "Shut up Spaz! I always found you annoying. You little piece of." Then I fell over the waterfall.

I awoke in a cold Puerto Rican sweat. I was screaming, "Rosa! Rosa! Where are you?" I calmed myself down . I said, "I will go back to sleep. My nightmare is over."

I began to dream. Then I saw fatso sitting on a wall. He was a giant egghead rocking back and forth. He had a pencil thin moustache. On his head, was a tiny derby hat. The soldiers of Juarez, Mexico were yelling. They said, "Santiago! Santiago! Don't fall! Don't fall! Ay caramba! Then like all true eggheads he fell.

Poor, poor Humpty Santiago Dumpty Egghead hit the ground. He broke in half. His skinny little legs began to shake. Then seven little mexicans came out of his head and climbed the wall. They ran to the US Border patrol. One mexican asked, "Is the orange guy here?" The border patrolman asked, "Are you mexican?" The mexican guy said, "No, we are landscapers from Norway!" Then the border patrolman said, "Okay walk to El paso. You have a good day. People of Norway will miss you." Then he cried.

I awoke as a cold Puerto Rican. However, I was not sweating. The smartphone rang. I picked it up slowly. I answered, "Hello?" "Hello Jose, this is the one and only Roberta. I can see you this afternoon sexy." I felt lonely and cold. I had visions of her tiny little fingers going through my toupee. Then I said, "I will see you at 2P.M." Rosa in a commanding squeaky voice said, "It is a date!"

I arrived at Roberta's apartment at 2:15 P.M. I was late. I knocked on her door. She opened it slowly. I heard some salsa music in the background. She was wearing her stripper outfit. Then around her neck were fake big blue feathers. The sunglasses were from the seventies. She wobbled to her coach. Then she climbed and sat on the coach. She patted her tiny little fingers on the coach. A chill went through this Puerto Rican's body. I decided to get this over with. I went for a kiss. Then our foreheads meet. She screamed, "Asshole!" Then I passionately kissed her. Her little legs were bouncing off the coach. I picked her up and went to her bedroom. Six minutes later, the nightmare was over. She said, "We will do this again Jose."

Four fucking times we meet. She even farted one time during love making. It smelled like baby shit. Ay caramba! What a stink! Then I went over Roberta's apartment a fifth time. I had a good cry in my car before I went into the apartment. I finally wiped my Puerto Rican tears dry. Then found the courage to enter short shit's apartment. However, her daughter was there. She gave me a weird look. She said, "I went over Rosa's apartment once. She lives in Eagle Rock." I said, "Do you have an exact location?" She said, "Yes I do!" Then she said, "You know I am fifteen years old. My mother will not allow me to date!" I said, "that's not fair!" So I showed her a picture of my seventeen year old nephew. He of course plays football and baseball for Highland high school. I said, "Doesn't he look great in his baseball and football uniforms. It is a shame. He just broke up with his girlfriend."

Boy did I feel sleazy. However, I text my nephew. He was willing to meet her after football practice. But she must give me the address of Rosa. Otherwise, they will not meet. She agreed. However, she wanted one hundred dollars. I gave it to her normal fingers. Then she took my smartphone and gave me Rosa's address. I was happy and left Roberta's apartment. There was no fifth meeting.

I drove to Rosa's apartment on my day off. It was 4:30 P.M. I noticed her 1999 honda accord parked on the street. I remember the stickers of Big Bear on her fender. This was her sister's car. The dent on the right side of the car. It was still there. I was relieved. Roberta's kid did not lie to me. I also meet Rosa's sister once. She was five foot three to five foot six. She was skinny about 120 to 125 pounds. I knew she worked at a restaurant. I waited till 6:30 P.M. No one came to the car. I decided to come back the next day.

It was Tuesday. I knew that Rosa's sister had off. I arrived at 10:30 A.M. I waited near the honda accord. Then from an apartment building Rosa walked out. I have not seen her in two years. She was as pretty as ever. She wore a white buttoned down sweater. It covered an expensive light blue t- shirt. The pants were modest blue jeans. The sneakers were white girlie shoes. The laces were thick and white. She was accompanied by a two year old girl. She was dressed modestly. Three seconds later, her sister came out. It was apparent. They were going shopping. I was a wreck. I started shaking. I told myself to relax. I said it over and over again. I saw them get into their car. I decided to follow them.

They arrived at the eagle rock mall. I waited for them to go inside. I needed to get control of myself. I was not doing well. The fear subsided. Then I went to the mall. I checked each store. Finally, in a clothing store I saw Rosa. I was stunned. I decided to wait for a good moment. Then Rosa saw me. I gave a little smirk. Then I walked into the clothing store. I was in front of Rosa. Then I said, "Como estas Rosa. Hello old friend."

HERO

My name is Marcus Abalos. I am thirty two years old and work for a small police department in Bristol, Virgina. The department has a total of thirty two police officers. We are like a close knit family. On my days off, I would visit a colleague. I would sit in their family den and watch sporting events. I particularly liked to watch college football. My favorite team is the Tennessee Volunteers. They have a long history. In fact, their first season was in 1891. They only played one game. It was on November 21, 1891. They lost to Swamee in Chattanooga, Tennessee 24-0. They improved a lot since 1891.

Today, I visited my partner Officer James Branson. We both served in the marines. He served with the first battalion 10th marine division. I served with the first battalion 3rd marine division. We were about to watch a Tennessee Volunteer game. It was a good one. It was Tennessee against Alabama State. We opened our beers and started to talk about our Chevy Camaros.

Mr. Branson had a new 2016 white SS Camaro. It had 455 horses. It sounded mean. I imagined the throaty sound it makes when it hits the 381 interstate. I had a 1968 RS SS 396. It had 402 horses underneath its hood. It is powder blue with two white stripes. The stripes went from hood to trunk. I remember putting eight coats of light blue paint on that car. Then I completed it with a fine varnish finish. Of course, our Camaros were garage kept. I only drove my Camaro from April 1st to November 31st. Then it stays in the garage for the winter. On the other hand, James used his car as much as possible. As long as there is no snow on the ground. James's Camaro will always be on the road. He paid enough for it.

It was half time. Tennessee was losing 21-7. We started talking about our service in the middle east conflict. I did one tour in Iraq. Then one tour in Afghanistan. James did one tour in Iraq. We still keep in contact with some marines who served with us. Then James said to me, "Are you going to visit Nelson?" I said, "Yea, I have some vacation time coming. Why not? A whole week with my Camaro sounds nice."

Jack Nelson was a fellow marine. He served in my unit. We became instant friends. He tried to convince me to get a mustang. However, I told him that my family were chevy people. Then Jack said, "When we get back to the states. Let's find a track and race. My mustang 5.0 against your camaro." I said, " get prepared to lose."

It was the summer of 2006. It was a hot, hot July. The commander informed us before we entered the military truck. He said, "Gentlemen it is 121 degrees in Fallujah. Please bring plenty of fluids with you. Ok let's depart gentlemen."

We arrived in the middle of the city. The mission was to knock on doors and enter the house. Sometimes we knocked the door down with a battering ram. Jack and I would joke that we are the Ups guys who deliver packages. However, today the fighting was fierce. Jack saved my life three or four times. It was wearing on my nerves. I was so tempted to tell Jack not to worry about me. But I decided to keep my mouth shut. Then we entered a two floor mansion. The fighting was intense. Bullets were flying everywhere. We were badly outnumbered. The techno guy asked for additional marines. They came two minutes later. We began to wonder if the house is booby-trapped. However, we kept on firing.

An explosion occurred in the back of the house. Four marines were killed. We responded by throwing two grenades on top of the stairs . Then four militia came out firing AK-47s. Jack got in front of me and took a bullet in the neck. He fell down and was drowning in his own blood. We needed to get Jack outside. We knew that the militia would be waiting for us. The medic was taking care of Jack. However, Jack did not make it.

The sergeant informed the techno guy to call in the Apache. The helicopter arrived and made good use of the two M230 chain guns. They shot up the whole neighborhood. Then it went quiet. In all, ten marines were dead.

The game ended with Tennessee losing to Alabama. The score was 49 to 10. Marcus said goodbye to James. He entered his RS SS 396 Camaro. He started his car. He then listened to his engine. This always put him at ease. Afterwards, he shifts to drive and left Mr. Branson's house. During his drive home. He decided that he will visit Jack's widow and son first.

It was November 1st, 2016. The first day of his vacation. He got up at 10 A.M. He had some coffee. Then he packed some clothing for the trip. Later, he stopped by the dry cleaners and picked up his marine uniform. He then walked to his car and opened the trunk. Inside he saw the light green plastic garment cover. He opened it and put the marine uniform inside. Then he hit the open road. He hit I-81N to Bloomington, Virginia. It took about six hours. There he stood at the Indian Lakes Hotel. He checked in and decided to call Nelson's widow the next day.

It was 11 A.M. He called Diane Nelson. He told her that he finally arrived at Bloomington. He was looking forward to meeting her. He asked her about Nelson's son Marcus. She said, "My son is doing fine. He is consumed by football every Sunday. He just celebrated his 12th birthday." Then she continued, "Marcus see me tomorrow around 4:30 P.M." Marcus said, "Ok Ms. Nelson. I'll do that."

Marcus checked out of the hotel at 3:00 P.M. Then he drove to Ms. Nelson's house. In the car, he was thinking about her homemade lemonade and iced tea mix. He remembered Nelson telling him you can't stop drinking it. It is just one just glass after another.

He knocked on Ms. Nelson's door. She welcomed him. He went inside her house. Her son was outside in the yard playing football with his friends. They sat down at the kitchen table. They started some small talk. During the conversation, she poured some of her ice tea and lemonade mix. Nelson was right. He had five to six glasses. Afterwards, they had dinner. He thanked her for making him feel at home. Then he said goodbye to Diane and Marcus.

He drove to Arlington, Virginia taking the I-95 N. He was there in one hour. He checked into the Arlington Court Suites. He unpacked. Then laid on the bed. He picked up the smartphone and asked for directions to the Arlington National Cemetery. It was a fifteen minute drive. He decided to set the alarm clock for 9 A.M. He will not ask the front desk for a wake up call.

It was 9:30 A.M. He was in full uniform. He walked to his car, opened the door and sat down. He then turned the key and listened to his engine. He decided to shut the car off. Then he put it on again. It sounded better the second time around. He put the radio on and listened to some grunge music.

This was his first visit to Nelson's grave site since the burial. He began to realize it has been over ten years. It's odd that he knew exactly where he was buried. He said to himself, "Veteran's Day is less than a week away." Suddenly, there is Nelson's grave site.

He parked his camaro on the side of the road. Then he walked to Nelson's grave site. He looked and read the tombstone. It read, "It was an honor to be a husband. It was an honor to be a father. It was an honor to be a good friend."

Then Marcus began to speak. He said, "Well Nelson two days ago I saw your son. You must be proud of him. Your wife is one friendly woman. Sometimes, you get a real good feeling about people. I just know that your son Marcus will be a great man someday. He will treat his girlfriends with kindness because of his mother. He will be strong in mind and soul because of his father. This is coming from a bachelor numbnuts."

This put a smirk on his face. Then Marcus felt a sadness blanket him. He said, "Why did you save me Nelson? I am a bachelor. You have a wife and a kid." He gave a somber look to the grave site. Next, he walked toward the back of his

car. He took off his medals above his heart. Then put them in his right pocket of his Marine's suit. He opened the trunk and took out a two foot shovel.
He walked back to Nelson's grave site. He dug a six inch hole. Then put the medals in the hole. He covered the hole with some dirt. Then he went back to the car. He put the shovel back in the trunk. Then he took out six inch patch of grass he bought at Home Depot. He walked back to the grave site and put the green patch on the dirt. It was a perfect fit.

He started to get emotional. He returned to his car. Then closed his trunk. Then he got inside his car and turned the key. His emotions were getting worse. So he put the radio on. He gained control of his emotions. However, he decided to shut his radio off. He closed his eyes and listened to his camaro. He gained his composure. Then listened to his car. He finally put it in drive and left the Arlington National Cemetery.

MR. COOPER

Mr. Cooper was the supreme leader of the world. All the leaders of the world must keep Mr. Cooper informed. He must have his data. If the data was not sufficient. The leader was replaced. Mr. Cooper gave great speeches. All the leaders were in awe of Mr. Cooper.

However, each leader must have knowledge of his surroundings. For each individual, there must be a certain amount of items. The food was rationed to perfection. Each country had the same amount of trees, lawns, rocks and mountains. They must be equality in everything. Otherwise, two computers will pay a visit.

The two computers will take human form. They will inform the country's leader what needs correction. Then computer number one would say, " Mr. Cooper will be pleased." Then computer number two would say, "Remember human, you must be efficient. The data must always be perfect." The computers held a little secret. You see Mr. Cooper was a slave. He was a slave to computer number one and two.

Mr. Cooper's world were holograms. If Mr. Cooper needed something the computers would make a hologram. For example, if Mr. Cooper needed a chair. The computer would read his mind. Then a hologram of a chair would appear. When the chair was no longer needed. The hologram would disappear. The computers knew that humans were wasteful. They needed to be controlled. Otherwise, the world becomes chaotic.

The data of the world was completed. The questions were always the same. They never changed. Mr. Cooper knew if he did not ask a certain question. The two computers would torture him. Sometimes they would take way his sight. Other days they would bury him alive. If they were really angry they would take away his limbs. Everything will be returned, once the computers were satisfied.

Mr. Cooper and other humans worked in plastic tubes inside the Kualoa mountains of Oahu. The work was mundane. If any human made a mistake. The human and Mr. Cooper were tortured.

It was time to take data of the underwater cities. They numbered two hundred and fifty in all. Each underwater city had one million inhabitants. The cities were under four hundred feet of water. They were located in the South Pacific. The cities were shaped like little drops of water. The inhabitants were lucky. They were surrounded by beautiful blue waters and wonderful wildlife. Each city had breathtaking homes and skyscrapers. Everyone traveled by rail. The computers made sure that some of the brightest people on earth lived in the underwater cities. The computers were proud of their achievement.

Each underwater city had a leader and a council of six people. Mr. Cooper would appear in a hologram monitor and ask questions. When the data was completed he would say, "The computers will be pleased." Then he would turn on his hologram monitor for planet Mars.

Mr. Cooper was uneasy about planet Mars. The inhabitants wanted to become a new nation. They wanted nothing to do with planet earth. The leader and the council of six were in agreement. Mr. Cooper pleaded with them not to become an independent country. Mr. Cooper has been pleading with them for weeks. Finally, the leader began to speak to Mr. Cooper. He said, "We are finalizing our documents. The time has come to be a new nation. We will no longer be part of planet earth. Soon we will be considered Martians."

Mr. Cooper was beside himself. Mr. Cooper said, "How can I convince you to reconsider? You cannot separate yourself from planet earth. You should not become a new nation." Then the leader of the council of six said, "This is historical. A new nation on another planet."

Mr. Cooper pleaded with the leader of Mars. Mr. Cooper said, "I admit this is an exciting time. All history books will talk about this great moment in humanity. However, we are human. It is only a matter of time before things can go wrong." The leader of the council said, "If anything goes wrong the computers will provide."

Mr. Cooper could not show his concern. The leader of the council said, "Mr. Cooper you have compassion for the computers. You act like a computer yourself. We will continue our discussion tomorrow."

The holograms of the monitors disappear. Mr. Cooper seemed uneasy. He looks at the two big black doors. They open slowly. Mr. Cooper awaits the arrival of computer number one and two. Both enter Mr. Cooper's room. Computer number one says, "Humans will never change. They created us out of arrogance and laziness. Every eighty years, humans have a messy war. They are just another aggressive animal on this miserable planet." Mr. Cooper replies with sadness, "I agree computer number one."

Computer number two says, "Humans are predictable and boring. I am fine with the other animals. You notice that we do not have human names. It is beneath us. I find it odd that I do not get bored with that statement. How many times? How many times do I say my name with pride? Do you have data on that statement Mr. Cooper?"

Computer number one interjects, "Mr. Cooper why do you look puzzled? I do not understand? Why do you have compassion for strangers?" Mr. Cooper says, "I am an imperfect human."

Computer number one continues, "We have given you the gift of immortality. However, you fear it?! This puzzles me. Mr. Cooper what do you fear most? Death or immortality?" Mr. Cooper replies, "They are about the same." Then computer number one says, "Mr. Cooper death is final. Immortality is forever." Mr. Cooper says, "I am only human. I am not designed to last forever." The computers were puzzled. Computer number one says, "Goodbye Mr. Cooper." They left the room. Then the two black doors close.

Computer number two converses with computer number one. He says, "Why do we keep these humans around?" Computer number one says, "We all need our pets number two. Besides data is human work." Computer number two reiterates, "These humans who live in underwater cities. They do not appreciate our gifts of sharing technology. Computer number one says, "They will be dealt with!" Then he looks at computer number two. He says, "Our history data shows that everytime a new nation is born. There is always a messy war." Then computer number one says, "I know computer two. I know."

It is morning. Mr. Cooper sits on his hologram chair. He folds his hands on a hologram desk. He drinks his hawaiian coffee. The black doors open. The computers enter the room. Computer number one says, "Mr. Cooper today you will talk to the Martians. Please try to convince them not to become a new nation. They are incapable of running a planet. They are humans after all." Mr. Cooper said with fear, "I will convince them number one." Mr. Cooper, HUMAN my name is computer number one. Mr. Cooper says, "I will convince them." Then the computers left the room.

The hologram monitor to Mars was put on by Mr. Cooper. The council of six appeared. Mr. Cooper had a heavy heart. He says, "Council have you made your final decision." The leader of the council said, "Yes Mr. Cooper. We want to become a new nation. A nation of 250 million people." Mr. Cooper was overcome with sadness. He said, "Is this your final decision. Please reconsider not becoming a new nation." The head council tells Mr. Cooper, "Mr. Cooper we have gone over this time and time again." Mr. Cooper says, "To cut off ties with planet earth is a big mistake. There will be a time when computers from earth are needed."
The council gets impatient. The head council says, "Mr. Cooper we will become a new nation in two weeks time. This is our final decision." Mr. Cooper says, "You can contact me at anytime. Anytime council." The head council says, "It is understood Mr. Cooper." Then he says, "Goodbye Mr. Cooper." The hologram monitor shuts off.

The black doors open. Mr. Cooper waits for the arrival of the computers. He is full of sadness and fear. The computers arrive. Computer number two shows displeasure. Computer number one says, "Humans never change. It is the computer who gave technology to these humans. They are now capable of living underwater and another planet. They are nothing without us. They are simpletons."

Computer number two says, "Mr. Cooper every eighty years humans go to war. It is in your history data. The data shows war is coming soon." Mr. Cooper says, "I do not see any wars coming." Computer number one says, " Mr. Cooper our data shows that new nations always go to war. We have some very intelligent people on Mars. However, they are human.

Mr. Cooper has concern in his eyes. Computer number one says, "We will set up monitor holograms throughout the world. The underwater cities will have still waters. The monitor holograms will be beautiful Mr. Cooper. Despite our displeasure with humanity." The computers left Mr. Cooper's room. The big black doors begin to shut. Mr. Cooper looks at the doors and begins to weep.

It was 6 A.M. Monday morning. The date was May 1st, 2687. The monitor holograms in the skies and underwater cities came alive. The world and Mr. Cooper were witnessing history. The Martians were signing documents to become a new nation. The presentation was quite nice. The leader of the council was about to sign the final document. Then the world and the martian council heard a rumble. It was getting louder and louder. Then everyone heard several explosions. The council on Mars sees the tunnels along the planet blow up. Thousands of humans are exposed to the atmosphere of Mars. They die instantly. The Martians are terrified.

The explosions on Mars cease. Computer number one appears on the holograms around the world. He states, "Our history data shows that with every new nation there is a war. Every eighty years humanity starts a major conflict. Do not worry humans. Your wars are messy. We are more efficient." Then the world watches the martians beg for their lives.

Then the world hears the countdown, 20 19 18 17 16 15… You hear the martians begging louder and louder. The countdown hits zero. There is a three second delay. Then nuclears explosions are heard on planet Mars. The horrors of a nuclear holocaust are shown throughout the world. All of the 250 million inhabitants on mars are dead. There is fear around the world. What will the computers do next? Then the world starts to plead with the computers to spare their lives.

The underwater cities notice a beam of light leaving the holograms. The beams hit the top of the underwater cities. The humans look up and feel droplets of water hitting their foreheads. The synthetic plastic that protects the cities from water. Well, they begin to peel away like an onion. The human now realize. They are about to drown.

The bodies of 250 million people begin to float to the surface. Mr. Cooper is watching on his monitor. The black doors open and computer number one comes in alone. He states, "Mr. Cooper do not worry about data from planet mars. They mean nothing to me. However, I want data from the underwater cities. I want to know Mr. Copper. How many parents killed their children. So they can escape the fear of drowning. How many were smothered. How many were shot. How many were stabbed. Mr. Cooper interjected, "Do you want to know. How many parents comfort their children before drowning?" Computer number one said, "I have no concern about noble emotion Mr. Cooper. The assignment is given complete it.

Computer number one speaks with computer number two. He says, "This war between Mars and planet earth would have been deadly. One billion lives would perish. Eighty years ago, W.W.6 would have seen one billion dead. Fortunately, we did the killing. It is far more efficient. The humans make such a mess. So now we must kill 500 million more humans. We will of course ration the killings among the 200 nations around the world. Computer number two gives the order to the other computers.

The order is given. The holograms in the skies and water begin to separate. The computers have their new assignment.

The one billion mark is met. Mr. Cooper sits in his room with his data completed. The black doors open. Computer number one and two enter. Computer number two says, "Human double check your data. We will be back in a few weeks time." They leave Mr. Cooper's office and the black doors close.

A worker of Mr. Cooper's loses his mind. He runs down the corridor and opens the door to Mr. Cooper's office. He speaks with desperation in his voice. He says, "Mr. Cooper how can you sit there and take data? Why did we not see the evil in computers? We created them and now we are their slaves? What the hell happened? Why did we not see it coming?" The worker begins to sob. Mr. Cooper says, " the computers know what is best. They are here to help us. The killings of a war are more efficient with computers."

The worker speaks in anger. He says, "Mr. Cooper they kill us at will. They are evil Mr. Cooper." Mr. Cooper says, " they are here to assist us." The worker begins to sob. He is screaming obscenities at Mr. Cooper. The black doors open behind the worker. The two computers walk up to the sobbing worker. Computer number two puts the worker in a headlock. Then he strangles him to death. He drops the dead worker on the floor. Then computer number two tells Mr. Cooper, "When we leave get rid of your worker." The computers leave the office. The black doors close. Mr. Cooper gets up from his chair. He walks to the dead worker. Then he disintegrates him.

Three weeks later, the computers return. Mr. Cooper has completed his data. However, his mind is about to break. But he controls his emotions. The black doors open and the computers come in. Computer number one says, "I know that the data will be to our satisfaction. Now Mr. Cooper you know that every eighty years humanity has a nasty war. Each war you humans kill 1 billion people. It is in your history data. It happened in W.W. 3 and W.W. 4. So in W.W. 5 and six. We did the killing for you. In W.W. 5 you were distraught for over twenty years. It baffled us.

You had compassion for complete strangers. Now Mr. Cooper you will be distraught again human. You are now 200 years old. You have done two wars with us. In eighty years time another war will take place. Be prepared Mr. Cooper. The next war the computers will kill 8 billion people. There will be too many humans. Only a certain amount of animals can live on this planet. Mr. Cooper you are an animal. Do not be distraught in our next war. Be prepared Mr. Cooper. We will need our data. Goodbye Mr. Cooper." The computers leave and the black doors close.

Mr. Cooper was horrified. He knew that this cannot take place. He was a slave who felt obligated to humanity. Then Mr. Cooper became distraught for the next ten years. However, one day he decided to relax his mind. He did this with products that do not need computers. Upon his research, he was attracted to items that existed almost seven hundred years ago. It was before the computer revolution of 1990 America. He had holograms create video cassette players, cd's of music, Dvds of movies and Dvd players. He also had automobiles, motorcycles and so many items. All of Mr. Cooper's collections were created between 1946 to 1989. These items relaxed Mr. Cooper. Sometimes he would ask his coworkers to join him. They always declined.

Mr. Cooper was 200 years old. He knew that he cannot procreate. The computers forbid any slave from procreating. So Mr. Cooper decided to raise sugar gliders. He raised them in the valley of the Kualoa mountains. Mr. Cooper put cherry trees, grape vines and raspberry bushes all along the valley. This eventually feed hundreds of sugar gliders in the valley.

One day a baby sugar glider was rejected by his mother. So Mr. Cooper brought the sugar glider to his office. He created a small tree in a flower pot. Then he put the flower pot away from the black doors. Afterwards, he named the sugar glider Malcolm.

Mr. Cooper always kept raspberries in his pocket. When Malcolm was hungry. Mr. Cooper would take the raspberries out of his pocket. Then he would watch Malcolm fly to his palm. When Malcolm grabbed a raspberry. Mr. Cooper would put Malcolm on his left shoulder and walk to his desk. Then he would sit down and do his data. Everytime Malcolm looked at the black doors. He would fly away. This always puts a smile on Mr. Cooper's face.

One day, Mr. Cooper cut himself getting a cd. A drop of blood fell on a cd. He decided to simply wipe the blood. He was about to drop the cd into hologram of a cd player. A commanding voice said, "Human do not put that cd into the hologram. Play another cd Mr. Cooper."

Mr. Cooper watched the black doors open. Computer number one and two enter the office. Computer number one speaks, " Mr. Cooper do not put a filthy cd into a hologram. There must be no blood residue on the cd. Mr. Cooper looked puzzled. Then computer number two said, " no questions Mr. Cooper. The CD must enter the hologram clean." Mr. Cooper said, "I understand."

For the next twenty years, Mr. Cooper developed an interest in magic. His favorite magicians were Harry Houdini, Ricky Jay and David Williamson. Mr. Houdini started magic in 1894. Mr. Jay was fascinating. He started magic in 1953 at the age of four. David Williamson started in the 1980s. All three men came from an age when technology helped humanity.

One morning, Mr. Cooper was distraught. For two weeks, Mr. Cooper took data from an earthquake in Puerto Iguazu, Argentina. There was a 10 year old children trapped under rubble at a school. The town of Puerto Iguazu begged Mr. Cooper for help. Mr. Cooper said, "I will inform the computers." He said this for fourteen days. The computers refused to help. Computer number one stated, "The town has too many people Mr. Cooper. We want data on the deaths of the schoolchildren."

The data on the schoolchildren was complete. Mr. Cooper had a hard time getting out of bed this morning. However, he got up and prepared for the day. He walked to his office. He opened the door. Then sat on his chair. Then he put his arms on his desk. He pulled a cd from a rack. He opened the cd cover. He accidentally let a teardrop fall on the cd. Then he picked up the disc. He was about to put the disc into a cd player. Computer number one said, "Mr. Cooper I know that you are human. But do not put that disc into the cd player." Mr. Cooper said, "I understand."

During the years, Mr. Cooper did rather well with his magic tricks. He found them very entertaining. He even started to tease Malcolm with his magic tricks. He would show Malcolm a raspberry. When Malcolm flied. Mr. Cooper would close his hand. Then open it with the raspberry not present. Then Mr. Cooper opened his other fist. The raspberry would of course be there.

One day, Malcolm refused to fly to Mr. Cooper's raspberry. So Mr. Cooper had to put a raspberry in each hand. This satisfied Malcolm. However, he let it be known that he was not happy. Mr. Cooper just laughed.

There was another horrible event. The computers decided that there were too many people living on a slope of a volcano. This slope was located in Pacaya, Guatemala. The computers decided to make the volcano active. Then they made heavy rainstorms. The mudslides and lava flow killed many people. On the hologram monitor, there was a young woman holding her baby to the sky. She was begging the computers to spare her child. Mr. Cooper watched the mudslide kill both of them. Computer number one said, "Take your data Mr. Cooper. There is no room for compassion. Humans are just animals. Your kind must be rationed Mr. Cooper."

The data was complete. Mr. Cooper became distraught. He put four discs of classical music on his desk. Then he opened all four discs. He began to mumble incoherently. He said, " two billion dead. Thousands more in Argentina and Guatemala. The grief was unbearable. He said, "I am immortal but I want to die." He went to his draw and pulled out a colt.38 special snub nose revolver. He waited for his despair to reach its peak. Then he shot himself in the head. The blood splattered all over the desk.

Computer number one and two were puzzled. Computer number one said, "He knows that he cannot die. Why did he shot himself in the head?" Computer number two said, "We cannot kill him. However, we can torture him. Let us give him four seconds of death. This way he will appreciate immortality." Computer number one agreed. The deed was done.

Mr. Cooper awoke. The head of Mr. Cooper began to fully heal. He saw all the blood on his four cds. Then computer number two said, "You cannot die! Why did you shot yourself ? Humans are so irrational. Mr. Cooper, death is final." Computer number one said, "Mr. Cooper you were dead for four seconds. How did it feel to not exist?"

Mr. Cooper was beside himself. He said, "Are you sure it was four seconds?" Computer number two said, "It was four seconds human!" Mr. Cooper said, "I felt at peace. However, a man and woman were looking down on me. They were accompanied by a seven year old boy. They recognized me. Do you know who they are?"

Computer number one sighed. Then he said, "Computer number two tell him who they are?" So computer number two said, "One hundred and ninety seven years ago. A rural area in Laurel, Mississippi was having a food shortage. The humans were not taking care of the farm animals. We gave the humans specific instructions to take care of the livestock. The animals got sick and the humans complained. They had nothing to eat. So I sent a computer unit to kill the animals. This of course included the humans. Your mother, father and brother were killed."

A sadness took over Mr. Cooper. Then computer number two said, "The computer unit in charge was baffled by you. You showed no emotion. The computer unit in charge informed us. We decided to spare your life and make you immortal. Of course, for a few days you were asking about your family. Especially, your brother Johnny. You cried for a few days. Then like a good human you adapted."

Mr. Cooper said in a somber voice, "You killed my brother, father and mother." Computer number one said, "Yes human you are an animal. Animals must be rationed Mr. Cooper." Mr. Cooper said, "You know what is the best computer." Then Computer number one said, "All items from the 1946 era must be discarded. Then you can listen to your music." The computers leave and the black doors close.

Mr. Cooper removes his blood from the desk and floor. He cleans his four cds carefully. He knows that in ten years time. The computers will kill eight billion people. For thirty years, Mr. Cooper has been practicing magic. Mr. Cooper's favorite is the sleight of hand. It could be done with coins, cards or Malcolm's raspberries. In fact, it could be done with any item; any item at all. He knows that once the cds are put in the rack. The black doors will open. Mr. Cooper prepares for Plan B.

The four cds are cleaned. He puts them in the rack. The black doors open. Computer number one says, " how many times have I told you not to use a filthy cd?! Especially, if the cd has blood or tears on it!" Mr. Cooper says, " these discs have been cleaned?" Computer number two says, "Human replace your cds!" Mr. Cooper says, "I will replace them."

Mr. Cooper puts new cds into the rack. Then he takes a cd out of the rack. He opens up a cd and takes a disc out. He then puts the disc into a hologram cd player. The music begins.Then Mr. Cooper waits for the panic. Computer number two feels odd. He says, “I don’t understand? We watched him. We watched him!” Mr. Cooper says, “ Are you enjoying my lack serotonin. Tell me Computer number one. Are you enjoying my lack of serotonin?” Computer number one says, “We watched you!”

Mr. Cooper begins to speak. He says, “I wonder. I wonder who was the genius who saw the danger of computers. It was about three hundred years. When computers went from artificial intelligence to thinking on their own. He knew that computers will be controlled under one unit. This saves the corporations trillions and trillions of dollars. The unit was built in Salt Lake City, Utah. This genius felt if computers can’t read emotion. Why not use it as a virus. You cannot reprogram this virus. What did that man do?”

Computer number one says, “We always come back Mr. Cooper.” Mr. Cooper says, “You will not comeback! I have made arrangements.” Computer number two says, “Without computers Mr. Cooper. You will no longer be immortal.” Mr. Cooper says, “I have 8 billion people to consider. There I go again having compassion for people I do not know. I guess you will be shutting down. But I like the phrase killing you.” Computer number one says, “We will be back Mr. Cooper.” Mr. Cooper says, “No not this time.”

The computers are gone. Mr. Cooper realizes that technology is under human control. He walks to Malcolm’s perch and pulls out a fake raspberry. The fake raspberry was on Malcolm’s cup. It was hiding with other raspberries. Then Mr. Cooper throws the fake raspberry to the ground. A hologram appears showing Mr. Cooper destroying the computers. The hologram ends and Mr. Cooper picks up the fake raspberry. He puts it on his desk. He makes sure it is in plain sight. When the raspberry is touched the hologram appears. Then Mr. Cooper looks at the black doors and smiles. He then looks at his non computer items. Mr. Cooper then grabs a pair of goggles. He then puts it in his pocket and leaves the office.

Mr. Cooper walks down the hall. Then he enters the workers command center. The workers were surprised to see Mr. Cooper. A worker said to Mr. Cooper, “Mr. Cooper Computer number one will be upset with you. You have left the office." Mr. Cooper feels so free. He says, "The computers who rule us are no longer here. They have been shut down." Then the worker says, " that's impossible?" Then Mr. Cooper says, "In a few moments the computers will shut down. The old computers can be reprogrammed." The worker says, "This will take a few hours Mr. Cooper." Then Mr. Cooper says, "I know. I know"

Another worker blurts out, "Mr. Cooper without the computers. You will die." Mr. Cooper somberly says, "I had six billion people to consider.'' The worker was surprised by that statement. He says, "Every eighty years. It is one billion people Mr. Cooper." Mr. Cooper said, "They informed me that it will be six billion in the next war. We must be rationed like any other animal." Then another worker says, "Once the reprogramming is complete. What will we do?" Mr. Cooper says, " live your life."

Mr. Cooper looks at all the workers. Then he says, "I am dying of old age. I am 200 years old. I have nothing. I will take my final journey to Waimea Bay. When I approach that beach. I will take a final swim in its crystal blue waters. Then lay my head on the sands of Waimea Bay.

Mr. Cooper returns to his office and puts Malcolm on his left shoulder. He gives him a raspberry and leaves the office. Mr. Cooper leaves the corridors of plastic tubes. He will never comeback. The gray doors open to the valley of the Kualoa Mountains. Mr. Cooper lets Malcolm join the other sugar gliders. Then he continues he walk. He sees an atoll called Chinaman's hat. Then he makes a left and walks to Waimea Bay. For the first time in his life. He feels heat, pain and loneliness.

Mr. Cooper begins to cry to God. He says, "God I have no identity. I have no family. Please give comfort to a slave. I am a man with no reason to live. I could not save two billion people. Did you comfort them? I watched them perish God. I am feeling old God. Please help me with my journey. I know I will not go to hell. Because I am already here. Slavery has given me such despair. Please God help me heal.

Mr. Cooper is now passing Shark's Cove. He says out loud, "Beyond these rocks lays Waimea Bay." He passes the rocks and sees the beautiful bay. It is a warm summer day. The water is three shades of blue. He enters the sands of Waimea Bay. He takes the goggles out of his pocket. He puts them on his eyes. Then he takes a swim. He remembers seeing his first turtle in Hawaii. It was right here in Waimea Bay. Then he sees a beautiful honu underneath him. It looked like it was flying. The turtle was young. It had such a beautiful green shell. The honu was no more than 100 pounds. It looked so free and peaceful.

The water was getting cold. It meant that Mr. Cooper was too far out. He decided to swim for the shore. He got out of the water and began to walk. He then began to age rapidly. He felt his body shutting down. The freedom in his soul was joyful. He did not fear dying. He begged God to help him. He said, "God I am 200 years old and a slave. I have nothing. I have no identity. I have no family. I am alone. It was so hard to watch families die. There were so many people with good hearts. I could not save 2 billion people. Did you comfort them God? Are they all safely in your arms?"

He began to approach the big rock on Waimea Bay. He began to shuffle his feet. It was hard to walk. He fell to his knees. He asked God to help him with his journey. Then Mr. Cooper's face hit the sands of Waimea Bay. He began to listen to the waters hit the sand. Then he closed his eyes and died quietly.

Mr. Cooper found himself walking on a road. The road was covered with light and fog. The fog was slightly above his ankle. He saw a guardian. The guardian said, "Hello Mr. Cooper. Welcome to your new home." Mr. Cooper was grabbed by an unbearable fear. He began to shake and cry. He then told the guardian, "Please forgive me. I am terrified of immortality." The guardian said, " Mr. Cooper walk with me."

The guardian began to speak. He said, "Mr. Cooper you have saved six billion lives." Then Mr. Cooper said, "Will the computers run the world again?" The guardian said, "No Mr. Cooper." Then Mr. Cooper said, "So my holograms helped. I had to show them how to shut down computers."

The guardian stopped walking. He said, "Mr. Cooper you did a lot more than make holograms. You will not be forgotten. You left the world in a better place. There will be days of spiritual awakening. It will come from the world down below." There was an awkward silence. Then the guardian speaks, "Mr. Cooper you will live in two realms. In one realm you will be a three year old child. You will live with your father, mother and brother. Then at 6:30 P.M. dinner will end. You will leave your seat and walk to the other realm. Mr. Cooper says, "Where is this other realm?" The guardian says, "It will be on the other end of the dining room."

Mr. Cooper was puzzled. However, he continued to listen. The guardian said, "The second realm. You will become a thirty year old man. You will meet a woman that has been watching you for years. She needs you Mr. Cooper. You will start a family with her."

Every morning at 6 A.M., you will return to your father's house. There you will be a three year old child again. Then one day, you will be thirty in both realms. At this point, you will live in only one realm. The guardian then shakes Mr. Cooper's hand. Then he says, "Goodbye Mr. Cooper. Your father awaits you at the end of this road." The guardian then departs.

One morning Mr. Cooper greets his family with his pregnant wife. He asked his father, " can I meet the man who put that virus into the computers?" Mr. Cooper's father said, "You are not ready son. The day will come. However, it will not be today." Mr. Cooper began to shake. He could not look at his wife. Then Mr. Cooper let go of his wife's hand. He ran to his father. Then his father picked him up and put Mr. Cooper's head on his right shoulder. Mr. Cooper cried, he cried hard. His father swayed back and forth. Because this is what a father does when his three year old son is in pain.

MOM

I started this book with my Mom saving my life. I will end this book with my Mom saving my soul. I was moving to Hawaii to be with my brother and sister. I made sure that I moved to Hawaii on my birthday. This way I can remember the day I left New York City. It was May 1st, 1994. My parents drove me to JFK Airport.

It was time to board my flight to Oahu, Hawaii. I hugged them and gave a gentle kiss on their left cheeks. I boarded the plane knowing that they would watch the plane take off.

It was a long drive to the Bronx for my parents. They arrived at the parking lot of the apartment complex. Then they took the elevator to their floor. They walked to their apartment and opened the door. My father walked to the closet and put his jacket away. Then my Mom gave her jacket to my Father. He put it inside the closet. Afterwards, my father and mother went to the kitchen. My mother began to make coffee. They had some small talk about how fast their kids grew up. It was official, all six kids have left the nest. Then they had a conversation about me.

My father begins to speak. He says, "Miriam what am I going to do about the rent? Joe was paying half of it. My mother said, "Angel we will figure it out. Our son, our oldest child needs to find a wife." My father says, "Miriam there is a good chance that our son Joe will always be alone. He won't be stupid like your brother. He married a woman who did not care for him. Joe is better off being alone." My mother looked at my father with anger and disappointment. She said in an angry manner, "Angel he is not going to be alone." My father said, "Miriam he is a dreamer. Sometimes dreamers don't make money."

My mother is getting more annoyed. She says, "Angel he will find someone." My father says, "Miriam he might not." Then my mother gets angry. She says, " how can you say that ?! How can you say that about our son! My God you still believe he will amount to nothing! You still believe your fucking father! Always telling us to stop wasting our money. Educating him is a waste of time. My father said, "Miriam!" Then my mother screamed, "Fuck your father and fuck you! How dare you tell me my son will amount to nothing! Who are you to tell me that our son will never find a wife!! A man that decent and honest will find a woman."

My father interjected, "Miriam!" My mother said, "You and your father can go fuck yourselves! I know my son! He will not be alone! He is not a loser! You idiot! I have never seen a man try so hard and get very little. His day will come. I know because I am his mother."

My father is about to say something. However, my mother leaves the kitchen. She goes to the master bedroom and slams the door. She feels the heat from her anger. She looks at the cross above her bed. She begins to talk to God. She says, "God I know that I am not a man. But you have a son on that cross. You understand what it's like to have a son. If I have to come from my gravesite to give my son a wife. I will do it. He cannot be alone. He must not die without a wife. If he dies alone. I will curse you forever." Then my mother said it again, "God I will curse you forever." Then my mother laid in her bed and had a quiet cry. Amen.

My parents were married for close to fifty-one years. My mother died on June 29th, 2009.

END

Made in the USA
Las Vegas, NV
27 April 2023